THE HAUNTED HOMECOMING

ANGIE FOX

Moose Island Books

Also by Angie Fox

My Big Fat Demon Slayer Wedding

Beverly Hills Demon Slayer

Night of the Living Demon Slayer

What To Expect When Your Demon Slayer is Expecting

SHORT STORY COLLECTIONS:

A Little Night Magic: A collection of Southern Ghost Hunter and Accidental Demon Slayer short stories

The HAUNTED Homecoming

The Southern
Ghost Hunter
Mysteries
Book 10

NEW YORK TIMES BESTSELLING AUTHOR

ANGIE FOX

This edition published by arrangement with Moose Island Publishing.

First Edition

ISBN: 978-1-939661-70-8

Moose Island Books

Chapter One

A crisp fall breeze blew in through the kitchen window as I cracked fresh-ground black pepper over my pecan and apple salad. With a final twist of the grinder, I smiled down at my pet skunk, Lucy. She turned a tight circle and stomped her feet in front of the door that led out to the back patio.

"Oh, now, sweetie. I just let you in." About ten seconds ago. Right after I'd slipped the tomato, cheddar, and bacon pie into the oven. I gave the salad a stir.

Lucy quirked her silky ears back and forth before she dashed straight for me, whipped around my legs, and head-butted me on the shin.

The jolt knocked a slice of apple out of my bowl. I popped it in my mouth. "I'm sorry, Lucy, but I have my hands full at the moment." And I was running behind.

I'd given in to a last-minute temptation and treated Lucy to a bubble bath and a brush-out before I'd started preparing a nice, fancy lunch for some long-awaited guests. My little skunk looked like a princess and smelled like peach blossoms, but it had put me behind.

My mom and stepdad would be arriving at any minute. In

true Sugarland tradition, I planned to show my love with food, and plenty of it.

They were back in town for the 106th annual Sugarland Homecoming Festival and football game. The celebration lasted four days—Wednesday through Saturday—starting with this afternoon's Welcome Home Jamboree in the town square. There'd be food booths, music on the main stage, a visit from the high school marching band, and a special performance of *106 Years of Homecoming Highlights*, a play written and performed by The Sugarland Players theater troupe.

And even bigger this year—we'd be opening the time capsule under the flagpole by the football field.

It was all anyone could talk about.

My mom's graduating class had been in charge of organizing the time capsule back in 1985. Now you may be thinking that's not long to keep the thing buried, and it isn't. That's the catch. The homecoming day newspaper and autographed football from the big game—along with Darcy Johnson's secret apple pie recipe—well, they were originally supposed to stay buried for a hundred years.

Only fate, in the form of a much-needed expansion to the Sugarland football stadium, got in the way.

Now in private, most folks would admit that the home of Sugarland football was more of a large field than a stadium, but we liked to think big. And thanks to Roan's Hardware, which had donated a small fortune to build an even larger scoreboard and stands big enough to fit most everyone in town, that optimism was finally paying off.

Too bad the school flagpole stood in the way.

A group of concerned citizens had banded together to save it, and coincidently keep the time capsule buried. The daughter of the late pie maker Darcy Johnson had spearheaded the effort. But there was no stopping progress.

Besides, the rest of us couldn't wait to crack open that time capsule, and not just to keep Darcy Johnson's daughter from dominating the Sugarland Bake-Off for the next thirty years. A good many groups and organizations—not to mention individuals—had kept what they had tucked in the capsule secret. There's nothing a town like Sugarland loves more than digging into someone else's secrets.

And now? It would all see the light of day.

It seemed like anyone who'd ever left Sugarland was coming back for the festivities. You could smell the family barbeque pits firing up for miles around. Streamers and bows trailed from cars cruising town, and many had soaped their back windows—for school spirit and all.

I'd done my part by lining my front steps with red and white geraniums, on account of our football team, the Sugarland Biscuits, wore red and white. I'd wound red and white holiday lights up the columns that graced the front porch and taped a pennant to the door. I'd also decorated my 1978 Cadillac with red streamers and balloons tied to the antenna.

When my grandmother had passed, she'd left me the car and the antebellum home. I liked to think I'd done her proud.

Lucy gazed up at me with those adorable eyes, and I flicked her a slice of apple. "I know you're excited, sugar. I am, too."

When Mom had heard about all the people from her class coming back, she'd decided to join in the fun. I couldn't wait to see her. Less than a month after my grandmother passed away, my mom had skipped town and rarely come home since. She'd used her inheritance to buy an RV and had crisscrossed the country with my stepdad at least six times that I could count. They called it wanderlust. I'd hoped it was a phase. How could they not see that they had everything they needed right here in Sugarland, Tennessee?

Evidently, they thought otherwise. Mom and Carl hadn't been back since my failed wedding two years ago.

"It's not like she stayed away on purpose," I told my skunk. At least I didn't think so.

Things had gone so wrong that day I could hardly blame Mom for wanting to hop into her RV and blow town as fast as possible. I might have done the same if I hadn't had the house and a job to consider.

And Lucy. She needed a big backyard.

Lucy ran straight into my leg and bounced off, but she didn't seem to notice. Instead she made a beeline for the back door.

"What the—?"

The crackle of car tires on my gravel side drive explained it all.

Lucy let out a loud grunt and waved her white-striped tail like one of the color guard girls in the high school marching band. She turned to me, her shiny black eyes imploring.

"I'll bet that's Mom and Carl, and you want to be the welcoming committee," I said, drying my hands and nudging the door open for the skunk, who took off across the white painted porch like it was on fire. I smiled as she toddled as quick as she could down the steps that led to our generous backyard.

My mom doted on Lucy whenever she saw her, and that skunk remembered.

I'd join them in a few seconds, but first I needed to grab the trifle dish out of the fridge. I arranged everything on the kitchen island before stepping back to take it all in. Lunch was fixing to look like a page out of the church cookbook and would taste even better. I wanted my mother's homecoming to be perfect.

"Mom?" I called, untying my apron and tossing it onto the counter as I banged out the back door.

I'd left my avocado green Cadillac out back by the rose-bushes, and my mom had parked her one-of-a-kind RV directly behind it. My stepdad had custom made their vehicle out of an old school bus. He'd painted it gray with silver trim, adding an awning and a nice pop-up camper on top. It was huge—a paradise on wheels, with plenty of living space down below and a lot of privacy up top.

Just then, Lucy came tearing out the open doors of the school bus, wearing a skunk-sized red and white Sugarland football cheerleading uniform. She was the picture of school spirit. Never mind that she managed to shake the matching bow off her head as she dashed to greet me.

"Look at you, gunning for homecoming queen," I said, scooping her into my arms.

"I'm so glad it fits," my mom gushed, laughing as she followed the path blazed by my excitable skunk.

"You always did like to push the accessories," I teased, holding Lucy up to show that she'd at least kept the bow on her tail.

Mom wore a pink tunic top over white jeans, her gold earrings jangling as she walked. Her platform wedges made her taller than me, even though we were the same height. "A lady must always look her best." She winked, repeating what my grandmother had drilled into both of us. "Speaking of such, I love your dress!"

"I found it last week at the resale shop," I managed as Lucy wriggled in my arms. My finances were looking better lately, but I didn't want to take my savings account for granted. Besides, New For You had some great bargains.

I let Lucy down so she could start jumping and chasing her tail all over my porch.

She knew she looked good.

Mom gave me a hug that smelled like roses. When she pulled back, she whipped off the pink and orange scarf that held back her long, graying blonde hair. "I think this would look great on you."

"I can't take your clothes," I said. And I certainly didn't want her thinking I needed them. "Honestly, it's fine," I insisted while she brushed off my objections, turning her scarf into a head-band for me.

"Oh, come on. It's so cute. I got it at a flea market in Denver, and ah!" She stepped back to admire her work. "I was right. It looks better on you."

"Thanks, then," I said, touching the silky fabric. I knew better than to argue with my mother. "Where's Carl?"

"I dropped him off at his brother's. They're behind on their float for the parade, and you know how Carl likes any excuse to wield a power saw."

Carl had been a custom cabinetmaker before he'd retired and taken off on the road with Mom. His family owned Roan's Hardware downtown.

"What's their float theme?" I asked, holding open the door for Mom.

"Building Sugarland," she said, breezing past me. "They would have been done last week if they hadn't gotten the hare-brained idea to make a double-decker replica of the original Roan's storefront."

"You know every one of those boys is in heaven," I said, glad they were using those power tools at the Roans' house instead of mine.

"Verity!" my mother gasped when she saw my spread on the kitchen island. "You made grandma's banana pudding."

"And your tomato bacon pie, but that's still got another twenty minutes in the oven."

She eyed the handmade white oak kitchen table that had been cherished by one of my grandma's dear friends. "I remember this," she said, making her way over to it. Jorie Davis's daughter had passed it down to me after I'd helped the family solve the mystery of Jorie's sudden death. I couldn't bear to hide the polished wood under a tablecloth, so I'd decorated the four-chair round-top with red and white place mats and colorful cork trivets. "You've done it up so cute," Mom gushed. "I like how you've made it your own." Then she sighed. "It's good to see you're recovering from that awful attempt Virginia made to bankrupt you."

"It wasn't easy," I admitted. Virginia had sued me for the cost of the wedding after I'd ditched her youngest son just short of the altar. Never mind the fact that he'd cheated on me.

"I love that purple couch," Mom burst out, looking past the table into the parlor. She strolled over to get a better look. "And wow. That rosebush by the mantel is growing like a weed. What are you using as fertilizer? Frankie himself?"

"Oh, my stars. Mom!"

Frankie was my ghostly housemate and sort-of friend. And his ashes were in that dirt, but that didn't mean…I didn't want to think about it.

Frankie was invisible to every living person except for me, and that was only because I'd accidentally tied him to my ancestral property. I hadn't meant to do it. I'd simply dumped some ashy soil from an old vase onto my late grandmother's heirloom rosebushes. Only it turned out that vase was actually Frankie's burial urn, and I hadn't realized my error until I'd hosed him in good.

So now he was trapped here with me until we figured out a way to fix my mistake. Only nothing we'd tried had worked.

"I think it would be nice if Frankie turned into a flower," Mom mused happily, fingering a deep red bloom.

"You'd better not tell him that." Frankie was upset enough that he'd been grounded onto my property.

I did try to make him feel welcome, though. That was why I'd dug up his rosebush and relocated it to an industrial-sized trash can in my parlor. My boyfriend had also built the gangster a wooden shed out by the back pond so Frankie could have a little privacy.

Mom waved off my concern. "In any case, I'm happy you've

made this house your home. And his, too." She turned her attention to the battered urn resting on the mantel. "Maybe you could make this a little nicer for him." She ran her fingertips over the dull green stones near the lid. "Maybe tie a bow around it."

"Mom—" I barked as she lifted the lid.

"What?" she asked, already peeking inside. "Is he in here?"

"No," I said, rushing over to her. "Well, yes. Some of his ashes are." A small portion had remained stuck along the bottom. In fact, the only way he could leave my property was if I took the urn—and that smidge of ashes—with me. "But Frankie doesn't live in his urn." This wasn't *I Dream of Jeannie*. "Besides, even if he was in there, you can't barge in uninvited. You have to treat ghosts like people." I retrieved the lid from her and placed it back onto my ghost's final resting place. "I mean, they *are* people."

"*Were* people?" she offered.

Heavens to Betsy. I sighed, making an effort to rein in the lecture. She was already pushing my buttons. I'd been missing Mom so much I'd forgotten what it was like to actually have her around.

"I'm sorry," she said, contrite. "I'm just interested in what you've been up to." She moved back to the rosebush, which seemed safe enough. "I have to admit," she said, running the tips of her fingers through the soil, "I can't wait to meet your friend. You know, I sometimes catch a shadow here or there out of the corner of my eye, and I wonder if I see ghosts."

"My situation isn't hereditary, Mom." More like an unhappy accident.

She caressed a silky rose petal. "Well, all the same, I'd love to say hello."

"You won't be able to see Frankie," I cautioned, hoping to manage her expectations. Besides, the 1930s gangster who haunted my property wasn't exactly the type to hang around and drink sweet tea with my mother. He preferred speakeasies, illegal racetracks, and the occasional armed robbery.

"Well, I bought your ghost a present," she announced. "Only —whoops—I set it down when I went to dress up Lucy."

"What did you get him?" I asked as she led me back out onto the porch. Frankie was notoriously hard to buy for, seeing as he couldn't touch anything on the physical plane.

"It's a little something I discovered at a roadside stand on the way into town," she said, heading down the back stairs. "I was hoping it would go with Frankie's homecoming decorations, but," she said, glancing at the shed by the pond, "I don't see that he's done a thing."

He hadn't. The mobster didn't give a fig about the big game. Even if he had, she wouldn't have been able to see his decorations anyway.

Mom led me inside the RV into a blue and white shabby chic living area.

"Wow, Mom. This is ruffle city," I said, taking in the floofy pillows on the couch, as well as the white painted antique chandelier over a hammered stainless steel table most likely salvaged from an old diner. "Carl lets you get away with turning your home into a girly-girl paradise?"

"Carl lets me do anything as long as I let him drive," she said, fetching a flower-encrusted wreath from a hook by the door. "Isn't it darling?" she asked, lifting it up. White magnolias competed with red footballs to escape a candy-cane-striped ribbon. The red and white fabric wound all around the wreath and made a huge bow at the bottom. "And look. I added little whiskey bottles," Mom said, pointing out the airline-sized bottles tucked into the straining bow.

Frankie might actually like that part, I decided.

"Let's go deliver some homecoming spirit," I said. "With spirits!"

"To the spirit," Mom added.

She knocked on the wooden door to the shed, and while we waited for the ghost to answer, she held up the wreath. It fit perfectly.

Frankie had no reason not to love it, but then again, Frankie was good at not loving things. And as the air temperature around us dropped like a rock, it became clear he wasn't thrilled to see us.

"Is he here?" Mom asked, shivering.

I had a feeling. "Frankie," I said, knocking on the door myself. It wasn't like he could leave the property. "Franklin Rudolph Winkelmann," I said, using his proper name. I heard something clatter to the floor inside. "I know you're in there."

He could at least be polite and answer the door.

"Franklin Winkelmann," my mom repeated, grinning.

A cold breeze whipped past, and I heard the groan of the ghost. "Why don't you yell my name again? I don't think the entire neighborhood heard yet."

Frankie appeared in black and white between me and the shed, his image transparent enough that I could see through him if I really tried. He wore a 1920s-style pin-striped suit coat with matching cuffed trousers and a fat tie. His shoulders stood level to my line of sight, which would have made him unusually tall if he weren't floating a foot off the ground.

He used his ill-gained height to full advantage as he glared down at me with those sharp features that made him look every bit like the killer he was.

"You have company," I reminded him, hoping he'd mind his manners.

"I'm laying low," he hissed, throwing his arms out like an Italian grandmother, "and you two aren't helping."

Oh dear. "What did you do now?" I asked.

"It's more like what I did eighty-five years ago," he said, looking over my shoulder. "If you see any Cuban gangsters, run."

"Do Cuban gangsters look different from the local mob?" I asked. As usual, Frankie wasn't giving me much to go on. "Should I be watching for a shifty-eyed rum swiller?"

"Don't look El Gato in the eye," Frankie warned, leveling a finger at me. "That's the easiest way to get iced. He'd kill you as soon as look at you and then kill you again."

"He's warning you about Cuban gangsters? Oh dear," my mom said, her shoulders slumping.

"It's fine," I rushed to reassure her. "He means ghost gangsters. You're perfectly safe."

"No, it's just that I was hoping I could see Frankie," my mom said, waving a hand in the general direction of the gangster. "Since he's tied to the land. I grew up in this house, you know."

And she'd been quick to leave it behind. "I don't think you have the same tie to the land that I do," I said diplomatically. Plus, I'd been the one to do the accidental ash dumping.

"It's bad enough Verity pesters me every waking second," Frankie balked. "I don't need two of you. Now get out of here and stop calling attention to my shed," he said before disappearing through the wall.

I glanced at my mom.

"Did he like the wreath?" she asked.

"Yes," I brightened, figuring I could be forgiven one little white lie. He hadn't said he *didn't* like it, after all.

She positioned the colorful homecoming decoration on the door. "Oh, look. There's already a nail."

Frankie's head whipped through the door so fast, I let out a yelp.

"Don't even think about it!" he said, his face framed by magnolias, toy footballs, and whiskey bottles.

Then he hit me with a blast of power that about knocked me sideways. My head spun as the cold energy prickled over my skin and sank down to the bone. I'd never get used to the feeling.

I could always see Frankie because it was my mistake that had grounded him, but when Frankie lent me his energy, I could see the ghostly realm the same as he did. Often, it felt like stepping back in time. At the moment, it was like standing outside a shed.

Only on the other side, my backyard lay bare.

Frankie stood in front of...open grass. At least that was how it looked from the ghostly standpoint.

"You made your shed disappear?" I marveled.

"It's right there," my mom insisted, pointing at the wreath that hung from the door on our side of the veil.

"I can decide how it looks on this side," Frankie said defensively. "And in this case, I like it invisible. Nobody can know I'm here."

"What about Molly?" I asked. "Your girlfriend is going to want you to at least take her to the homecoming dance."

The kids had their homecoming in the school gym, but because we had so many Sugarland High graduates living in town, there was also a formal alumni reunion dance in the town square. It was always a huge fundraiser for the PTO, but this year, they'd sold almost fifty more tickets than usual.

Not that ghosts needed tickets.

"Now that you have a girlfriend, you really should go," I advised Frankie. He could be so clueless in the love department. "I'm sure Molly is expecting you to ask."

He looked at me like I'd suggested he take up macrame. "What part of laying low don't you get? No one goes in or out, *and no visitors.*"

Goodness. "You really are in trouble." Frankie had never tried to hide his shed before. And he adored Molly.

Frankie cocked his chin. "You're looking at the guy who pulled off the great cigar heist of '36."

"What was that?" I asked.

"Only the most famous cigar heist of all time," he pointed out.

Amazing. "I never heard of it." Maybe I needed to watch more History Channel.

He dragged a hand through his hair. "I also set up El Gato's baby sister with a rumba dancer. They eloped."

"Aww," I crooned. "I'm all for true love."

"Yeah, well, you're not a gangster," Frankie scoffed.

As if I could forget.

He rested a hand on his hip and nudged back his jacket to reveal the ugly black revolver at his belt. "Then there was the small incident where I accidentally told the police how El Gato stole the frame off the *Mona Lisa*."

He had to be kidding. "Why the frame?"

"He's crazy that way," Frankie insisted. "He also opened a dog track with puppies. The guy is nuts. Completely unpredictable."

Wow. "I can see where a murderous gangster with no limits would be dangerous."

Frankie gave a quick nod. "I'm number twelve on his revenge list, and he just polished off the guy at number eleven."

That didn't sound good. "Maybe he'll take a break." I hoped.

"Maybe I'll wake up at the bottom of the river, wearing cement shoes," he said, eyes narrowing.

"You'd be fine." It wasn't like the gangster could kill him again. Besides, the only things Frankie could permanently keep were the objects he'd died with, so the cement shoes would fade over time.

"You don't get it," Frankie said, glancing over my shoulder once more. "El Gato specializes in torture. He toys with you. He takes his time. The guy takes pride in his ability to make grown men scream."

I chewed my lip. "Okay, that could be bad." If this ghost wanted to hurt Frankie, he could make him suffer.

He took off his hat and wiped the sweat from his brow. "He tortured number seven for two decades before the guy escaped into the light. I don't want to go to the light." His voice creaked. "I'm not ready."

Nobody should be forced to make a choice like that. And I didn't want to lose Frankie yet—not unless he was willing to go. This was starting to get scary. "Are you sure he's coming for you?"

He planted the hat on his head once more. "Suds and some of the gang saw El Gato this morning in the town square."

Right in the heart of Sugarland.

Frankie lowered the brim of his hat. "He was asking questions about me."

"We'll keep you safe," I vowed, taking the real-world wreath off the door. It wasn't entirely necessary. Frankie could make the wreath disappear in the ghostly realm, as he had the shed. But I wanted to show him I was willing to do my part.

"What's going on?" my mom pressed. "He doesn't like the wreath?"

I'd almost forgotten she was there.

I glanced to Frankie. "Well, Frankie ticked off a Cuban gangster."

"By pulling off the greatest cigar heist of all time," he added, as if that justified it.

"And now El Gato is in town for revenge, so Frankie can't have a homecoming wreath."

"That's a shame," my mom said.

"We'll put it on my front door," I said, glad for one problem I could solve.

"So Frankie isn't coming to the time-capsule opening tonight?" my mom asked, hesitating when I made a move to leave the gangster to his hiding.

"I am a time capsule, lady," Frankie shot back. "Besides, I'm working on a plan," he assured us, his image fading. "I'm talking intrigue. Explosions! And little tiny Cuban gangster bits."

Could you even blow up a ghost? I didn't want to know. Frankie's last big plan had ended with him in a ghostly prison on my property. I'd scarcely survived what it had taken to get rid of it.

"Don't do anything rash," I warned the ghost.

He just laughed before his voice faded away entirely.

"I think it would be a nice gesture if you helped him with this El Gato," my mom said, taking the wreath off my hands. She began to fluff the ribbon and straighten the whiskey bottles. "I could pitch in too if you'd like."

Normally, I was all for showing I cared, but... "Frankie's plans have a way of getting out of hand. Besides, trying to solve Frankie's problems for him only leads to worse trouble." Been there. Done that. Barely survived the car chase. "Let's just enjoy homecoming."

"And trust Frankie to do the right thing," she agreed.

"Riiiight," I said, hoping I'd made the correct call.

Chapter Two

"Did you hear if Ashley Starling has made it back into town yet?" Mom asked as she brought the pecan apple salad over to the table. "Now that I've met Frankie, I can't wait for you to meet *my* best friend from town."

"I haven't heard," I said, handing her the salad tongs. So many people were back in town. "And Frankie's not my best friend."

"You do seem to spend a lot of time with him," she mused, watching me draw the tomato bacon pie out of the oven. "No offense to your ghost friend, but it sounds like Frankie is more of a troublemaker than I imagined."

She had no idea.

"Well, he did try to stash his take of the Memphis crawdad heist in my upstairs bathtub," I admitted, carrying the pie over to the hot plate on the table. "Those crawdads were a rotten, stinking mess, but try convincing Frankie to let go of a haul."

The saving grace was that it had taken his deadly catch less than a day to disappear, which was good because the smell had driven me from the house.

"And what about that illegal racetrack he opened in your

backyard?" Mom countered, fetching the drinking glasses. "I told Elladee at the farm stand all about it when I was buying Frankie's wreath."

My fingers tightened on the knife as I cut the pie. "You didn't."

Elladee was nice enough, but I was half-convinced she'd opened that farm stand as a drive-by gossip station.

Mom poured the sweet tea, oblivious to my distress. "And then Elladee said Frankie couldn't possibly be stuck in your grandma's rosebushes, so I showed her pictures of the trash can in your parlor."

I yanked the knife out so sharply that a tomato wedge flew across the table. "Mom." I recoiled in horror. "Those pictures were only for you."

She went to fetch the ice. "Well, you decorated that trash can so nice this past Christmas. Oh," she added from behind the freezer door, "Elladee helped me pick out some homecoming decorations for your trash can, too."

Of all the... "Mom," I grated out. Now Elladee didn't only know about it, she was picking out bows and garlands and no doubt—a wreath.

My skunk nudged my leg. It seemed Lucy had scarfed down the wayward tomato and was licking her chops for more.

"No more treats. You got lucky," I told the skunk. "And you," I said, addressing my mother, "have you forgotten how fast gossip travels in Sugarland?" It practically galloped.

"I'd never gossip," Mom said, placing the sweet tea on the table. "I just like talking to people."

And Frankie called *me* naïve.

I took a deep breath. This was no way to start our reunion. I'd missed my mother, and despite the fact that we were two very different people, I was glad to have her here. She was family. And that meant she'd sometimes drive me crazy.

Heaven knew I'd been a handful for her at times. Like when I was out in the backyard sandbox as a child and thought I'd discovered dinosaur fossils. I'd proudly showed her my discovery, but it turned out my "rare artifacts" were just old dried-up cat droppings.

She'd laughed until I told her I'd hidden my treasure all over the house. I'd been too excited at the time to remember all the places. For months on end, poor Mom would find random cat poo in her planters or tucked behind her favorite throw pillows.

I took a sip of sweet tea and willed myself to remember nobody loved me like my mother. And I loved her.

At least I was pretty sure I still did.

I ignored the tension crawling up my back and focused on how good it felt to have her home. I smiled to myself as I tucked the pie server under the crust of the pie. My family had been serving this same recipe since, well, before my grandmother.

"I can't get over this spread," my mom said, sitting down. "You did a wonderful job, Verity. It feels so good to be home."

"Well, I missed you," I said, my heart warming as I served the first slice. My mom might be free with her opinions, a little too trusting, and a lot too chatty, but she was one of my favorite people in this world.

"Anyhow, the decorations are in the RV," she said, placing the napkin in her lap. "I told Elladee I'd send her a picture of your dolled-up trash can when we were done."

I dropped the pie server. "Absolutely not. You can *not* tell Elladee any more stories, much less show her one more picture of how I dote on my ghost."

She seemed genuinely puzzled at that. "Why not? You're showing him Southern hospitality, and that's a good thing."

"Mom…" I began, fighting the urge to rub at the ache beginning to pound between my eyes. "Some things are private. The entire neighborhood doesn't need to know my business."

She gave me the same interested, yet uncomprehending look Lucy did when I cut her bananas and explained the intricacies of skunk nutrition. She wanted to get it, but she simply couldn't fathom what on earth I was going on about.

Or how it applied to her.

I passed her a small salad bowl. "I'm starting to gain some acceptance as a ghost hunter." I'd done a lot of good and even solved some mysteries along the way. I was slowly becoming an asset instead of the crazy girl who talked to thin air. "The people in this town don't need to know how I do what I do, and they absolutely don't need to hear the entire story of how I dumped Frankie's ashes in my rosebushes," I explained, willing her to understand.

Her eyes widened. "Whoops."

The bowl thudded to the table. "What do you mean, 'whoops'? Who did you tell?"

"Oh, nobody," she said, with a weak wave of the wrist, not fooling me for a second. "Have some salad," she said, serving me from the big bowl.

"Mom..." I pressed.

"Only Elladee and her cousin at the farm stand, along with a few customers," she had the grace to wince, "and Bob at the gas station."

I'd solved plenty of murders, but I never understood why people killed until now.

She started serving me extra apples, as if that would make up for it. "Oh, and Carl's brother and the guys from Roan's." More and more apples piled on top of my greens. "Donald's wife, Peggy, who stopped by with sticky buns."

"Mom—" I didn't even know where to begin. Not only about her complete lack of discretion in the ten minutes it should have taken her to drive through town, but also if she served me one more apple, they were going to start toppling out of the bowl.

She gave up on the salad service. "Well, I think it's wonderful how you tried to free your gangster by dumping the soil mixed with his ashes into that baby pool in the backyard." She pressed her hands together and brought them to her chin. "And how you added water and tried to skim his ashes off the top. That's so sweet."

"You told them that, too?" I asked flatly.

"Yes," she said, hastily grabbing her fork, as if this were a normal conversation, as if we were just having lunch. "I mean, not many people would do that."

"That's my point," I told her.

I hadn't even told my best friend, Lauralee, why I'd needed to borrow her kids' turtle-shaped pool. Or why I'd commandeered the sand shovels. I'd been desperate to free Frankie, and it hadn't worked anyway.

Mom stared guiltily at the tomato pie in front of her, the one I'd worked so hard to make. "I also told them how nice you were to take Frankie to see all his friends at the speakeasy." She placed her fork on the table. "You're good for him. You're *good*, period. I don't know why you're ashamed of that."

She was going to be the death of me. Or at least my fledgling reputation as a serious ghost hunter. "Why didn't you just tell them about the time Frankie and I broke into the First Bank of Sugarland?"

She blinked hard. "Did you tell me about Frankie robbing banks? I don't remember."

To be fair, Frankie tried to rob a lot of things.

"In any case, I told them only the nice things," she said, waving the fork like she could use it to clear the air. "Like how you take him to visit his ghost friends in Resurrection Cemetery. About that proper 1930s gentleman who died wearing only his underwear."

"He was a hit man." And hardly proper.

"Well, what about his sweet girlfriend who died holding the bar cart," she said, stabbing her pie so hard a chunk of tomato went flying. It fell to the floor to the sound of scrambling skunk claws. "I mean, I'm not a big drinker, but how lucky is that?"

"Stop," I ordered. She couldn't just tell stories and fling tomatoes and have her way whenever she decided to buzz into town. "These are not your secrets to tell." This was my life, not another one of her crazy adventures.

"Fine. I'll won't share anything new or exciting in our lives," she said, taking her fork and poking at her uneaten tomato pie.

"My life," I corrected.

"I don't mean any harm. Honestly, I don't," she said, spearing a bite. "I'm only being social. I mean, there's only so many times I can tell them how when you were little, you called 911 because the clown on *The Wiggles* stole a cake."

That again? "Dad taught me to call 911 if I saw someone doing something illegal," I said tightly.

"And you listened," she said, startled as Lucy jumped up in her lap, still wearing her cheerleading uniform.

"Why do you have to tell stories at all?" I demanded.

"They just pop out!" she shot back, as if she had no control whatsoever.

Lucy flinched, and my mom went soft in an instant. "I'm so sorry," she said to my skunk, stroking her silky ears as Lucy gobbled up the bite of tomato pie that had fallen from her fork. "Honestly, Verity, you worry too much what other people think."

Easy for her to say. "I have to live in this town. *You* left."

She stiffened, her lunch forgotten. "Is there something you'd like to say?" she asked, trying—and failing—to cover the hurt in her voice.

I think on some level, she always felt bad about how she'd up and left me and my sister so soon after my grandma died. It was as if we'd lost our entire extended family support network in the space of a few weeks.

But I didn't blame her. Much. In any case, I didn't expect her to sacrifice her life or her happiness for me.

I returned my unused fork to the table. This wasn't how I'd wanted our lunch to go, with the salad ignored and the pie going cold.

I took a sip of ice-cold sweet tea. "I'm glad you're back," I said, gently returning my glass to the table. I meant that, even if she did like to overshare. "And I do wish you lived here, but I know how much you love your travels, and I'd never want to clip your wings."

She nodded, her gaze flicking to mine. "Are you happy?" It was a quiet question.

"Yes." It was the truth. "I love my life. I love it here in Sugarland."

"Then that's all that matters," she said, reaching out to cover my hand with hers. "The rest of it's only window dressing, darlin'."

That simple gesture, that touch felt good.

"Let's start over," she said, patting me on the hand.

I found myself nodding. "I missed you, Mom."

"I miss you every day. Your sister, too. You and Melody are the only reason I come back at all." She drew away. "I don't mean to interfere with the relationships or the reputation you're building here in town," she said, taking a sip of sweet tea. "It's just that I'm proud of you."

"But—"

"But I won't share anymore," she promised. "I'd never want to upset you. But I want you to enjoy your life for you and not for anybody else."

"That's exactly what I'm doing," I said, picking up my fork.

"Good," Mom stated, finally trying a bite of lunch. "This tomato pie is divine," she added. And she was right about that. The basil crust was crisp, the cheese melted perfectly with the bacon and tomatoes.

I smiled. "We both forgot our salad."

"Well, you know I always go for the pie first." Mom winked. "Life is short." Tomato pie was her favorite, and she wasn't shy about it.

Maybe she had a point about letting the crazy flag fly, or at least letting go of some of my secrets. When it came down to it, I didn't always need to worry as much as I did. I had a wonderful home. Friends. A boyfriend who loved me.

Why should I care if people thought I was one banana short of a bunch?

The cold truth wound in my stomach.

Because my ghost-hunting adventures were real and dangerous, and I deserved to be taken seriously.

I also wanted to fit in more than she ever had, and some things—private things—made that harder. I didn't want to air my business, or my rosebush trash can decorations, all over town.

"This pecan apple salad is perfect," Mom said, digging in.

When we couldn't eat another thing, Mom helped me pack up the substantial leftovers.

"We should take this to your sister," she said, sealing the lid on the Tupperware pie keeper.

Melody was working today, manning the library booth at the Welcome Home celebration. She probably hadn't found time for lunch.

"Ellis is down there, too," I said, packing up the rest of the banana pudding, eager for my mom to spend some time with my guy.

"The last time I was in town, you were about to walk down the aisle with his brother," she said, opening the cabinet under the sink.

My thumb went into the pudding. "Certainly don't say that to him."

"You think he's not aware?" she asked, drawing out a hemp bag to store the leftovers.

Maybe I didn't want her to spend time with my guy.

"Anyhow, I can't wait for you to meet my friend Ashley," she said, shaking out the bag. "Ask her to tell you about the time she thought she had study hall and ended up skipping math class for the first week of the semester." Mom giggled to herself. "I was horrified for her. But in true Ashley fashion, she waltzed into math class like nothing happened. She got an A, too."

She sounded like she could be friends with Frankie. "What's she doing now?"

"Something fabulous, I'm sure," Mom said, fetching the leftovers.

"Wait. She's the one who left town instead of being home-coming queen, right?" I asked, licking the pudding off my thumb.

"Oh, she was crowned queen at the football game." My mom let me past to wash my hands. "No girl worth her salt would miss that. But the crown was barely on her head and she skipped town to start her new life," Mom said sadly, still amazed. "On the night of the big dance, too. I mean, yes, she kept talking about her secret love—how they were writing letters and how they were going to run off to Vegas together, but I didn't think she'd actually do it."

"And I can't believe anyone kept a secret around you," I teased.

"I know, right?" she asked, tossing me the dish towel. "But that's Ashley. She'd get an idea and—poof—she'd go with it." She leaned a hip against the counter. "I always wanted to be like her."

I'd say she was succeeding.

"And I'd like to see who she ended up with," Mom said, packing the leftovers in the bag while I dried my hands. "All I know is it wasn't anybody from Sugarland."

"Well, the party's started already," I said, rehanging my dish towel nice and neat. "Let's go."

Chapter Three

A s we drove up Main Street, we hit a traffic jam—an actual backup of cars leading to the town square. It was wonderful. I'd never seen so many people eager to celebrate Sugarland.

Homecoming was always a big deal, but this year, it bordered on epic.

"Phyllis!" My mom cranked down the passenger window of my car and waved to a woman walking past the historic brick storefronts with her family. She had short dark hair and wore a red and white scarf.

"Tilly!" The woman waved big, and I half-thought she was gearing up to set off through traffic to see us. Then one of the little boys she was with shouted, "Grandma!" and pointed to the cakes in the window of A Bun in the Oven.

Phyllis settled for another excited wave as traffic started up again, and Mom nearly fell out the window greeting a bearded Abe Ryther, who'd pulled up beside us on a motorcycle decorated with red and white Christmas lights. He had tied helium balloons to his helmet. He looked ridiculous—and wonderful.

"Abe married my friend Niki." Mom craned back toward me.

"I know all about Abe and Niki," I reminded her as she nearly fell out the window again.

"How is Niki?" she asked Abe.

"Already in the square," he said, "probably looking for you. Glad to see you back." He leaned his head down. "Hey, Verity," he said, acknowledging me.

"Looking fine, Abe," I said.

He winked and responded with a tug on a balloon.

We drove on and barely found a parking spot in front of one of the fancy old houses a few blocks north of downtown.

The crisp fall air swirled leaves around our feet as we set off down a sidewalk shaded by thick oak trees. Music echoed from the town square, and I couldn't help humming along to Garth Brooks's "Friends in Low Places."

Everybody and their brother packed the blocks leading up to the square, and I reveled in walking with the crowd as we made our way to the heart of Sugarland.

The buildings in this part of town had been constructed at a time when every door and window was considered a work of art. While they'd used brick and wood for Main Street, the town square had been done in white limestone.

Mom scanned the crowd like she was Tommy Lee Jones hunting the fugitive. "Keep an eye out for Ashley," she said, waving at a pair of ladies her age, who honked at us from a passing convertible.

"I'm not even sure what she looks like." I'd seen high school pictures and that was it.

"That's okay. I'll introduce you," Mom said, following the crowd left off Main and toward the lush, green town square. "I'm sure she's back in town by now. She was head cheerleader as well as homecoming queen, and it's not like the chair of the time-capsule committee could skip the opening."

I loved that there was an actual crowd to search.

The scents of baking dough, fried corndogs, and fresh popcorn almost made me forget I'd just eaten.

"Ashley gave me this necklace," Mom said, fiddling with the gold pendant at her neck. "I know it sounds crazy, but I always thought I'd see her even before today. Like I'd turn around at the Grand Canyon or in some little shop in Maine and she'd be there."

Mom always loved an adventure. And I supposed Ashley had too, or she wouldn't have run off.

Food and craft vendors ringed the square, with a main stage set up in the middle, near the statue of our town founder on a horse.

"Weren't you friends with Colonel Larimore's three-times great-grandson?" Mom asked.

"I was," I hedged, "until that day I invited him home for fresh-baked sugar cookies and lemonade."

"What boy doesn't like lemonade?" Mom scoffed, pausing at the Band Boosters fried corn stand.

She really didn't remember. "Sixth grade. We barely even knew how to flirt. His mom took us to the movies and then agreed to drop us back to our place, and do you remember what he saw flapping in the breeze on the old laundry line? Right next to where his mom parked the family station wagon?"

"My laundry," she ventured, fighting the crowd in order to slip a few dollars into the Band Boosters' donation jar.

"My training bras," I reminded her. Pinned in a line stretching from the front porch post to the walnut tree. "His mom made him get out of the car and pretend not to notice. If the wind had blown wrong, he would have gotten thwacked in the head."

Not only had I been a late bloomer, but she had advertised it to the neighborhood. Not to mention my budding first boyfriend.

"Everybody does laundry," she said, poo-pooing my junior

high drama and leading me over to the Rotary Club fried pickle booth.

"I never invited Cyrus Larimore over again," I said. In fact, I'd avoided him entirely.

Who shows a boy their bra on the first date? Not to mention a bra lineup.

"You always did worry too much about what other people think," Mom mused.

And she didn't worry enough.

"If I wasn't so stuffed, I'd suggest we try the fried pickles," Mom said, artfully changing the subject.

"Or the PTO funnel cake stand," I said, going along with it, determined to have a good day out with my mom. She always tried her best, and so did I. "In the meantime, let's get these leftovers to Melody," I suggested. The hemp bag slung over my arm was starting to get heavy.

It took nearly an hour to make it across the square to the library booth. Between us, we saw everyone we'd ever wanted to see from grade school, the First Baptist Church of Sugarland, and the old neighborhood where I grew up.

The clock tower on city hall had begun to chime three o'clock by the time we made it to Melody.

They'd set up in front of the historic Sugarland Library, which was a slice of town history in itself. You could still see the Civil War cannonball embedded in the white limestone wall to the right of the wide steps leading up to the front door.

Melody's blonde ponytail—tied with a red silk flower—was easy to pick out among the small squad of librarians manning the display on *Sugarland Homecoming Throughout the Years*. This year's crown jewel stood on a podium at the center—a football signed by every member of the current team.

Melody dodged it as she ran to give Mom a hug. "You made it!" A second later, she eyed my hemp bag. "And you brought me tomato pie!"

"How on earth did you know?" I asked, handing her the bag.

"My neighbor Sue saw you shopping yesterday," she said, digging through the bag. "Ohhh...pie and salad and pudding! I'm taking a break," she called to a woman with short gray hair and red glasses, who told her to go.

"I'd have figured you'd fill up on fair food," I said, joining her on the wide concrete steps leading up to the library.

"This is healthier," she said, cracking the lid on the tomato pie.

Technically. Although come to think of it, Melody was always a size smaller than me. Maybe she knew something I didn't.

Mom sat on the other side of my sister, and we chatted while Melody dug into lunch like she'd never tasted food before.

"Maybe I should try to cook more often," I said, watching Lucy plant her front paws on Melody's leg and do the "I'm too cute for you to ignore" dance.

I made little delicacies for my skunk all the time. But for real human people? Not so much.

"Well, you haven't been baking for him," Mom said as my police officer boyfriend strolled up. His tan and black deputy sheriff's uniform fit over his broad shoulders like a dream, and excuse me if I got a bit of a thrill from the gun belt around his lean hips. "No tummy on that one," Mom added as she stood to greet him. "You grew up real handsome, Ellis."

"Thank you, Tilly." Ellis grinned, showing off the dimple in his chin. "It's good to see you back home."

"My home has six wheels and an escape hatch out the back," Mom said proudly.

"I'm starting to envy you there," Ellis said, running a hand through his short dark hair as two boys dashed through the library display, nearly toppling the football off its stand.

"Watch it!" the librarian with the red glasses called after them.

"I'll have a talk with them, Jean," he said to her before turning back to us. "What is it about homecoming that makes this town go nuts?"

"I think it's nice that people are so happy," I said. A dad and his son had taken a seat next to Melody, and I watched him show the boy how to bite into a caramel apple.

Ellis was less enamored. "The mayor's convertible for tomorrow's parade went missing, and you know who had it? His son. We caught him drag racing it down by the river with half the class of 2021."

I hated to say it, but that was kind of a homecoming tradition, too.

He rested a hand on his hip. "On the way over to talk to you, I caught a group of high school kids drinking Fireball behind the Baptist church bake sale booth."

"I remember when we used to smoke back there," my mom mused happily.

"And Tonya Jefferson's goat ate the entire C and L off the garden club's *Class of 2021* display," Ellis said, exasperated.

My mom snickered at that, which set me off, too. "I'm sorry, Ellis."

A grin tickled the corner of his lips despite himself. "All I'm saying is homecoming hits and every kid in this town under eighteen goes nuts. Half the parents do, too." He reached down to pet Lucy. "I had to cite David Cornell and Fred Portman for having a bottle-rocket duel by the soon-to-be-demolished flagpole, and they're both in their forties. Everybody is a teenager this week."

I caught a flash of white and brown through the crowd behind him. "I think I just spotted Tonya Jefferson's goat." Wearing a Sugarland football jersey, no less.

"See you later," Ellis said, jogging over to have a chat with the goat, and probably Tonya, too.

"You understand why I need banana-pudding therapy," Melody said from the steps as she tipped the lid off dessert.

Lucy danced on her hind legs, her front paws planted firmly on my sister's leg. And I could see why—there was no hiding the tomato pie crust crumbs in Lucy's whiskers.

"I think the crazy makes it more fun," Mom stated with a grin, her smile fading as Ellis's brother, Beau Wydell, snapped our picture.

"It would be a lot more fun without your ex-fiancé," Mom grated out, not too quietly, either.

Beau was almost as handsome as his brother, only blond instead of dark. But the main difference was that Beau was the type who was born on third base and thought he'd hit a triple.

"He's actually okay now," I murmured back, making sure to greet him nicely.

Beau was trying to be a better person. Although change didn't always stick when it came to the charmed youngest son of the Wydell clan, I was willing to give him the benefit of the doubt—especially after the way he'd helped me explore a haunted theater on my last adventure.

"Where's Virginia?" my mom asked him, by way of greeting.

Virginia Wydell, the ice queen of Sugarland and mother of both my boyfriend and ex-fiancé, had nearly ruined me after I'd called off my wedding to Beau. And she didn't appreciate me dating Ellis, either.

Beau hitched his camera up on his shoulder. "My mom is boycotting the events entirely. Officially, she's above all this silliness. But if you ask me," he said, leaning conspiratorially close, "she's just put out because she was never elected home-coming queen."

Yet another reason to love homecoming.

Tonya's goat ran by, chased by the president of the garden club and a half-dozen elementary school kids. Beau ran off to take a picture.

The goat cornered and clipped the edge of the library display, sending pictures toppling. "Vincent van Goat!" Melody exclaimed. "I already warned Tonya twice about him."

"Finish your lunch," Mom ordered as we dashed to go rescue my sister's display.

"It's not bad," I called back to Melody and Lucy. Mom and I retrieved a half-dozen photos and began setting them back on the table.

"At least you're well behaved," Melody said to Lucy, flipping her a bit of tomato.

I righted the Class of 1972 group photo, straightened a few homecoming queens, and... "Hey," I said, looking at the last framed photo. "Look, it's you, Mom." She wore a metallic green dress with a black lace overlay and large poufy sleeves. But it was the mass amounts of blonde permed hair that truly caught my eye. "Your bangs are six inches tall!" It was unnatural.

And a little scary.

"It was the style." She plucked the photo from me. "I'll have you know, I was almost entirely responsible for Aqua Net's record profits that year."

"And the hole in the ozone," I added. "Who's that blonde next to you?" I asked, pointing to a girl in a blood-red dress with even poufier sleeves. If my mom had used half a can of Aqua Net, this girl had used the rest.

"That's Ashley." She ran a finger down the glass. "I forgot we wore matching blue eyeshadow," she clucked. "Bought it at the dollar store. Sparkling Indigo Mist."

I checked it out, and it was very...blue.

"We listened to the *Dirty Dancing* soundtrack over and over while we got ready at my house. Now your house," she gushed. "We ran out of power outlets and had to plug in the boom box in the hallway."

I could just imagine both of them crammed in my upstairs bathroom.

Mom brought a hand up to her cheek. "Goodness. I still feel like the girl in this picture, but I sure don't look like that anymore. How's Ashley going to recognize *me*?"

"Well, we can always stop by the drugstore and pick up a can of hair spray," I teased. "We can fan your bangs up and she'll recognize you, no problem."

"I've been meaning to change up my look," Mom said, almost daring me as she placed the photo back on the table.

She would, too.

We kept Melody company until she finished her lunch and then said our goodbyes for the moment, fully intending to wander the square.

In actuality, we ran into more friends and neighbors and didn't make it much past the library display. After an hour or two, I found Lucy a clump of bushes at the side of the library while my mom stood out front, chatting with a friend from her days answering phones at the *Sugarland Gazette*.

I shook the wrinkles from my skunk's outfit while she took care of other things. She was on her way back over to me when she froze in her tracks.

I felt it, too. The chill of a ghost.

It took me by surprise, mainly because I'd forgotten Frankie had left his power on.

"Hello?" I asked, the hair on my arms prickling.

I tried to prepare for whatever I'd see next, but I wasn't ready for it when an orb shot up from the ground at my feet. "Whoa there!" I jumped back.

The gray, swirling ball of light surged toward me, hovering right at my eye level, flickering with bits of color. "Um, hey," I managed, wishing I could have this one day off.

A wet, ghostly gasp pierced the air as the image lengthened into the gray, swirling shadow of a young woman.

"Molly," I said, relaxing as Frankie's girlfriend took form in front of me. I hadn't seen her in ages.

"Verity?" My mom called, a hand braced on the corner of the library. "Who are you talking to back there? Is it a ghost?" she asked, with relish.

"Just Lucy," I promised. "Why don't you go talk to Kay Roan?" Carl's aunt always had something to say. "I think I saw her by the autographed football."

Mom wandered off while I turned my attention to the apparition.

She wore a black Civil War-era dress with lace detailing on the long sleeves and high neck. Molly had always been exceptionally pretty. Delicate, too, with an upturned nose and perfect bow lips.

"I didn't mean to be rude." She blushed, bringing a hand to her sweet, roundish face. "I've been trying to get your attention, but you've been...distracted."

"There's so much to see and do at homecoming," I said, by way of explanation. "I'm always glad to see you, though." Even if it meant, in this case, that Frankie had left me plugged in.

She gathered her composure. "I need to speak with you in private."

"Whatever Frankie did, he didn't mean it," I said, cutting her off. The gangster had been pushing her away lately, even though she was the best thing that had happened to him since I'd lost his ashes under a rosebush.

"The issue with Frankie is...well," she said, wringing her hands. "He hasn't done anything. He never stops by to see me. He doesn't invite me over." She gulped. "If he wants to end it, he needs to say so."

"No," I said quickly. Losing her would break his heart, even if he was too dumb to realize it at the moment. "He can't stop by without me, and I've had him busy on too many ghost-hunting cases." Not to mention the heartbreak he'd recently been through with his brother. "Give him time to make it up to you."

She closed her eyes. "I've given him too many chances

already." She glanced down at the skunk, who passed straight through the folds of her dress while sniffling the grass. "He's broken too many dates, too many promises. I know when it's over," she added. "Although I will miss him." Her voice broke. "I'll miss coming to see you."

This was worse than I'd thought. "Frankie cares about you," I insisted. He just didn't always remember what was important until it was right in front of him. "He's hiding out now," I explained. "Some gangster's after him."

"How horrifying." She drew a hand to her chest.

Yes, well, she'd have to get used to gangster drama if they were going to stay together. "I'm sure he wants to see you." He always enjoyed it when she stopped by, even if she was too old-fashioned to pursue him without an invitation. "Come by tomorrow. You'll see." Frankie always came around when he spent time with Molly. They could make up. Talk out their issues. "He'll be so glad to see you."

Hope shone in her eyes. "I could bring him a picnic lunch," she said hopefully.

"He'd love that." He would. "Don't give up on him."

She deserved to be happy, and so did the cranky gangster.

"All right," she said, growing excited. "I accept your invitation. I would be most pleased to visit you both."

Both? About that… "It's so sweet of you to include me, but I'll be heading to the Sugarland High School open house," I informed her. It started at noon. "So you and Frankie will be alone."

"Oh my," she said, her ghostly pale cheeks flushing a darker shade of gray.

I knew that look. She was more intrigued than scandalized.

Lucy pulled at her leash, eager to rejoin the party. "I'd better get back. But I'm glad you could talk to me," I added.

"Me too." Molly pursed her lips together. "Thank you, Verity," she added before she faded away.

"At least we know Frankie doesn't have homecoming plans for tomorrow," I said to Lucy as I slipped her back into her cheerleading outfit.

Perhaps he'd have fun at home after all.

Lucy twitched her tail in agreement while I double-checked the bow on her head. "Let's go."

When we at last found my mom again in the square, she was telling Joyce Guo from the *Sugarland Gazette* about the time I fended off an angry spirit from Chicago by showing him my ghostly peach orchard. "I think it's time to go," I said, leading her away.

"You told that story yourself," she reminded me, waving goodbye to Joyce.

"To you," I clarified. "I need to be able to trust you, or I won't be able to tell you anything." And that would be terrible because she was mostly out of my life anyway with her traveling. If I couldn't tell her the honest-to-God's truth about what was really happening with me, then we'd be no better than small-talk acquaintances.

I stopped walking. I took her hands and looked into her eyes. "Promise me, Mom."

It was clear I'd startled her. "Of course." She nodded sharply. "I promise. I simply forgot," she added quickly, by way of apology.

I released the breath I'd been holding. "Okay." I hoped that would be the last time we'd need to worry about it. "It's about time to see the opening of the time capsule anyway," I added, moving on to a more pleasant topic as we worked our way over to the high school with the crowd.

This was where you could tell the locals from the out-of-towners. While a half-dozen or so people struggled to work their way back to Main Street to start going north and over to Second Street to the high school, the locals went the opposite way, toward the thick line of trees beyond the east edge of the square.

There were several cut-throughs, although it did take a bit more time with everyone taking turns. Once we made it through, then all we had to do was stroll past the bleachers and the Sugarland Biscuits scoreboard to the flagpole that stood between the church of football and the high school.

"The school looks so nice," Mom gushed, admiring the bunting along the stone-trimmed windows of the red-brick high school.

Built in the early 1900s, Sugarland High had been built to last.

The high school marching band formed a semicircle behind a small wooden grandstand built next to the flagpole and played "Walk Like An Egyptian."

"This song's from my graduation year," Mom gushed as we joined the crowd. "Class of 1986!" she hollered to nobody in particular.

"Class of 1986!" scattered voices answered, like mock-ingbirds.

"We need to have our own reunion," she said, sighing with satisfaction.

"You did. Every five years." She'd skipped them all.

A hastily hammered fence made of two-by-fours kept the onlookers at a distance, even as they signed their names on the wood and wrote all kinds of homecoming messages.

I picked Lucy up and hugged her close so she wouldn't get stepped on in the excitement.

The time capsule had been a hit from inception. They'd origi-nally planned for a modest-sized box of mementos, but Sugar-land did nothing modestly. The town hall staff alone had filled the original box.

Then the school collected donations—a box from each class. Add to that donations from the Elks Lodge, the Downtown

Business Association, the Silver Seniors Club, the four main churches, the Rotary, the Kiwanis, Lions, Optimists, Betas, and Jaycees. Luckily, Abe Ryther's construction company had not only been the low bidder for the time capsule build, but Abe was just starting out and eager to make an impression. He'd taken charge of the job and gone the extra mile for free. Instead of digging a cubbyhole, Abe had poured a vault.

"There's the mayor," Mom said, pointing out the bald head of Mayor Crews as the band launched into "The Final Countdown" by Europe. "It should be starting soon."

"I can't see a thing," I confessed. For the first time, I envied my mom's platform heels.

Ellis slipped in next to me as the mayor took to the podium to welcome the crowd.

"Taking a break?" I asked, my heart warming to know he'd found me amid the crazy.

He drew an arm around me, and I could smell his spicy aftershave. "Everyone's in one spot for the moment," he murmured into my ear. "Besides, you're harboring a wild animal. I thought that called for a personal investigation."

I smiled up at him. "You have something on your lip."

"What?" he asked, surprised as I gave him a sweet kiss.

I caught my mother beaming at us when I pulled back.

I leaned into Ellis as he laced his fingers with mine. I'd found a good one, and it pleased me to no end that my mom knew it.

Maybe now she'd be glad she visited.

The band finished their song, and Mayor Crews straightened his red and white bow tie and raised his hands. "Welcome to the 106th annual Sugarland Homecoming Festival and time-capsule opening!"

I clapped as hard as I could, and the crowd went wild as Barry from the electronics store and his son unveiled a huge television monitor to the right of the mayor. "That's so you all can see everything I do as we dig into this thing."

The crowd laughed and applauded as Mayor Crews donned a thick headband with a camera attached. "I'm going to use this to clean my gutters later tonight," he added, to more guffaws.

"Maybe you'll find your hair in there!" someone shouted.

"Seriously, folks. I know how pumped you are about the new football stadium, and I am, too. But I'm just as excited about tonight. We're gathered here to celebrate our past, even if it is as recent as 1985 And while we're sorry to disturb it so early, we can't wait to see what's inside."

The monitors showed blurry shots of the crowd as the mayor walked down the steps of the podium to join a smaller group inside the barriers. "Jean Norwood and Melody Long from the library are going to assist me and record our findings for posterity," he said as my sister, along with the librarian with red glasses, stepped up next to him. Melody wore white archivist gloves and stood close to a table covered in white cloth. "Is your library team ready, Jean?"

"Ready, Mayor," she said as Melody nodded.

My sister flashed a smile as she caught my eye.

The concrete had been jackhammered away from beneath the flagpole, leaving exposed a rusted hatch, wide as a cellar door.

The library janitor used a bolt cutter to slice open the padlock, and Melody stepped in wearing a pair of archivist gloves to retrieve the vintage lock.

My mom snorted. "If that's a relic, what does it say about me? I had one just like that on my locker in high school."

"Well, you know…" I said, not willing to commit to anything of my mom's being old enough to archive. "It's for posterity."

Several men on either side of the hatch used crowbars to pry it up and ease it open.

"I bet we're going to find lots of goodies inside," the mayor teased as he shone a flashlight down into the hole.

The monitors blurred for a moment as he gasped.

"What is it?" someone shouted as the crowd pressed forward.

The mayor's light passed over a rusting lockbox, a bundle wrapped in cloth, what appeared to be a discarded homecoming crown.

And fell on the body of a long-dead girl wearing a red taffeta dress.

Chapter Four

Ellis dropped my hand and rushed through the crowd, toward the time capsule. Mom followed in his wake.

The camera had come to a halt over the body, the television monitor glaring with the image of rotted skin over white bone.

The body looked like it had been in the capsule a long time, and I stood stunned because I'd seen that dress before. It was the same dress Mom's friend had worn in that photograph at the library display.

I clutched my skunk and dodged my way to the front. With the wide sleeves on the gown, not to mention the crown and the wisp of blonde hair that clung to the skull, I had to admit the figure looked a lot like the picture I'd seen of Ashley Starling.

My mother had never run into Ashley at the Grand Canyon or seen her old friend on any of her adventures. Ashley had never made it out of Sugarland.

By the time I got to the front, Ellis had taken control of the crime scene. I stood behind the wooden barrier fencing with my mother while Ellis charged up to the podium and took the microphone.

"Stand back, everyone," he ordered. "No pictures or video,"

he added to the dozens of people who'd whipped out their phones. And as Ellis pulled his own phone out of his pocket to call in our gruesome discovery, he added, "Think of how you'd feel if this was your sister or daughter."

The woman next to me lowered her phone. "He's right," she said, erasing the footage. "That poor girl."

Mom stared down into the time capsule in disbelief. "Oh, Ashley," she murmured.

"I'm so sorry, Mom," I said, wrapping an arm around her shoulders, letting her lean on me for a change.

"They sealed it up the night of the big dance," Mom said, unable to remove her gaze from her friend's body. "That was the night she said goodbye to me." She shook her head, unable to comprehend it. "She was so excited. She was going to run away and be happy." Mom pulled away and turned to me. "What happened?"

"I don't know," I said, shaking my head.

I hoped Ashley hadn't been buried alive in that time capsule.

Lucy wriggled in my arms. She didn't like being held when there were interesting smells to investigate all around. I absent-mindedly readjusted her, focused on Police Chief Royce and Senior Detective Pete Marshall making their way up to the scene.

Mom shook her head. "When she wouldn't give me details, I simply thought she was dating a guy from the wrong side of the tracks, like a football player from Jackson." She sniffed and dug into her pocket for a tissue to dab her eyes. "I should have pressed harder. I didn't realize we were running out of time."

Why hadn't Ashley shared her secret? I wouldn't keep that kind of thing from my best friend, Lauralee. Although I hadn't told her everything about my ghost hunting.

I looked down into the hole to where poor Ashley lay. The camera was still on her, broadcasting her terrible fate over the big screen.

"This is my fault," Mom said grimly. "I never should have let her leave the dance by herself."

"You can't blame yourself." I wouldn't let her. "You were just a kid at homecoming."

Her eyes grew glassy with unshed tears. "I was too wrapped up in slow dancing with your father to worry about what was happening to my friend. I should have been watching out for her."

I understood girl code—never leave a soldier behind. Still... "You never could have expected this. I'm sure she wouldn't blame you."

Mom gasped and closed a hand over my arm. "You can ask her."

"Possibly, but I can't promise—" I began.

"You can let Ashley tell you what happened. You can tell her how sorry I am that I let her down."

It wasn't that easy. "Just because she's passed on doesn't mean I can contact her," I explained.

Mom had endured enough trauma for one night. I didn't want to build her hopes up that I had some kind of direct line to everybody who ever died.

Ghost hunting was complicated, to say the least. Ashley might have gone to the light years ago. And even if she hadn't, she might not be in Sugarland, even for homecoming.

Spirits only appeared when they chose. I didn't get to decide when or where—or even who.

It wasn't as if I could call up Ashley on my ghost phone.

And I really wished they'd get that camera off her. It was awful.

"Look around," Mom pressed, scanning the crowd surrounding us. "Can you see Ashley now?"

"Mom—" I began, willing her to understand.

The main camera flipped off, and the big screen went dark. Thank goodness. Deputy Officer Duranja had made it to the front and was working to keep people back while Ellis talked to the chief and the mayor.

We cooperated with the police directive and stepped away from the barriers.

"Please look," Mom pressed. "For me."

"All right." I stood on my tiptoes as we moved with the crowd, struggling to see around as many people as I could. "Ghosts have to be extremely careful among crowds of the living," I explained, scanning. As I'd expected, I saw no entities at all. "They feel icky if they touch us." It was equally as bad for me if I was tuned in and touched one of them. "But I can keep an eye out," I promised as Lucy tried to climb onto my shoulder.

I tugged her down. Unfortunately for her, she was not a parrot.

"Maybe we can get Frankie working for us, too," Mom said, taking Lucy from me as my little skunk attempted a nosedive into the crowd.

"It's been known to happen from time to time," I hedged, although usually after negotiations, threats, and at one point the building of a ghost shed. "You have to remember, at the moment, he's hiding out from the Cubans."

On the plus side, I hadn't seen any Havana-style gangster ghosts so far...not that I knew for sure what one might look like.

"Appeal to his better nature," Mom coaxed.

"He doesn't have one," I pointed out. When her face fell, I added, "I only want to keep your expectations realistic." Frankie wasn't the cooperative sort, even when he wasn't lying low. He wasn't overly keen on homecoming in general. And the only reason I could see ghosts now was that he'd been twitchy lately and neglected to shut his power off. "Frankie is an entity unto himself."

"So are you," she reminded me.

"I appreciate that." I did. Mom had always believed in me.

"But remember that you have Ellis on the case, and he's a great police officer. There's also Senior Detective Marshall and Officer Duranja." Those two might not like me much, but they were good at their jobs. "Lots of people in Sugarland want to help."

The crowd had stopped retreating. In fact, many had begun to circle around us and back toward the murder scene.

"Ellis is lovely," my mom said, catching my arm as she stumbled over an uneven patch of ground. "I trust him with my friend's life. I do. But we need to use every resource we have."

Microphone feedback screeched over the crowd as Detective Marshall stepped up to the middle of the podium. Behind him, the chief stood with the mayor, their heads close, talking intensely. Ellis joined them, frowning.

Marshall ran a hand through his sparse hair, his cheeks ruddy. "Ladies and gentlemen, please vacate the crime scene in an orderly fashion."

"Good luck with that," I said to myself.

The crowd had dug in like ticks. It was to be expected. A gaggle of at least a hundred had gathered to watch the Shelby Funeral Home burn down last year. Now Detective Marshall had five times that many people in a festival mood, and a dead body in a time capsule.

In fact, if I wasn't mistaken… I stood on my toes and craned to see. "I think there are more people coming down Second Street toward us."

Word must have spread.

"Please," the mayor said, nudging his way in front of the microphone. "Folks, we need you to disperse. This is someone's child. Let's show some respect to the family."

My mom hugged Lucy tighter. "I wish we could talk to Ashley's mom." She gasped. "Maybe we can. She passed five years ago this past spring."

I was not the Psychic Friends Hotline. "We're going to do our best, but please don't get your hopes up."

But Mom wasn't listening. "Now she's gone, and Ashley's gone, and there's nobody even left. Ashley really doesn't have anyone else to watch out for her."

"We'll do everything we can," I pledged, which wouldn't be much unless I could get Frankie on board.

Ellis grabbed the microphone off the holder. "Anyone who doesn't clear the high school property in the next fifteen minutes is banned from the rest of the homecoming celebration."

The crowd froze.

Ellis looked at his watch. "Starting...now."

That got them going.

The good citizens of Sugarland retreated like a slow wave, dragging us along with them.

"Let's get you home," I said to Mom, who'd buried her chin against Lucy's fluffy head.

She paused, looking back at the hole in the earth. "Goodbye, Ashley," she said softly before walking away. "We'll make this right," she promised as I led her down Second Street toward Main. "I won't let you down again."

We'd do our best. "At least we found her," I said, hoping to offer some comfort. "Her body, that is." At least we knew she was gone.

"We'll find her again, Verity," Mom vowed.

"I hope." Still, lots of ghosts went to the light and never returned again. I'd never seen my grandmother or my father. It had been a thrill enough to meet my great-grandmother's long-lost love. Never mind the fact that he'd scared me out of my wits and driven Frankie to try to live out of my coat closet.

Mom let a struggling Lucy down to the sidewalk, and the skunk darted ahead on her leash, reveling in her freedom.

"Ashley's *got* to be here in Sugarland," she said. "I felt her this afternoon. I can't explain it," Mom said, tossing her hands up. "But I know she was near."

"I understand," I said as we reached the car. "I do."

Who was I to doubt her? I knew firsthand how our loved ones could come back to us.

But I couldn't talk to Ashley unless she revealed herself. I also had to make sure I kept Frankie's power. I opened the door, and Lucy hopped in, completely bypassing the crate I had for her in the back.

"I've got her," Mom said, sliding into the passenger seat and gathering the skunk into her arms. "So let's do this," she said, slamming the door. "How do we find a ghost?"

"I usually look in the places that mean something to them," I said, firing up the engine. "Where did Ashley live?"

"It's gone now," my mom said sadly as I looked for a way to pull out amid the mass exodus. "It was torn down when they made that overflow lake by the river."

I ran my hands along the steering wheel. "Her old property is at the bottom of a lake?"

That would make it hard to talk to any ghosts lingering at home.

"It was for conservation," she said.

"Okay," I said, pulling out onto North Main. "Is there any place in town that Ashley especially enjoyed? A favorite restaurant or ice-cream parlor you'd visit together?" I asked, pausing for a family to cross the tree-lined street.

Mom rubbed Lucy as the skunk settled in her lap. "Ashley didn't have a lot of money, so we didn't hang out in town very often."

"We can try the school," I suggested. After all, she'd been seen last in the gym. Even if she wasn't there, the ghosts at Sugarland High might know more about what had happened the night she disappeared. "We'll also check the flagpole once we're allowed back on the property." Ghosts tended to haunt their death spots, and as much as I hated to think it, she might have died in that time capsule.

"They're giving homecoming tours of the school tomorrow," Mom said, stroking my skunk. Lucy had fallen asleep in her lap. "It's the annual open house."

"We'll go tomorrow. As soon as it starts." I doubted we'd get my ghost's enthusiastic help, but with any luck, Frankie wouldn't have an issue with me keeping the power on. He would be having a picnic with Molly, which should give him plenty to spare. He always had more energy when he was around her.

I gave myself a mental pat on the back for my matchmaking skills earlier.

I'd scored a point for true love and made it easy for Frankie to help out.

What could possibly go wrong?

Chapter Five

✦

An hour later, I stood in my kitchen, facing down an angry ghost.

"You lent me out," Frankie said, pacing straight through my kitchen island. "You volunteered me and my power without even asking. You know I hate it when you do that."

"Mom's friend died," I explained. He had to see reason. "At least we think it's her," I added. "In any case, there's a poor girl forgotten in the time capsule. Who would we be if we didn't do anything to help?"

Frankie gaped at me. "We'd be minding our own business!"

"I'm not sure I see the value in that," I admitted. "Not when it's a matter of life and death.

"You're not exactly saving a life, doll." He yanked the cigarette case out of his jacket pocket and flipped it open. "In case you haven't noticed, the girl's been dead for thirty-five years," he added, shoving a smoke up onto his lip.

"No smoking in the house," I said quickly.

"I think I earned it," he said, whipping out a lighter. "First, you want to blow my cover with El Gato—"

"Mom was trying to do something nice for you." And he could easily hide the wreath on the ghostly plane.

"Then you want to borrow my power when I need every bit of it to get my revenge on El Gato."

As if he hadn't forgotten and left it on today. "You'll have more power if you spend time with Molly," I reminded him. Romantic happiness seemed to give him more juice. "Plus, why are you getting revenge on this El Gato guy when you're the one who stole from him?"

"I'm teaching him respect," he said, as if it were obvious. "Besides," he said, lighting up, "revenge is fun."

"Well, I'll feel good when I help my mom and her friend," I informed him.

He took a drag. "She treats me like a sideshow, and you? You want to traipse all over Sugarland, blowing my energy on interviews with ghosts who probably don't even care about this dead dame."

"Only the high school," I clarified.

For starters.

Smoke trailed from his nose. "You want to burn through my power," he said, pointing his cigarette at me. "You want to jam your nose into everybody's business while you promise not to drag me into it, but of course you're going to drag me into it." He strolled straight through my back wall and out onto the porch.

Dang it. "Frankie—" I banged out the screened door and found him blowing smoke rings next to the white painted porch swing. "It's not like you haven't done it before."

He groaned and took a long drag.

Frankie blew the smoke out the side of his mouth as he turned to face me. "You want me to hang out at the high school. Molly wants me to take her to the homecoming dance."

"Told you so."

He gave me a long look. "Doesn't anybody care about my

delicate plan for vengeance and destruction? Or that I could get nipped by the Cubans?"

"Of course," I said, "but you've always been able to take care of yourself." It was what Frankie did best. "While you're at it, you need to pay more attention to your girlfriend," I added as he took a quick, angry drag. "She's feeling neglected and upset. Enough to pop out and scare me half to death by the library."

"What?" he asked, smoke trailing out of his nose.

"You left your power on this afternoon. Imagine my surprise when I saw her today."

He didn't appear too happy imagining it.

"I can't believe it," he said as a tingling surge whipped down my body.

"Hey—" My bones felt like liquid, and my joints went slack. I gasped and bent over, clutching my knees as he yanked his energy out of me in one fell swoop. "Real nice." He could have at least given me warning. With a shaky hand, I checked my hair, hoping it hadn't gone all staticky. "Ow!" I exclaimed as I gave myself an electric shock. Darn it. If we didn't do so much good with his power, I'd never want it again.

"Anyhow," I continued, a little light-headed as I straightened up, "I invited Molly to visit tomorrow. You two can spend some quality time together and work out your issues."

"Stop. Helping. Me," he gritted out.

"You've been ghosting her, and that's not right."

"I am a ghost!" he shouted.

I ignored his tone. "You'll thank me later," I stated, patting my hair, wincing at the way it crackled under my fingers. "Molly doesn't want you to be lonely, and neither do I." Even if he deserved it.

Frankie's eyes bugged out. "I don't want Molly anywhere near me or El Gato! And what if the Cubans show up while you're out running around the high school? I'll be trapped on this property. If Molly won't leave, I'll be stuck defending her, too. We'll be sitting ducks!"

I hadn't seen any Cuban gangster on my property so far. "You can't simply put your girlfriend on a shelf and talk to her only when it suits you." I wouldn't tolerate that kind of treatment from Ellis.

"I can if it keeps Molly out of trouble," he snapped.

I sat primly on the porch swing, and he eyed me as if I'd decided to sit in his lap. He couldn't ignore me or Molly and expect us to go away. We were both independent women who could take care of ourselves.

"Listen." He dragged a hand through his hair. "Molly can't be involved. What if the Cubans take her hostage and hurt her? Or worse." His face fell. "El Gato is a legendary ladies' man. He seduced the wife of el presidente with his sexy salsa dancing."

"Salsa isn't overly sexy," I countered. It was a fast dance.

"The ladies swoon when El Gato does it," Frankie insisted. "When he was arrested for rum running, el presidente's wife threatened to leave her husband unless he granted El Gato a full pardon, and invited El Gato to dance with her at Club Havana."

How terrible. And insulting. "Surely he didn't?"

"What else could he do?" Frankie flung his arms out. "He was up against El Gato."

I crossed my legs. "Well, he could have found a woman who treated him right and loved him more than a salsa-dancing gangster," I said as Frankie hunched against the porch rail and began chain-smoking again.

"El Gato would just seduce the next wife. That's how he operates."

Yes, well, Frankie didn't have to play that game. And Molly certainly wouldn't. "Molly would join the circus before she'd let El Gato seduce her."

He gazed at me doubtfully. He'd smoked his cigarette down to a nub.

I planted my feet flat. "Molly loves *you.*"

"For now," he said stiffly, tossing his smoke into the yard.

Frankie turned his back and lit up another one.

How had this gotten to be such a mess? Just this morning, I'd been so excited for the perfect homecoming weekend with my mom and Ellis and everyone I cared about. Even Frankie.

Now I had a dead body under the flagpole, a mother bent on investigating, and a ghost who qualified for a slot on *Dr. Phil.*

Still, he did have a point. If he were trapped on this property when the Cubans arrived, he could be in trouble. And Molly was the type who would stay and try to help defend the shed.

Light shone from the RV parked in my back lot. Carl had arrived home shortly after my mom and me. It hadn't taken long for word of the dead body in the time capsule to travel to the guys working on the Roan's float.

Mom was hurting, and there wasn't a thing I could do about it except help her learn what had happened to her friend. I didn't relish it, but I couldn't avoid it, either.

Carl was in the RV with Mom now. She'd squired him inside as soon as he'd arrived home. It seemed he could provide her the kind of comfort I couldn't. I'd offered to let them stay in the house. They could even have my futon. But Mom wanted her own bed.

Frankie leaned back against the porch rail, watching me as he took another drag. "Molly's really coming by tomorrow?" he said, like a man facing the gallows.

"She's bringing a picnic lunch," I said. Ghosts didn't need to eat or drink, but they enjoyed it. "It was supposed to be a surprise. Maybe I could find you a secret place to meet. We could take your urn to the park or even the cemetery." I'd have to hide his remaining ashes well if I left them in a public place. Still, a covert rendezvous would be romantic—and Frankie wouldn't have to worry about El Gato sneaking up on them.

"Nothing's secret around here." Frankie took a drag. "And with you gone, I'd be stuck wherever you decided to leave me."

"Or you could zip back here." But we'd already discussed the dangers of him being unable to leave my property if the Cubans found him there.

The gangster sighed. "We got lucky today. Very lucky. If my guys hadn't spotted the Cubans in town, if I'd let Molly drag me downtown today instead of staying home to plot my revenge..." He crossed his arms over his chest. "It could have been lights out, Frankie."

I leaned back in the porch swing. "But now you know to be careful," I said, giving the swing a nudge. "None of the dead residents of Sugarland will give you up." It had been one of the reasons the mob did so well down here—the citizens of our small town protected their own. "The point is the Cubans have no idea where you live or they'd have found you already."

"True." Frankie ran a hand over his chin. "That means the weak link is you."

"Excuse me?" I sat up straight. I was one of his staunchest supporters, as evidenced by the rosebush climbing the wall in my parlor.

"It's no secret that I lend you my power." Frankie pointed his smoke at me. "Even if the dead don't say a word, the Cubans will hear the live people talking about it. Face it, the live people never *stop* talking."

He did have a point.

Frankie took a drag. "El Gato and his men will keep an eye out for the girl who sees ghosts. You draw attention to yourself, and they'll follow you straight home to me."

"Then we won't investigate the high school." I folded my hands in my lap, resigned. "I'll have to find another way to help Mom."

"We'll go," Frankie said, surprising me. "For a price."

I glanced up at him, not sure if that was good news or bad

news. Frankie wasn't the most reasonable guy to make a bargain with. "What do you want?"

The bright moon shone straight through him. He took a final drag before flinging the ghostly cigarette into my backyard. "You keep Molly away from me and out of danger until I get rid of El Gato."

I wasn't sure how I could babysit a ghost, but... "Sure," I said before he asked for anything else.

"And I want you to take the blame when I stand her up for that surprise tomorrow."

"Seriously, Frank?"

"Don't call me Frank."

"She'll be so disappointed."

He flinched. "That's on you," he snapped. "I'm not the one who made the date."

"I was trying to save your relationship!" Somebody had to.

"Do you want to take my power to the high school or not?" he prodded.

Dang. The tours began at noon, and I did want to start right away. "I suppose I can leave her a note," I said and hoped she'd understand. "But you can't keep ducking out on her like this. There's only so much disappointment a girl can take before she gives up and starts looking for a nicer guy."

Frankie pointed a finger at me. "Don't tell her where we're going. Don't help her find me. And for God's sake, talk her out of that crazy homecoming dance."

"I'll do my best," I promised. "Although I think you're making a big mistake."

I didn't know how we'd fix his love life after all of this.

Frankie chuckled low under his breath.

"What?" I asked.

"You're frowning," he said, ashing his cigarette. "Means I made a good deal."

I wasn't so sure of that. But I also didn't think he'd appreciate me worrying about him.

The lights flicked out in my mom's RV. Good. I hoped she could get some rest. With any luck, we'd get some answers for her tomorrow.

I'd have to do it without drawing attention, and then I had to figure out how to help Frankie with his gangster situation—as well as his love life.

First things first.

I stood and straightened my dress. "I just hope the high school is haunted."

Frankie cocked a grin. "Oh, it's haunted all right." He hitched a thumb in his pants pocket. "Not exactly my crowd."

"Finally, some good news."

His grin never wavered. "We'll see about that."

I heated up some soup for a late dinner and tried to call Ellis, but it went to voicemail. No doubt he was busy. So I left him a message telling him what Mom had said about Ashley Starling and her homecoming disappearance, ending it by promising I'd do what I could to help.

The police usually hated when I assisted their efforts, but Ellis understood the good I could do.

Mom declined to have breakfast with me. She'd slept in, which wasn't unusual. But she was quiet on the way to the high school, which worried me something fierce. Her hair had lost some of its fluff, and red rimmed her eyes. I snuck a glance at her as I parked my vintage Cadillac in the side lot and killed the engine.

"How are you doing?"

"Better, I think," she said, gazing up at the side entrance to Sugarland High.

Perhaps a ghost hunt would cheer her up.

Nobody ever went in the fancy front doors overlooking the wide, two-acre lawn. We all took the narrower stairs off the student parking lot to an old door that led straight into the first-floor hallway.

Today, a handmade sign taped to the brick wall next to it read: *Welcome alumni!* in red bubble letters.

I dropped my keys into my bag, where they clanked against Frankie's urn. My ghost never hung out inside the urn, so I didn't have to worry about ringing his bell. When it came right down to it, I think it squicked him out to look at his ashes.

But Frankie did have to stick fairly close to me and his remains. He'd been quiet on the ride over, but I knew he was here somewhere.

Probably plotting.

I was under no illusion that he'd agreed to this trip only to help me or merely to avoid Molly and the Cubans. Knowing Frankie, I'd bet my last nickel it had something to do with his revenge plot against El Gato. I only hoped I could search the high school before it all blew up on him.

Mom hesitated as I opened the door for her. "Ashley and I used to come this way every day on the way into school," she said, tentatively crossing the threshold. "She'd pick me up in her 1980 Impala. We called it 'the Beast.'" I let the door close behind us as we breathed in the old wood and booky smell of the school. "I can't believe she's gone."

With any luck, we'd see her again.

Or at least I would.

"I'm so sorry, Mom," I said, walking her past the metal lockers on both sides of the hall. I couldn't imagine her pain—or how I'd feel if it were my best friend, Lauralee, down in that hole beneath the flagpole.

"We'll find her," she vowed. "Just tell me what to do."

Sugarland High had been built in 1912, with wide hallways

57

and tall ceilings. The wooden doors to each classroom were original to the school, their transoms open to let in the air. Scattered voices echoed down the hall, and each classroom door stood open, welcoming visitors.

We'd start simple. "Where did you and Ashley make most of your high school memories?"

"Everywhere," she said, pausing to run her hand down the front of a locker.

"Was this hers?" I asked quietly.

"No." Mom sighed. "I shared it with Sharon Thompson. We had a huge senior class, and some of us were forced to double up. Every time I opened our locker, her old test papers would come flying out. It drove me nuts," she added with a wistful smile.

"Where were Ashley's favorite spots?" I pressed as Mom spotted an ancient teacher who couldn't have stood more than five feet tall waving from a doorway down the hall.

"Mrs. Callaway!" Mom gushed, rushing for her.

"Chantilly Garber!" The teacher clasped her hands together. "You're old enough to call me Brenda," she said, enveloping Mom in a hug.

"Tell your mom to hurry up." Frankie shimmered into view next to me, frowning. "If I get nipped in this place, I'm going to be the laughingstock of the South Town Boys."

"I know you're up to something," I said, not bothering to sugarcoat it.

"I'm always up to something," he countered, glancing up and down the hall to make sure the coast was clear before he hit me with his power. It prickled over me like a thousand tiny glass needles. Then it sank into me, down to the bone.

"I don't think I'll ever get used to this," I cringed.

"Good," the ghost said, gliding down the hall away from me, "because it's happening way too often."

It wasn't as if it was always my idea.

"I do appreciate it," I called after him, wondering not for the first time exactly how many rules Frankie was breaking by lending me his energy.

Too late to worry about it now, I supposed, flexing my tingling fingers as the pain eased and the ghostly side opened up in front of me.

I looked around slowly, taking in every dent in the old lockers, the shine of the gray marble floor. When I was tuned into Frankie's power, the ghostly side appeared in black and white over the real-life version of a place.

From where I stood now, I couldn't detect anything different.

"I thought you said this place was haunted," I called after him.

"Maybe not this particular hallway," Frankie said, never breaking his stride.

I didn't know where he thought he was going.

Maybe he was looking for ghost friends. Frankie had dropped out of school in junior high in order to pursue a life of crime, but that didn't mean he didn't have friends here. "Did any of your mob buddies go here?" I asked, catching up to him.

"Maybe the late bloomers," he said, wrinkling his nose at a homemade poster advertising tickets for the big dance.

"Oh, come on." He had to see what a special place this was. Sugarland High had launched hundreds of wonderful citizens into the world. And with any luck, they stuck close. How could they not? "Let me show you something special," I said, leading him past the classroom my mom had ducked into and down to where the hall emptied into the atrium. "This was my locker in senior year," I said, stopping in front of number 199.

He did not appear impressed.

"Only seniors got lockers on the first floor," I explained. It was a privilege. "Lauralee would wait for me by my locker, and then we'd cruise the halls before school." It was the best social time. I couldn't hold back a grin.

Frankie ran a hand over his jaw. "Yeah, my life was just like that. I used to cruise the pool halls, trying to spot the ringers. Suds would wait in the parking lot so we could stuff them in the trunk of my car."

He didn't have to mock my fun. "I was eighteen at the time."

"So was I," Frankie mused.

Fine. I peeked into the atrium. To the left stood the triple set of French front doors at the main entrance to the school. The gray marble floor was original, with an eight-pointed gold star at the base of the wide stairs leading up to the second floor.

"That's the senior star," I said, working a little too hard to impress the ghost. "Only seniors could step on it." I remembered being so proud and excited my first day of senior year, I practically danced on it. "Everybody else had to go around."

"Kind of like how you couldn't walk in the front door of Morty's Steak House unless you were a made man," Frankie mused, although I had an inkling he was making fun of me.

"Were you ever a made man?" I asked brightly, trying to relate.

"No," he said, gliding straight over the senior star.

At least he hadn't stepped on it.

"This isn't a competition," I reminded him.

"Yes, it is," he countered.

"Frankie," I began. I wanted him to understand how special this place was, but it wasn't his history—it was mine. Still, he'd shown me an entire new world these past few years, and I felt obliged to return the favor. "It's okay to have a life. You know, where you care about traditions, people, things that matter. It's not too late to make up for all the things you missed."

He removed his hat. "I'm only going to say this once. I'm not missing anything. I'm not missing high school. I'm not missing a dance. I'm *fine!*"

"People who are fine don't yell," I pointed out. "You can look on the bright side of life without giving up being a rough and tough gangster."

He looked at me as if I'd asked him to eat his hat. "Or I could be happy living in my shed, having poker nights with the guys, maybe build a nice moonshine still out by your pond—"

"Are you happy?" I broke in.

"No," he said, planting his hat on top of his head, "because you're dragging me through a high school while I'm trying to lay low. Meanwhile, you're not even watching for the Cubans. You don't care that El Gato has a bullet with my name engraved on it. Or that it reads *Frank* instead of Frankie, which you know I hate. Instead, you're trying to kumbaya me when I'm perfectly capable of—"

My phone rang, and I saw it was Ellis. "Hold that thought," I said. Frankie muttered something about thumbscrews and mental torture techniques while I answered.

"Hey, I can't talk, but I thought you should know we identified the body." Ellis's warm voice hesitated ever so slightly. "You were right. It's Ashley Starling. She had her student ID in her pocket," he added softly. "You can tell your mom, but not anybody else. Tell her I'm sorry, Verity."

Me too. "Thanks for calling." I could always count on Ellis to take care of me.

"Also tell your mom we'll need to talk to her before she leaves town. I'll be in touch."

"Of course," I said, and Ellis let me go. Mom had seen Ashley shortly before she disappeared. She might be able to shed light on the case.

Then again, maybe I could, too.

"What is it?" my mom asked, entering the atrium and skirting the senior star.

"You can walk on it," I said, putting off the inevitable. "You graduated."

"See, the way my class did it, you could only walk on it if you were an actual senior," she said, as cheerful as she'd been before yesterday's gruesome discovery.

And I was about to ruin that.

"Ellis called," I said simply. "They officially identified Ashley as the girl in the time capsule."

"Oh." She brought her hand to her mouth. "Well, I knew the moment I saw her, didn't I?" The weight of it settled over her, slumping her shoulders as she joined me at the stairs.

"Let's go look inside the gym," I suggested. It had been the last place Mom saw her friend. Maybe we would run into Ashley's ghost there.

"I'll stay here," Frankie said, trying to blend into the wall.

"I'd love it if you could come along," I said as we approached the double doors on the other side of the main staircase. "We could use you." He was still my expert on the other side.

"Sure. Because it's all about you two, and a high school gym offers plenty of cover," he said, disappearing into the plaster until only the brim of his hat poked out. "I'll make sure everything looks good from here."

Somehow, I doubted he'd be keeping an eye out for a ghost in a taffeta homecoming dress. "We made a deal," I reminded him. "I'm taking the blame for breaking your girlfriend's heart, and in exchange you promised you'd join me on this investigation."

The brim of his hat tipped toward the sky. "I guarantee this is worse than El Gato's torture," he groaned as he emerged from the wall.

Well, if that was true, it was a good thing.

"Ready?" I asked Mom.

She nodded as I opened the doors to the scent of basketball rubber and sweat.

"Aww..." I cooed. This year's dance theme was a throwback to 1985, in honor of the time capsule. Students were busy hanging a large neon pink and green banner that screamed the *Sunglasses at Night* theme in streaky black letters. Round tables decorated with pink and green tablecloths sported clear cube centerpieces filled with Pop Rocks, candy necklaces, Pixy Stix, Ring Pops, Razzles and… "Candy cigarettes?" I asked, grabbing a pack off the nearest table.

"This is what's wrong with society today," Frankie stated, reaching into his jacket pocket for the real thing.

"I always preferred the bubblegum cigars," Mom stated, pointing out a pack of pink ones.

"Maybe the Cubans have been here," I said, teasing Frankie, who had opened up his cigarette case only to find it empty.

"Can I lend you a smoke?" I asked, offering him the candy pack I held.

He lowered his hat over his forehead. "You two think you're funny, but you're not."

Mom was giggling. "Oh, I think we're a little funny," I said, nodding to her.

A group of students hung vinyl records along the back wall, which made Mom snort. "This isn't a sock hop. We had cassette tapes," she said as I watched two students hang a poster advertising Pepsi Clear.

Mom caught my stare. "It tasted like Pepsi, but it looked like Sprite."

"Why…?" I asked, trying to understand the appeal.

"I'm not sure, but I thought it was cool. You probably had to be there," she added.

I supposed so.

More students sat along the wall at the back, manning an assembly line to blow up red and white helium balloons, tying them off with silver string.

Mom led us to an area on the right, about thirty feet from the door. "This was the last place I saw Ashley," Mom said in a hushed tone so as not to attract too much attention. "She left through the main double doors as she hurried out of the dance."

"She took one look at this crazy tradition of yours and bolted," Frankie said, wrinkling his nose. "Makes perfect sense to me."

I ignored him. The Sugarland homecoming dance was the event of the year, especially for high school seniors.

"Do you…?" Mom paused, as if she was afraid to ask. "Do you see any sign of Ashley's ghost?"

"Not yet." In fact, I didn't see anything out of the ordinary unless you counted the way the current high school boys wore their hair combed over their eyes. How did they even see?

A tour group banged through the door at the back of the gym, near the stage, startling one of the balloon handlers into letting one fly.

"Maybe Ashley isn't the type to return to the gym," I suggested. She had fled the place, after all.

Mom chewed her lip and kept scanning the room, as if she'd be able to see.

"Where would you go right now if you wanted to find her?" I pressed. "What place reminds you of Ashley most of all?"

Mom snarked out a laugh. "The cafeteria," she said on a sigh. "We'd sit in there and do cross-stitch during free periods."

"Seriously?" I asked, walking her out of the gym.

"And you mocked me for joining the mob," Frankie's voice sounded from the wall.

"I was an only child. Your grandma and I would do it together," she said as my ghost slipped free to glide behind us, eyes peeled. "I taught Ashley when she came over to watch MTV. Which was all the time. We were one of the first houses in town to get cable," she added proudly.

My grandmother had possibly doted on my mom too much, I mused as we bypassed the main stairs for a smaller set that led down to the lower-level cafeteria.

Mom led the way down the steep, rubber-lined stairs. The space smelled like cooking grease. Or perhaps that was the ghostly side, because a moment later I started smelling fried chicken and okra...and was that chocolate cake?

Perhaps they were serving refreshments as part of the open house, although I hadn't seen any mention of it in the paper.

"Do you smell that?" I asked, turning the corner at the bottom of the stairs. A short hallway led to a wide set of double doors.

"Yes, they really bleached the heck out of this place," Mom mused.

"That's not it," I said, stopping short as we entered the main cafeteria. Plastic chairs lined either side of two dozen large rectangular tables. To the left stood a long serving station, the hood drawn closed to hide the kitchen behind it.

A pot clanged loudly and made me jump.

I heard a muffled curse, followed by a woman muttering in the kitchen behind the serving station.

"Is anyone here?" I called.

My mom leaned close and grabbed my arm. "Do you hear something?"

"Yes." And now I saw it. The serving station glowed in shades of gray, and an unearthly silver light streamed from around the closed hood.

"Never," a woman's voice growled. "Never, never, never!"

I glanced to Frankie. "Is she friendly?"

"She's not one of the Cubans," he said, eyeing the ghostly glow emanating from the kitchen.

What a comfort.

"Let me check it out," I said to my mom. "And if it's Ashley, I'll call you."

Not all ghosts were friendly, and if this one had a chip on her shoulder, I'd have to watch my back. My mom was perfectly safe on the mortal plane, but when I was tuned into the ghostly realm, ghosts could touch me, hurt me, or worse. I had to go into this with one hundred percent concentration and focus.

"I'd like to be there to support you, honey," my mom offered.

"Just...go sit at your old lunch table," I suggested. "Concentrate real hard on Ashley."

Her eyes widened. "Will that call her to me?"

It couldn't hurt. "Go," I urged.

A low, slow dragging sound echoed from behind the metal hood.

"All right," my mom said, hesitating as she walked me to the door of the kitchens, then kept walking farther into the cafeteria. "Yell if you need me."

I sincerely hoped there wouldn't be any yelling on my part. Or screaming. Or running. But you never could tell. So I braced myself as I opened the door.

Chapter Six

The industrial kitchen glowed with an unearthly silver light, like a photographic negative on top of the "real" world, our world. And in an instant, it became clear to me—this space hadn't been renovated in a long time.

"What do you think?" I murmured to Frankie, who trailed a step behind me.

He'd never gotten into ghost hunting like I had.

"I can think of about ten other places I'd rather be hiding," the ghost said under his breath, his hand on the gun inside his jacket.

He needed to stop looking for trouble. It found us enough on its own.

An aqua-painted metal table, dented over many decades, stood to my right. Ghostly desserts crowded the surface, slices of chocolate cake with white icing covered over with plastic wrap.

A screech of metal and a muttered invocation made us turn.

On the other side of a long prep table, behind an industrial standing mixer almost as tall as me, I saw a ghost.

At least I saw the back of her white smock top. She hovered

a foot off the ground, her hair snared in a round bun under a crisscrossed net. She cursed under her breath as she rooted through a white 1960s-era industrial-sized refrigerator.

I exchanged a look with Frankie, who didn't take his grip off his revolver. He was fine. We were fine.

"I don't think she's armed," I whispered. Or Cuban, judging from her lack of accent.

"There's a knife missing," Frankie said, flicking his gaze to the block on the prep station. One large slot stood empty.

"That's not good," I said as the kitchen ghost jerked and turned around, her eyes glowing with a strange silver light. I gasped as I recognized that piercing stare, the plucked and slanted brows. The way her teeth showed when she frowned, like a bulldog.

"Mrs. Gremmelter," I managed. Surely Mrs. Gremmelter had been too mean to die. She'd run the lunchroom like a wartime prison camp, rationing napkins, demanding exact change for the milk line, and raining down holy terror if she saw too many buttered peas in the trash. She'd worked at the school for as long as any kid could remember, and we'd suspected she never left the lunchroom. We'd apparently been right about that. I wasn't sure if she was scarier dead than alive.

She held a large kitchen knife in one hand and a loaf pan in the other.

Okay, maybe dead was more terrifying.

For a split second, I stood dumbfounded. Then my manners kicked in. "It's lovely to see you, Mrs. Gremmelter, ma'am." Commandant. General. Whatever would get her to stop glaring a hole through me. "Sorry to pop in on you like this."

Her eyes widened, and the loose skin on her neck quivered. "You can see me…"

"Yes," I said, mustering up some friendliness to go with my manners, "I can see any and all ghosts," I said breezily, hoping to put us both at ease. "It's a talent."

"Is that what they're calling extortion these days?" Frankie said over his shoulder as he slunk off down the hallway at the back.

"I'm Verity Long," I said, pasting on a smile, focusing on the surly ghost in front of me instead of the one abandoning his post. "And he's…"

"Heading for the boiler room," the lunch lady grated out. "Good. Because I don't serve nonstudents in my cafeteria." She drifted toward me. I really wished she'd put down the knife. "I remember you, Verity Long."

She said it like an accusation, even though I ate all of my peas. Most of the time. And was careful to hide what I didn't eat in my milk carton.

"Students aren't allowed in the kitchen," she barked, looming over me.

Despite every instinct I had, I held my ground.

"Oh, I graduated," I said, forcing a grin. I was here to talk, not to run. Most people who knew me liked me. Although I wasn't sure Mrs. Gremmelter liked anybody.

I'd feel better if the General would cast aside her weapon. And perhaps if she would blink once or twice.

She drew close, too close, the chill of her sending goose bumps up my arms. She snarled. Or hopefully that was a grin. Sometimes, it was hard to tell. "You sure got big."

"You…never change," I said brightly. Although the more I looked at her, I realized that wasn't true.

She'd aged since I'd seen her last. She'd also lost weight. Her broad cheeks had sunken in and her eyes had hollowed. Now that I thought on it, I recalled she'd fallen ill shortly after I'd graduated.

"You're in luck," she said, waggling the pan at me. "Today's meat loaf day."

Mrs. Gremmelter knew so much it was scary. Meat loaf day had always been my favorite. That and chicken fried steak day.

69

There were no chicken nuggets or industrial pizza slices in the General's kitchen. She and her staff made real food. It had been both the bane and pride of Sugarland High, depending on who you asked.

Still, I declined her offer of lunch. "I couldn't," I said.

Quite literally.

"It's lunchtime, isn't it?" she asked, ever practical as she grabbed a rectangular-shaped plastic plate from a shelf underneath her prep table. "You're lucky the food's ready. Ever since I died, nobody puts things back where they belong." She turned to the industrial stove behind her, and a pot appeared a second before she grabbed it. "Today's veggie is succotash," she added, as if daring me to resist.

"That's lovely." If you liked lima beans with your corn. "But I'm afraid I'm here for more than lunch," I explained as she fetched a tray of buttered noodles. "Ashley Starling has died, and I'm looking for her. Have you seen her here in school recently, perhaps near the flagpole? Her death wasn't exactly natural."

She looked at me like I was a wagon wheel short of a gravy train. "I fix you kids lunch and I go to church," she stated, slopping down a generous portion of noodles above the sections with meat loaf and succotash. "I don't have time to pry into other folks' business or make judgements on their deaths, and you shouldn't, either."

"Oh, I'm not gossiping," I said, quick to correct her. "Ashley was killed, and I want to learn who did it so we can bring them to justice." This was my chance to investigate in a way the police could not. There was no telling what the crime scene would offer in the way of evidence after all those years, but if I could give Ellis a lead, while at the same time doing right by my mom and poor Ashley, I had a moral obligation to do so.

The lunch lady stared me down. She didn't seem surprised at

the fact that Ashley had been killed, nor did she seem extremely bothered.

"You do remember Ashley, don't you?" Nothing escaped Mrs. Gremmelter, at least as far as I knew.

"Oh, I remember," she said with absolute certainty as she added a plastic-wrapped slice of cake next to the noodles. "She was joined at the hip with your mother."

"Yes!" Exactly. "Mom wants to learn what happened to Ashley, too."

The ghost was not impressed. "Those two girls liked their homecoming cheers. They'd do them all through lunch. They wouldn't let up until they had the whole cafeteria chanting homecoming songs."

I grinned. "That sounds like my mom."

"Nobody finished their spaghetti and pineapples," she said, resting a fist on her hip. "The drain was white with wasted milk. And worse—those rhymes stick in my head something awful." She huffed. "But that never stopped those girls."

"Well, it was for school spirit and all," I reasoned.

She frowned.

"Have you seen Ashley here at the school?" I ventured. "I mean, since she died."

For better or worse, it seemed Mrs. Gremmelter was quite attached to her old job. If she spent any amount of time in the school, I needed to get her to talk to me, or at least point me in the right direction.

The lunch lady looked me up and down. "Maybe. But first, you look like you could use a good meal. You kids play too hard, and you never stop to eat," she said, placing the ghostly plate on a tray and sliding the whole thing toward me. "Now take this out to your table. Eat, don't cheer. And don't let me catch you dropping food on the floor."

"Um…" It seemed Mrs. Gremmelter hadn't had much

contact with the living, or she'd know it was a really bad idea for me to touch her ghostly meal.

While I was tuned into the other side, I could handle ghostly items. Sort of. Touching them felt like plunging my hand into an icy lake. After a few minutes, I'd lose feeling in my fingers. Plus, it hurt. And that was merely handling a ghostly object. I had no idea what would happen if I tried to eat one.

I didn't want to learn.

"Go on," she ordered when I refused to lay a hand on the lunch tray.

I'd rather not. I squared my shoulders and faced down the General. "It's important that I find Ashley now. I can come back and eat later."

"Go take your seat." The lunch lady pointed to the door. "Ashley doesn't need you chasing after her. That poor girl has problems enough."

So she *had* seen Mom's friend! "What kind of problems?" I pressed.

Mrs. Gremmelter held her hands up, as if to ward me off. "I don't gossip," she stated, as if that were the end of it. "Now take your tray to the cafeteria. Clear your table after you eat. The janitors are long gone, and I don't need to be picking up after you."

She began to fade away.

"No," I said sharply, earning a disapproving grunt from the ghost. Well, sorry. She couldn't leave. Not when I'd almost gotten her talking. I didn't know where or if I'd find another ghost around here. And if I could convince Mrs. Gremmelter I wasn't after idle gossip, I stood a chance. "Will you eat with me?" I pressed before she disappeared entirely. "I mean, I'm the only kid here."

As soon as the words left my mouth, I regretted them. For one thing, I'd never seen her eat with a student unless it was to torture any kid who sat alone at a table toward the end of lunch.

For another, Mrs. Gremmelter was going to want me to scarf down every vegetable on my plate, and I had no idea what would happen to me if I ingested ghostly succotash.

Would it burn an icy hole in my throat? Probably not. Ghostly objects didn't burn my skin, even if they felt like touching dry ice. Once it hit my stomach, could I even digest it? Doubtful.

Eventually, it would disappear, right?

I swore I heard her cluck as her image came into sharper focus. Or perhaps it was a snort of derision.

"I do miss seeing you kids eat a good meal," she said gruffly. "The students today gobble down pizza slices delivered frozen in a box. Hamburgers shipped from clear across the country that don't even resemble the fresh meat I had delivered from our local farmers. And the worst part is, I don't even think they know the difference."

Hold on. Did Mrs. G...care? It was hard to believe, considering the way she'd ruled the cafeteria.

I considered the years and decades she'd spent carefully preparing homemade food for thousands of kids. And it had been good. Even the buttered peas. I couldn't remember any students ever thanking her. Mostly we'd speculated about her escape from a Russian gulag.

Maybe there was more to Mrs. G than I thought. "Thank you for looking out for us," I ventured.

"Somebody had to." She waved me off, as if embarrassed by my appreciation. "Now, do I get to feed at least one person today?"

"Yes," I said quickly. "Of course," I added, gathering my courage to touch the lunch tray, bracing against how bad it could be.

"About my mom's friend—" I began.

"We'll talk all about your mom's friend as long as you promise to eat everything on your tray," she said, bustling over to a basket by the refrigerator and drawing out an apple. She added it to my plate. "There."

Okay, time to temper some expectations. "As a living person, I can't eat ghostly food," I told her. "It could hurt me."

"Nonsense," she said, as if I were simply one more child refusing to eat a healthy meal. "Try one bite. I made it special."

"I'll eat what I can," I hedged, trying not to wince at the gray, glowing meat loaf. "But just so you know, I'm not hungry."

My stomach picked that moment to growl.

"Don't fib," she said, taking the tray for me. She opened the door to the cafeteria and ushered me out ahead of her. "Your mamma raised you better."

My mom stood at the far side of the cafeteria, holding the double doors closed. "I'm sorry," she called to whomever stood on the other side. "You can't come in," she insisted as the doors rattled on their hinges. "Verity is doing some very important ghost work."

Oh, my goodness. "Mom," I pleaded.

I mean, I appreciated her keeping the cafeteria clear, but she didn't need to tell them *why*.

Mom opened the door a crack, and I could see bodies—lots of bodies. "I don't care if it's the twelve-thirty tour," she called through the crack in the door. "Verity and her gangster ghost have determined this cafeteria is haunted."

Mom gave me the thumbs-up as Mrs. Gremmelter glided over to a small refrigerator on wheels where they kept the milk. She plopped a carton of chocolate onto my tray before I could protest that I truly didn't want it.

The General then ordered me to my old table.

Meanwhile, Mom slipped out the cafeteria door. "Ovis Dupree!" she greeted the investigative reporter who had dogged me more times than I could count. "What's Verity doing now? Well…" The door closed behind her.

Lovely.

I turned to find Mrs. Gremmelter standing over me.

At least Mom couldn't tell them this part. I could hardly believe it myself.

I didn't know how I was going to taste my ghostly lunch, much less eat it. I'd never forget the first ghostly object I'd ever touched—an antique necklace that had left my fingers smarting before it disappeared completely.

Meanwhile, Mom was spilling my secrets. Frankie was holed up in the boiler room. And I didn't know how I was going to get Mrs. Gremmelter to talk if I couldn't choke down a bite of her ghostly food.

I was still wondering how I'd gotten myself into this mess as Mrs. Gremmelter sat across the table and slid the ghostly tray in front of me.

"About Ashley—" I began.

"You always liked ketchup," the lunch lady stated, a ghostly glass bottle of Heinz ketchup appearing in her hand. "Here you are." She plunked it onto the table next to me. "Now you have no excuse."

If she only knew.

I looked down at my meal. It would have been quite delicious—a decade ago when the cook had been alive.

"I—" I really couldn't eat it.

"I'll give you an extra cookie," she rasped. "You don't even have to ask."

Oh, my word. I remembered getting extra cookies on my tray when I'd had the occasional bad day. Mrs. G snuck me free cookies? Just because? I'd assumed I'd been lucky.

I glanced up at her.

"How about this?" she asked, resting her arms on the table across from me. "I answer a question for every bite you take."

"Can't we just talk?" I asked, getting a little desperate.

"Not until you eat," she said, taking the fork and holding it out for me.

There really was no way around this. Unless I was willing to leave without answers.

"All right." I could do this.

I'd have to make each question count.

I took the fork and tried not to cringe as the chill of the ghostly metal bit into my fingers and radiated down my arm.

"Have you seen Ashley recently?" I asked quickly.

The lunch lady pointed at my meat loaf.

"I really can't," I protested. Holding the fork felt bad enough. "As a live person, it's not good for me."

"Meat loaf is always good for you. Eat."

"I—"

"Eat or I'm not saying another word," she declared.

I stared down at the ghostly, glowing plate of nutrition.

How bad could it be?

Frankie would know the answer to that, but he'd taken off, most likely to find ways to blow up the Cuban gangsters who couldn't die again anyway and who had no reason even to set foot in the hallowed halls of Sugarland High.

I forked as small a portion as I could and braced myself for the icy cold as I brought it to my mouth. I tried to block out her expectant gaze as I shoved it in and swallowed it whole.

It was like gulping an ice cube, only worse. The meat loaf radiated a ghostly zing that burned the back of my throat and my esophagus, searing a trail all the way down to my stomach, where I swore it gnawed a cold, vaporous hole. I tried to smile and failed.

"There!" the lunch lady said, pleased. "That wasn't so bad, was it?"

Somewhere along the line, I'd dropped the fork. A major ice-cream headache welled up. I wasn't sure if I could speak, so I simply nodded.

She ran a hand down the side of her face, dislodging the net cap from over her ear. She adjusted it back into place and sighed, crossing her arms over her chest. "I saw Ashley about an hour ago, here in the cafeteria. She was cheering instead of eating again. I only see her during homecoming week, so at least she can't drive me completely out of my mind."

Wait. "She only appears during homecoming? Why?" I choked out, throat raw. "Wait," I corrected before she could answer. "That's not my next question." I had to make them count, and I suspected I knew why Ashley picked this week. She returned on the anniversary of her death, possibly even to relive a part of it. I'd experienced enough of the ghostly side to recognize some of their habits by now.

That meant we only had this week to solve Ashley's murder —unless I wanted to wait another full year to talk to her and hope we hadn't lost key evidence in the meantime.

"Have you talked to Ashley?" I asked. "Do you know how she died?"

Mrs. Gremmelter pointed to my plate.

I rubbed my fingers, trying to get some feeling back from the last time I'd touched the fork. Being lost in there for more than three decades was bad enough. "She needs justice, Mrs. Gremmelter. But more than that…" If poor Ashley had been stuck all this time, if she appeared only on the anniversary of the week she'd died, she needed more than her killer brought to justice. "I want to help her find peace."

"Try the succotash," she suggested. "I added radishes today."

"I'm not trying to gossip, if that's what you're afraid of," I promised. I never sought to feed the Sugarland rumor mill. I knew what it was like to be on the receiving end of it, and I wouldn't wish it on anyone. "I want what's best for Ashley. That's all."

"The noodles are also quite good today," the lunch lady said, as if she could tempt me.

"All right," I said, finding the fork I'd dropped on the table. Two of the prongs were starting to fade, a casualty of my touch.

That didn't make it sting any less when I took hold of the fork once more.

"Someday, you'll learn to love all your vegetables," Mrs. Gremmelter said as I scooped up a diminutive portion of succotash and shoved it into my mouth before I could think about it.

I swallowed hard, feeling the individual pieces go down like dry ice pellets.

"I don't know how Ashley died, but the poor girl doesn't know she's dead," the lunch lady clucked. "Ashley haunts the second-floor science classroom and the flagpole most often, but I've seen her all over the school. She was a very active student."

I remembered the second-floor science classroom, or at least I thought I did. It was hard to think with my second ice-cream headache blooming.

"Mr. Norwood's class?" I managed.

She nodded, giving me a freebie.

I'd had him for both earth sciences and chemistry. Mr. Norwood had taught at the school forever—at least in student terms. In real life, that meant at least twenty years, perhaps longer.

Hopefully, he'd been there long enough to remember Ashley's last homecoming.

Mrs. Gremmelter looked at my plate. "You've hardly touched your meat loaf."

Never mind. There was another way to find out.

"I have to go," I said, standing. "Thanks so much for lunch, but I have to get back to class."

"You kids," she scolded, "always running somewhere."

"It was so good to see you," I said, feeling bad about my tray.

Not bad enough to touch it again.

"At least you didn't try to hide your vegetables in your milk this time," she muttered as I dashed for the stairs.

Chapter Seven

I made it as far as the first-floor lobby and was about to cross the senior star on my way to the main staircase when one of the front doors flew open. Mom, of all people, edged inside. Her red midi dress swirled around her legs as, with a furtive glance around the lobby, she closed the door behind her.

"Where were you?" I asked, making my way to her. She was supposed to wait for me outside the cafeteria.

"I'm sorry," she said, peering out the arched door, her features pinched with worry.

"What's the matter?" I looked past her and tried to follow her line of vision. Several groups of people milled on the lawn out front.

"It's just…Jake Everett," she said with a sigh, pointing out the hulk of a man wearing a red and white letterman's jacket. He laughed and one-arm hugged a giggling, skinny blonde, while a balding, middle-aged man hooted wildly and bashed his ample stomach into Jake's.

"I tried to talk to him, but Jake and his entire group blew me off," Mom said. "Me," she added, clearly not used to being ignored. "I mean, I was on the cheerleading squad. I hung with the football players."

It would be unkind to point out that more than three decades had passed. Still, if anything could hold up that long, it would be a high school clique. Perhaps it was simply the fact that Mom had been gone for so long.

"I can't believe that still fits you," the guy said, circling Jake, tugging on the jacket, beer sloshing out of the can in his other hand. "You're still a rock star, man."

Not quite, but it seemed Jake hadn't let himself go completely.

"The old football team got together to take a picture on the front steps. It's in the program," Mom said, holding up a clipping from the *Sugarland Gazette* with the high school open house schedule.

"I've been...distracted," I admitted.

"Well," Mom said, refolding her newspaper clipping, "it seemed like a good time to accidentally run into some of them. Jake was our star quarterback." She slipped the clipping back into the pocket of her jean jacket. "I was hoping to ask him about the night Ashley disappeared. He was her boyfriend, after all."

Oh my. "Wait. Was he the one she was supposed to run away with?" But that didn't make sense. If it had been Jake, you'd think the town would have noticed if he didn't leave with her.

Mom stiffened. "Jake wasn't her secret love. He was just the guy she thought she should date since half the school worshipped him."

"That doesn't look like it's changed much," I said, judging from the attention he was getting, and considering football was practically a religion in the South.

Still, we needed to talk. "Did this Jake guy know Ashley was interested in someone else?" I hadn't asked Mom as many details as I would have liked last night. She'd been so upset. "Let's try again," I said, opening the door.

"As long as you hold his admirers back," Mom drawled, accompanying me out onto the wide concrete landing. We were too late. Jake Everett and his entourage had moved the party to a cherry red convertible with streamers trailing from the side mirrors. He revved the engine while his beer-swilling buddy tumbled into the back face-first. The blonde slid into the passenger seat, and three more grown men hooted and piled in as well. "They're drunker than Cooter Brown."

"Ah." Homecoming.

Everett's friend spotted Mom and about fell out of the side of the car as he waved his hands at her. "Tilly! Sweet Tilly! We're going to the caves! I wish there were room for you!"

Mom shooed him off as Everett and the packed convertible sped off, trailing streamers.

"Jake will be back," Mom promised. "If not, I'll hunt him down."

"Were they always that jerky?" Not that my mom wanted to swill beer down by the caves, but I don't think she would have minded being invited.

"They haven't changed much," she said, stone faced. "And I didn't always hang out with them back then. I preferred your father." We watched the convertible grow smaller and smaller as it sped away down Second Street. "Your dad played baseball and basketball with them, so he knew them all like I did, but your father was sweet and considerate. He didn't do the kind of drinking they do at the caves. And he didn't let his athletic status go to his head."

"Did Ashley go off with those guys?" I asked.

"Often enough," Mom said stiffly.

So maybe there'd been something happening in that group that Mom didn't know about. "When was the last time you saw Ashley?"

The faint lines around her mouth deepened. "It was the night of the big dance. Everett had led the team to victory, and it had been a great weekend. We held a ceremony to dedicate the time capsule, and we were all so excited. Ashley made sure the box for the Class of '86 was the last item added, for drama's sake." Her eyes flicked to mine. "They closed up the time capsule, and we went to the dance."

They hadn't closed it well. "Then what happened?"

"We celebrated," Mom said. "The gym was done up like a masquerade ball. It was so magical." She played with her gold pendant, pausing as a group of out-of-towners walked past us into the school.

Mom smiled wistfully. "Ashley wore her red dress with a gold feathered mask and, of course, her crown. I was with your father. He looked so handsome in his dad's suit and tie." She grew misty, and I drew an arm around her. "You know how much I loved him," she said, patting my arm.

"I know." I'd seen it every day.

"Anyhow," she said, gathering herself, "Ashley wasn't being very nice to Jake, which I could see coming. She'd been getting little love notes and gifts from her admirer every day for the past week. Every morning she opened her locker, it held something new. We never locked our lockers back then."

"We didn't either," I said. Heck, most days I didn't even lock my front door.

"One day it was chocolates from the sweets shop on Main," Mom mused. "Another day, it was a bracelet. The Monday of homecoming week, her admirer decorated her entire locker in crepe paper and balloons. She lied to Jake and said I did it." Mom bit her lip. "Ashley was so smitten."

"And she never told you who he was?" I wouldn't have been able to hold off telling Lauralee or Melody if I had a secret love.

"She said he wanted it that way," Mom said helplessly.

"Then he was a jerk." Any guy who didn't want to get to know her friends and family was bound to be bad news.

"I don't know what he was because I never got the chance to meet him." Mom threw up her hands. "We were eighteen. We didn't ask questions. We thought we knew everything already." Mom crossed her arms over her chest. "Ashley was secretive to the end, although it was obvious at the dance she was on edge. It confused the heck out of your dad. And Jake." She frowned. "We all danced a slow song, and when Jake and your dad went to get us punch, she told me it was time for her to go. We never saw her again." Mom wiped a tear. "It hurt to lose her then. Now that I know what happened, it hurts so much worse."

"We'll find out who killed her," I promised. "We'll set it right." Or as right as we could.

"Maybe we can get a minute alone with Jake at the pep rally tonight," Mom said, trying to look on the bright side.

We could hope. "I also want to find out who was in charge of closing up that time capsule."

"It had to be somebody local." Mom nodded. "I'll ask my friend Niki Ryther. Her husband Abe was the one who dug the vault for it back then."

"Good." That would help us put together the timeline of Ashley's disappearance, or at least tell us when someone would have had the chance to hide her body without it being discovered. "In the meantime, I have an idea where Ashley's ghost might be. Word has it, she haunts the second-floor science classroom."

"That actually makes sense," Mom said as I held the door open for her. "She took every chemistry, environmental science, and geology class Sugarland High had to offer."

"So she was a sciency girl." I liked that.

"Yes," Mom said, tilting her head. "She also had a huge crush on Mr. Norwood."

"The science teacher?" I asked. Ick.

"Mr. Norwood was a cool glass of water back in 1986," she said, prancing up the stairs like someone half her age. "He was a year or two out of college and charming to boot," she added when my jaw went slack.

"But he's...old," I said, trailing her up, still trying to get my mind around it.

"You're no teenager yourself," Mom reminded me as I joined her at the top.

Well...technically, she was right. I was nearly a decade older than Mr. Norwood had been when he taught my mom.

I wasn't sure how I felt about that.

Luckily, I didn't have too much time to ponder it. Mr. Norwood's room was the second on the right, overlooking the practice field in the back. We arrived at a classroom door covered in ghostly construction paper. It glowed with an eerie gray light and featured a cutout of a Sugarland football player. Bubble letters, stapled to the paper underneath, read *Can't hide our Biscuit pride!*

"At least it's haunted," I murmured, earning an excited eyebrows-up from Mom as she pushed open the door.

Giggles erupted from inside the classroom.

"Now, girls..." a man's voice chastised.

We walked into the science lab and found Mr. Norwood surrounded by a gaggle of women my mom's age, all blonde. I didn't recognize them, which meant they must be returning home from wherever they lived now.

The skinny one in the white pantsuit twirled her hair as she laughed, while her gangly friend with the curled-under bob tried for center stage. "Remember that short pink miniskirt I always wore?" she asked the other ladies while looking at Mr. Norwood.

"Where's the eyewash station?" I murmured to my mom. I needed to scrub that image out of my head.

"Let's get to ghost hunting," Mom whispered back.

"Shouldn't that be my line?" I wondered.

"I'll show you Ashley's lab table," she added, leading me down a row of high tables near the door.

The third lady giggled. "Oh, Mark," she trilled, "I can't believe I asked you to the homecoming dance. I was just a baby!"

"I can't believe a ghost actually haunts this room," I murmured to myself. I wanted to leave, and I'd just gotten there.

Mr. Norwood smiled fetchingly at his admirers, and I had to admit he might have been attractive once upon a time in a Hugh Jackman sort of way. Still, it was hard for me to get my head around. I never saw him as anything but my teacher.

Instead, I focused on the ghostly side. The room glowed with unearthly light. It was definitely haunted. A spectral wall calendar showed October 1985.

Every lab table glowed. Spectral paper stars hung from the ceiling, each one with a handwritten message on it.

Roses are red, bromothymol is blue. There's no endpoint to my love for you. Jim & Angie, Homecoming 1985

Think like a proton and stay positive! We will WIN this weekend! Kim, Vickie & Aileen

Let's Bunsen burn the Jackson Cavers! Steve Long

"That's Dad's!" I said, way too loud. Quickly, I stopped pointing. Mom couldn't see the ghostly star dangling from the ceiling. "Dad made a star," I said, in a reasonable tone this time, glad to see Mr. Norwood and his court hadn't noticed me.

When I explained to Mom what the stars looked like and what Dad's said, she smiled. "I don't remember it, but that sounds like Steve."

"He was the king of dad jokes," I said, feeling the pang of loss. I'd barely made it to fifth grade before he'd had his heart attack. I admired the silver star once more, the corny joke, the familiar slanted handwriting. At least I'd had a good dad, for as long as it lasted.

I caught up to my mom, who had stopped at a lab table halfway to the back.

"Wait. This was my table..." my mom said, scanning the room. "I moved to be with your dad. He liked to play with my hair during class."

"Too much information, Mom."

"Ashley switched so she could be up front," Mom said, remembering. "She always sat first row in Mr. Norwood's classes."

I kept an eye out for Ashley's ghost as we made our way up front to an old soapstone lab table visible over the pristine, newer model. "These are lined up pretty good," I remarked, noting the similarity in the sinks. I bent and checked inside the cabinet right below the table. It contained a shelf with a Bunsen burner as well as an assortment of lab equipment, both on the ghostly side and in the mortal realm. Nothing out of the ordinary. But what I saw next made me pause.

The newer work surface covered the lab table, but I could see the original desktop in the ghostly realm. The soft, heat-resistant soapstone had withstood the lab spills that had darkened the wooden legs of the table. But that wasn't the interesting part. On that desktop, below the sink, a student had carved a heart. Inside, the letters A&M intertwined.

Ashley and...?

"What do you see?" Mom whispered.

I wasn't sure yet.

"Graffiti." A snapshot of the past. "There's an A&M, which...doesn't look good, considering she was hot for the teacher."

"That doesn't necessarily mean Ashley and Mark," my mom murmured, going a little pale.

It would explain the secrecy.

Still, Mom was right. There could be plenty of couples with those initials. Lots of kids had sat at this table.

I glanced up at the beloved teacher basking in the attention from his former female students.

Then I noticed something else.

"There's a lot of other stuff etched in this desk," I said, running my fingers over it, working it through in my mind.

"There always was," Mom said fondly.

More hearts, stars, names, and initials. From the days when the rules were obviously laxer than when I went to Sugarland High. Only these carvings and pen marks were smudged on the ghostly plane, unreadable. That had to mean something.

Now would have been a really good time to get Frankie's opinion.

"Frank," I whispered, acting casual as I tried to get his attention. "Frank?"

"Quiet," he rasped in my ear. And I caught a faint, piercing whiff of cigar smoke.

A *Cuban* cigar? Oh, poor Frankie.

I lost all slyness as I scanned the room for a cigar-puffing Havana gangster or, more importantly, for my ghost.

I didn't see either.

"Goodness." I resisted the urge to whisper to him again, if only to make sure he was okay.

At least he'd spoken to me. Evidently, he was too busy hiding to say more.

Perhaps we'd better think of clearing out of the high school. But before we did, I looked at the desktop once more. "The only thing that stands out is the A&M," I told Mom. That had to mean something.

I glanced around the gray glowing science room. "Whenever you have a haunting, there is always a dominant ghost. That ghost controls what things look like." Our ghost was from 1985 most likely, because that was the year we were seeing. "And if our ghost is showing us the A&M on Ashley's desk, and nothing else matters…"

My mom gasped. "It's important to the ghost."

It sure appeared that way.

"A spirit I met downstairs said Ashley haunts this classroom."

And if she did, she could be the dominant ghost. Which meant she could still be in teenager puppy love with—or at least interested in—someone whose name began with an *M*.

I glanced at the teacher who'd attracted too much of the wrong attention from his students. Mr. Norwood stood by the door of his classroom, saying goodbye to his admirers, effortlessly flirting with them.

Why had I never noticed it before?

Because I hadn't been looking. I'd seen him as a teacher and nothing more. But Ashley had been a vulnerable kid, in more ways than anyone had imagined. And Mr. Norwood had been barely out of college.

Had the science teacher flirted with her? Led her on?

My stomach tightened. Had he done the same thing to those ladies when they'd been just children?

I glanced at Mom, who seemed to be wondering the same thing. "Remind me to tell you a story after we leave," Mom said cryptically.

I had a feeling I wouldn't like it.

"I sure wish Ashley could tell us a few stories as well," I said, scanning the room once more.

"Do you see her?" Mom pressed.

"Not at the moment." I, of all people, knew you couldn't simply conjure up a ghost at will. "I think we should go," I said. Even if Frankie was safe for now, he had to be a little on edge.

"Give me a few more minutes," Mom said as Mr. Norwood treated the last of his fan club to a long, lingering hug at the door. In the same smooth movement, he turned to Mom and me, all smiles. "Why, is that Tilly Garber? Aren't you a sight for sore eyes! And Verity Long. It's so good to see you both!" He came over and gave my mom a bear hug, but treated me to a handshake. "How are you?" he asked, his attention on my mom.

"Glad to be back," she said, stepping back and keeping her distance. "A little shocked after yesterday," she added honestly.

His expression immediately went grave to match hers. "It's terrible, isn't it? Poor Ashley was destined for such great things."

Wait. "How do you know it was Ashley?" I asked. Ellis had told me in confidence.

"Oh, I'm sorry," he said, taken aback. "I assumed you would have heard. Everyone is talking about it."

The Sugarland grapevine strikes again.

"When was the last time you saw her?" Mom asked, not even trying to sugarcoat it.

At least she wasn't wasting any time.

Mr. Norwood took a moment to answer. "Ah, well, Ashley was my student, so I probably saw her in class Wednesday. Thursday is always open house."

"But didn't you award her the homecoming crown at the game on Friday night?" Mom countered.

"That's right," he said quickly, surprised. "She asked me to do the honors. She said I was her favorite teacher," he added with a grin.

"I'll bet you get that a lot," I mused.

"I do," he gushed, completely misinterpreting my attempt at sarcasm.

"Mom was telling me that Ashley had a secret admirer," I said, watching the science teacher frown. "Do you know who it might have been?"

He dropped the frown and gave an indulgent laugh. "I have a hard enough time keeping my students focused on their school-work. I don't worry about who they date. Except when the kids get engaged at graduation," he said, winking at my mom.

She blushed, thinking of my dad.

Yes, my parents had gotten married very young. And they'd had a happy life, but Ashley hadn't been given that chance.

"I think something may have gone wrong with Ashley's secret admirer," I said, eyeing the science teacher, watching for a reaction.

He gave none. "I admire your mystery solving, Verity, but this wouldn't be the first time you've assumed murder and been wrong."

My mom let out a gasp while I swallowed my irritation and remained a lady. "Well, if you've been following my career, Mr. Norwood, you'll also realize that I'm quite good at righting past wrongs. Nobody gets away with anything once I'm on the case."

"I'd expect nothing less," he said tightly.

"Are we still talking about Ashley?" Mom asked.

"Of course," Mr. Norwood said, a bit too indulgently for my taste. "I suggest you approach it scientifically. Start with facts. All we can say for certain right now is that Ashley died too soon."

"Yes," I said pleasantly. That was all we could say.

For now.

Chapter Eight

"I don't like him," I said to my mom as we hurried down the main stairs.

"Your dad didn't either," she admitted, her fingers skimming the bannister.

"Is that so?" I asked, slowing.

She kept going. "Oh, well, Mr. Norwood told me and some of my friends he'd give us extra credit if we wore short skirts on test days."

"That's gross, Mom," I said, catching up.

She ventured a glance at me. "It was a different time. We didn't think much of it." As if that excused it.

"Dad obviously thought a lot about it." My dad had been a kind man, but he didn't suffer fools.

She shrugged it off. "Your father was overprotective with me, kind of like Ellis is with you."

"It's not the same thing." Dad had his eye on a predator. Ellis couldn't even see what threatened me. Although my boyfriend did try his best to keep me away from angry ghosts and the occasional live killer.

"Believe it or not, I can handle my own problems," Mom said

tartly. "I did well enough in class without 'extra credit.' And Mr. Norwood obviously saw the light and stopped doing it if it didn't happen to you."

Darned straight. "I would have reported him for harassment." I couldn't believe she seemed more irritated by my questions than she did about Mr. Norwood's impropriety.

"He's harmless now," she said pragmatically. "I'm sure that all stopped when he settled down and married Jean from the library."

"Poor Jean," I said as we reached the bottom of the stairs.

My mom tossed a disbelieving look at me. "Don't say that. It's unkind."

She didn't say it wasn't true.

I rested my hands on my hips as we headed toward the senior hallway. "I can't believe something like that happened in Sugarland."

"It happened everywhere," Mom said, skirting the star.

I stopped walking as a terrible thought occurred to me. "Did something bad happen to you while you lived here? Is that why you left?" It made sense. Mom must have had a darned good reason for just…leaving.

Mom caught up to me and gave me a big hug. "No, sweetheart," she said. Yet her breezy tone felt forced, her hug a little too tight. She wasn't giving me the entire truth.

"You can tell me," I pressed. "I promise I won't judge."

"I wanted to get out of town, explore different places, different ways of life," she said simply.

There was more to it than that. I could feel it in my bones.

It also didn't appear as if she was going to confide in me quite yet. Pushing wasn't the answer.

"All right," I said.

For now.

But I'd be paying closer attention. If there was something else keeping Mom from Sugarland, I'd suss it out.

In the meantime… "Have you seen everything you wanted here at school?" I asked, slowing as we passed the classrooms by the senior lockers. I didn't want to rush her, but I had Frankie to think about.

He was being way too quiet, which worried me.

"Oh, I've been everywhere," Mom snorted. "I ended up taking the tour. It was the only way to guide that group away from the cafeteria."

"About that—"

"I also locked the door behind me so you could talk to your ghost in private," she added proudly. "So tell me. What did you learn?"

"I saw Mrs. Gremmelter. She's the one who sent Ashley haunts the science lab. She also said we might find Ashley at the flagpole."

Mom paled. "I can't get over the idea of Ashley haunting anything. Not to mention poor Mrs. Gremmelter. Baking giant sheet cakes for the rest of eternity."

"Wait. She baked those herself?" The cake was always good, but then again, as a kid any cake was amazing.

"Made from scratch using her mother's recipe," Mom said.

I should have known. "I don't think you need to worry about Mrs. Gremmelter. The General was in her element," I said. But Ashley might not be. The homecoming queen had not gone peacefully.

"Where's your personal ghost?" Mom asked, looking around as we walked, as if he might materialize and greet her.

"Trying to pretend he didn't hear that," Frankie's voice echoed from above. I looked up and saw him skimming the ceiling.

"Oh, thank goodness," I said, watching him pass through a hanging Sugarland Biscuits banner. "You're all right?"

"Now you care," he mused, adjusting the tie at his neck.

"I did care. I always care." I stopped, realizing I'd lost Mom.

She'd ducked into a nearby classroom. "Although, I could have used some help in the cafeteria."

At the very least, a distraction so I could shove my vegetables into the ghostly milk carton.

Frankie flung his hands up into the ceiling. "My job is to get both of us in and out of here, dead or alive. You're supposed to handle the questioning!"

"How comforting." And then I noticed something chilling. "Oh, my word, Frankie. Your left hand is almost gone." Disappeared up to the wrist. Whenever I drained too much of his power, he tended to lose body parts.

"It's fine," he gruffed, shoving the hand into his pocket, which meant it must be worse than I thought. "At least it's not my shooting hand. I can't afford to lose my trigger finger."

Frankie never enjoyed losing parts of himself, and I didn't blame him. It had been a huge issue before he'd met Molly. She'd stabilized his energy, made him feel whole and well, to the point where we'd solved several cases without him so much as losing a toenail.

That had sure been nice.

But now he was using his energy hiding and plotting and helping me, while at the same time avoiding her—and the energy drain was becoming a problem again.

I could see why he worried about being left alone on my property with her but not why he was avoiding her completely. "What on earth is going on with Molly that you'd rather lose your hand than talk to her?"

Frankie frowned, digging his disappearing hand deeper into his pocket. "I'll figure it out later."

Yes, well, I hated to pop his balloon, but… "Molly's going to want an explanation today. Remember, you stood her up in order to come here."

His left ear began to fade. "Stop stressing me out." He followed my line of vision and his eyes widened as he clamped a nonexistent hand over his questionable ear. "It's hard enough following you around while avoiding El Gato's boys. You're lucky no Cuban gangsters went to Sugarland High, or the place would be crawling with them."

"If it makes you feel better, we're almost done with the school." Unless Mom had discovered something.

So far, she hadn't returned.

"Then it's just an entire football field and the flagpole," Frankie groused.

"Hmm…I suppose that isn't any better," I offered, not quite sure how to avoid it.

But first, we had to find my mom. I started backtracking, trying to figure out which classroom she had ducked into.

"Sorry," Mom said, popping out of the arts and crafts room. "I saw Elladee from the farm stand. You know, the woman who sold me Frankie's wreath."

Frankie and I groaned in unison. "Please say you did not tell her that we're about to do a ghost hunt at the flagpole."

"I didn't even tell her you saw Mrs. Gremmelter haunting the cafeteria," Mom insisted as a red-haired woman stepped out of the classroom behind her and gasped.

"Whoops," Mom added.

Elladee clapped a hand over her mouth, too late to hide her delight. "Your secrets are safe with me," she promised.

Sure. Safe to be spread far and wide. And most likely embellished, practically guaranteeing the Cubans would follow me home.

"Did you know the more you talk about a ghost, the more likely he is to haunt you?" I asked Elladee, gratified to see her face pale.

"Not in a million years," Frankie drolled.

Elladee didn't need to know that.

"We have to go," I said as Elladee toyed with the cell phone she'd drawn out of her bag. "Think about it," I added as she stuffed it into her pocket. With any luck, we could conclude our business at the flagpole before Elladee gathered her courage to group text the town.

"Nice seeing you," Mom called over her shoulder as we hustled down the hall. "That escalated quickly," she added to me.

Story of my life.

"Are we doing this or what?" Frankie's voice echoed from above.

"We're on it," I said as we pushed out the side door.

"There are parts of me disappearing that I'd like to have," Frankie stated dryly.

"We'll make this as quick as we can," I promised.

The hard part was over. We were done navigating the school and trying to track down Ashley's haunting spots. Now we were out, and we were down to the last place we thought she might be.

Of course, the flagpole could be her death spot. It was terrible to think that poor Ashley could have died next to—or even inside—the time capsule. But if she had, that would be an excellent place to locate her ghost.

For better or worse, spirits who had died unexpectedly tended to linger in those places.

"Ticktock," Frankie prodded.

"Keep your pants on," I said.

Provided he still had pants.

We crossed the parking lot, and my heart sank as we headed down to the area between the school and the football field.

This...would not be easy.

More than a dozen people milled around the flagpole, including a woman with a stroller, a small Boy Scout troop, and a gaggle of seniors wearing Shady Acres branded homecoming sweatshirts.

Ellis stood nearby, arms crossed, in front of an area cordoned off with police tape. He looked real handsome in his

Sugarland Sheriff's Department uniform, tan with black trim and a gold badge. He stood at least a foot taller than everyone there, with broad shoulders and bulk in all the right places. Yet they still tried to weasel past him.

"Gawkers get banned from homecoming," Ellis warned from the other side of the barrier.

"I lost my glasses somewhere around here," a spry woman in her eighties insisted.

"They're on your head, Harriet," Ellis replied, unamused.

"My *other* glasses," she said, craning her neck to see past Ellis and into the crime scene.

Ellis looped a thumb under his utility belt.

Police tape stretched over the plywood barrier obscured my view, but I could make out a live person at work down in the time capsule.

"It's Melody," Mom gasped.

She was right. Behind the barrier, Melody stood down in the hole, wearing a white smock and gloves.

"We've removed the body to the morgue," Ellis told us. "Melody and Jean are archiving the contents of the time capsule," he added, glancing up at Jean, who was walking down the hill from the parking lot. "We had to put a police guard on the library van to make sure nobody decides to make their own memories with the time-capsule findings."

"Hey, Mom, hey, Verity." Melody appeared in her element, carrying a metal box like it held the crown jewels.

"Look at you," I beamed with pride. One of the reasons Melody worked at the library was that she loved preserving the town's history. But to get to do it in such a personal way? I was tickled for her.

"What is it?" Harriet asked Melody.

"We'll have to see." Melody winked. She'd wrapped the box in a clear archival bag and didn't even bother using her hands as she climbed the stepladder out of the hole. "First it has to be catalogued and organized," she added with relish.

"Let her through," Ellis ordered, and the lookie-loos parted. Reluctantly.

"Can we get closer to the hole?" one of the Boy Scouts pleaded. "I'm really good at climbing down into holes."

"Not this one," Ellis countered.

"I dropped my pen," claimed a weathered man with short-clipped white hair as he inched around the fencing toward the entrance to the podium.

"Yeah," Ellis said. "You dropped it over my barrier while Harriet tried to distract me." He glanced back at the glasses lady. "Nice try, Harriet. Do you kids want to get banned from homecoming?"

"Ellis Wydell, I taught you Sunday school," Harriet admonished.

"I remember. Bother ye not in the affairs of others," Ellis said drolly.

"I don't think that's a real verse," she scoffed.

Ellis shrugged. "And I know you wear contacts."

"Give an old reporter a break," the man said, edging past the barrier as if he only wanted to talk to Ellis.

Ellis blocked his way. "The VFW newsletter isn't exactly known for its crime reporting, Bert, and you'd better retreat before I call in reinforcements."

"Can you tell us more about what's in the time capsule?" Bert asked, trying to see around Ellis.

"I heard there was gold," one of the Boy Scouts piped up.

"Better," said a lady wearing a hand-knitted Sugarland Biscuits sweater. "The 1985 Homecoming Bake-Off winners put their recipes in a box. There's Gloria Wallice's secret salad dressing, Louise Burk's fried chicken recipe, and Claira Reynolds's heavenly grits. And don't forget Darcy Johnson's apple pie. Those crafty ladies took their recipe books to the grave, but that time capsule is about to spill their best secrets."

"And we will get to it in time," Ellis insisted. "But right now, we're cataloguing the artifacts."

"And autopsying the body," one of the Boy Scouts chimed in. "My dad said so."

"Maybe the dead girl was trying to break in and got trapped," the woman with the stroller suggested.

"Ashley Starling was not a thief," Mom declared.

"Then what happened?" one of the Boy Scouts asked.

"We don't know, sweetie," I told him. I couldn't imagine how Ashley had ended up in the time capsule. "We're going to do our darnedest to find out."

"She means the police will find out," Ellis added tightly, but he wasn't fooling anybody.

All we knew was that Ashley had been in charge of the class of 1986 box. Maybe she'd seen something go into the capsule that shouldn't have been there. Or could she have intercepted a thief?

But none of that explained why she'd left the dance in a hurry, or why she'd be out this way in the first place.

I tried to see past the milling crowd to locate any ghosts, but the area around the flagpole didn't even glow gray.

Neither did the football field or the stadium stands.

"Are you almost done?" Frankie's groan sounded in my ear.

"We haven't even started." I'd expected at least one haunting. At the very least, I'd hoped to meet a ghost who could give us a lead on Ashley.

"Yeah, well, in the meantime, you've got me out in the wide open while you make a show of looking for any ghost you can find," Frankie said, as if I were trying to get him caught.

"Hide where you hid before," I suggested.

"I am *not* melting into my urn again," he declared. "It was disgusting in there."

It was him. "Nobody can tell I'm ghost hunting," I informed him. "So far as the Cubans are concerned, you might not even be here."

"You're ghost hunting?" the Boy Scout gushed. "Can I help?"

Frankie slapped his forehead.

I went for damage control. "I'm finished. There are no ghosts here," I assured the little boy.

"Except Frankie the gangster," he said, in a voice clear as a bell. "My mom told me all about him."

Perhaps I did need to tone it down a bit.

I turned to my mother. "If Ashley does haunt this spot, she's not here now. I think we'll have to try again later."

"Cubans!" Frankie shouted in my ear.

Oh no. "Where?" I asked, swiveling my head, praying they hadn't heard my earlier conversation.

"You're making it worse!" Frankie hollered.

I was zeroing in on the threat. Or trying to.

"You're not supposed to be able to see them!" Frankie hissed as I spotted a ghost with a zebra-striped feather in his hat emerge from behind the pack of Boy Scouts.

He was a squat bulldog of a man, and he looked mean.

I stared into his sharp, beady eyes.

Whoops.

"Is he carrying a cane?" Frankie demanded. His energy rippled hard, making me dizzy for a second as he shrank into an orb and zipped straight into my purse. "El Gato carries a bamboo cane with a dagger inside and poison in the handle," Frankie cried, his words tumbling over each other.

I couldn't see. "He's still got one Boy Scout in front of him."

"Are you okay?" Mom gasped, holding me steady as Frankie's urn knocked against my keys with a muffled clang.

"I think so," I said, bracing a hand on her shoulder, ignoring the open-mouthed stare of a Boy Scout in an oversized uniform shirt. Now I had Frankie in an urn in my purse, and the ghost with the feather hat eyeing me funny.

He clutched a bamboo cane as he stepped out from behind the oblivious Boy Scout.

Oh, my stars!

I tried to stare past him.

I don't see you!

But all I could see was the cane. With the poison and the dagger and... "Tell me what to do," I whispered to Frankie. "Frankie!"

"Stop. Talking," my ghost grated out.

I could do that.

I gripped my purse tightly as I straightened. Maybe the terrifying and lethal gangster legend hadn't noticed Frankie. I wouldn't put it past my ghost to be a little stealthier than I'd been.

"Let's get out of here," I said under my breath. "Now," I added, sparing a wave for Ellis, who was busy deputizing a couple of Boy Scouts to lead people away from the barriers.

I just hoped the notorious mobster didn't follow us.

Because I had no idea what I'd do then.

Chapter Nine

"What's going on?" Mom pressed as we hurried away from Ellis and the flagpole and the Cuban mobsters.

"We caught El Gato lurking behind a pack of Boy Scouts," I gritted out, fighting the urge to glance over my shoulder. "He might have seen Frankie."

"Stop. Saying. My. Name." The gangster's urn knocked against my side as it clanged around in my bag.

"Right," I agreed.

Be casual.

Nothing to see here.

I tried to fast walk like I would if there *wasn't* a vengeful Cuban gangster on my tail.

We'd made it halfway across the football field when I couldn't stand it any longer and looked over my shoulder.

El Gato stood behind the flagpole, glaring at Ellis.

None of the gangsters liked the fuzz.

"Thank goodness." I sighed, slowing. "It looks like he was focused on Ellis instead of me."

"He's probably trying to figure out how to buy him off," my ghost said. "Beware if Ellis receives any fruit baskets. There could be a deadly scorpion inside. Or there could be his grand-ma's cinnamon capuchinos. With El Gato, you never know."

Yes, well, there was the small matter of Ellis actually seeing the gangster's bribe.

"If El Gato's on his own, that means he has his henchmen spread out. I'll bet they have guys all over town looking for me," Frankie said, his voice an octave higher than usual. "Keep moving. I won't feel better until we're out of sight."

"Gotcha," I said, kicking up the pace as we walk-ran across the football field. "I'm not sure when we can go back," I said, breaking the news to Mom.

"We'll manage," Mom vowed. "You tried your best," she added as we reached the trees on the edge of the property. "I'm certainly willing to do my part, too."

"Like what?" I asked, holding a branch back for her to pass. Only at the same time, she was trying to hold a branch for me.

"Like figuring out what happened the night Ashley disap-peared," she said, as if that were the reasonable thing to do.

"You don't need to be investigating on your own," I told her. Someone had killed Ashley and stuffed her into the time capsule. Or worse, left her there to die. For all we knew, that person was still in Sugarland and eager to cover up the crime. "I know firsthand the trouble you can stir up by actively investi-gating a murder."

"Because you do it all the time," she pointed out, not moving an inch as I tried to usher her ahead of me.

"I look at things from the ghostly side," I corrected. "The police do the investigation. I simply give them information they wouldn't have otherwise."

"Somebody, please move!" Frankie pleaded.

"Fine." I let Mom hold the branch for me.

"She was my friend," Mom said as we wove through the trees. "And if I couldn't save her that night, you can be damned sure I'm going to bring her killer to justice."

"Oh, great. Now there are two of you," Frankie said, not helping at all.

I stopped and turned to her as we broke through the trees. At least I didn't see any Cubans trailing us. "Let the police handle the real-life investigation. Ellis is better at that than you or I will ever be."

"I'm not so sure I buy that," Mom insisted. "I mean, he seems real sweet, but—"

"Yes, he's also a great police officer. Going after murderers is dangerous."

"Believe me, I know," she said as we made our way toward the crowded square. "But this is the first time you've actually admitted that to me."

Oh, for Pete's sake. I never wanted her to worry. "You don't need all the gory details." That didn't mean she could fancy herself an amateur sleuth.

"Look at you," she said. "You keep flinging your hands like an Italian grandmother. Where did you learn that?"

"Don't change the subject," I said, pointing at her, realizing too late I was picking up way too many of Frankie's bad habits. "Let me handle this," I urged. "I know what I'm doing." I didn't want her in the sights of a killer, and I didn't want Frankie to get nipped by El Gato, and right now, I'd had enough of both of them. "I'm in charge, and I say we take Frankie home." We'd calm down, regroup, and consider our options.

"No," Mom and Frankie said at the same time.

Truly?

"El Gato is right over there," I said, pointing to the line of trees that hid the football field and the flagpole.

"El Gato is staying put," Frankie pointed out. "And I'm in a good hiding spot."

"You hate the urn."

"I found a nice spot under your wallet."

"Lovely." I mean, I did love homecoming, and despised missing any of it, but under the circumstances...

"You do realize Molly might still be at your place."

That wasn't a bad thing. "I can be there to get you out if things go south."

"Things are going fine right here," he declared, to my utter astonishment.

"I'm sure there are plenty of people at today's Bonfire Celebration I can talk to...about non-murder topics," Mom said, not fooling anybody.

"The bonfire doesn't even start until dark," I pointed out, although that hadn't put a dent in the party on the square.

I massaged the spot between my eyes that had begun to ache and tried for logic, as if that would work with these two.

""You said yourself there are other wiseguys staking out the town," I said to Frankie.

"I'd like to know who they sent and how many there are," Frankie said pragmatically. "And I can guarantee they're not looking for me in a lady's purse," he added, the urn in my bag jiggling against my side. "Unless... You. Keep. Talking to me."

How had my life gotten so weird?

"Cooping me up in the RV isn't going to keep me from using the phone," Mom stated, as if it were a challenge.

Unbelievable. "So you two just want to traipse around homecoming."

"Of course," Mom said, as if it were obvious.

"Well, I wish it wasn't homecoming," Frankie admitted. "But have at your crackpot party. Forget I'm here."

A Dolly Parton cover band had taken the stage next to our town founder's statue and started up a lively rendition of "Coat of Many Colors." And that wasn't the only temptation. The smell of fried dough and kettle corn made my stomach growl.

I'd neglected to eat any real food today, and ghostly lunch didn't cut it.

"I suppose we could mingle a bit," I said, spotting a woman walking past with a plate of shrimp and cheddar grits. "Excuse me, where did you get that?" It was one of my best friend's signature recipes.

"There's a food truck parked in front of town hall."

"Behave," I said to Mom, but she didn't hear me because she was already running off toward the crowd to greet BreSha Wallice, who'd lived next door to us when I was a kid.

"It's just you and me," I said to Frankie.

"I told you to stop talking," his voice clipped.

Fine. Then it was just me.

I bustled straight through the party, keeping an eye out for tropical mobsters as I veered toward the town hall, with its red limestone accents and arched windows. The small clock tower at the center top acted as my beacon as I navigated the thick of the crowd.

And there, parked by the curb next to the mayor's office, Lauralee's battered yellow food trailer stood like an oasis of peace in the chaos that had been my day so far. She was saving up for a real food truck. In the meantime, she served everything out of a converted cargo hauler that read The Fork in the Road Food Truck.

"Order up," she announced from behind a folding table. Lauralee handed over two mini buttermilk chicken and waffle plates to a balding man in a too-tight vintage Sugarland Biscuits football jersey.

She saw me and grinned like she was having the time of her life. She'd tied her auburn hair up into a pair of playful twin braids, and wore her mother's large pearl earrings with a sleeveless red shift dress.

"Verity!" she said, leaning over the table for a hug while her husband, Big Tom, took the next order. "I've been looking for you."

"We were on the other side of the square," I explained, my stomach rumbling at the smell of fried chicken.

"Did you eat?" she asked, not waiting for an answer as she turned and began serving me up a plate of chicken waffle sliders with a side of shrimp and grits. "What's the matter?"

"Nothing."

She shot me a look.

"Everything," I admitted. "My mom is driving me nuts."

Lauralee handed me a sweet tea. "Of course she is, she's your mother."

"And family is messy." Big Tom laughed as seven-year-old Hiram wiped chalk-dusted hands on his shirt.

The Fork in the Road Food Truck was truly a family affair. Lauralee's oldest son, nine-year-old Tommy Junior, stood up front, counting change. Hiram manned the standing chalkboard menu, answering questions and telling customers what he liked best. And the two youngest sat a little ways back from the trailer, at a plastic kiddie table, stabbing each other occasionally with the forks as they wrapped utensils in paper napkins.

"I'm taking five," Lauralee announced, earning a wink and a playful swat on the rear from her husband.

"Looks like you're having a good day," I teased as we headed over to an empty spot on the curb so I could sit and eat.

"Business has been...amazing," she said, holding my tea while I folded my sundress under me and sat. "If this keeps up, we'll have saved up enough by the end of homecoming to buy a real food truck."

"Oh, sweetie, that's wonderful," I said, giving her a little hug as she sat down next to me. She'd been working toward that for a while now.

"So what's this with your mom?" she asked, stealing a shrimp off my grits.

"Well, for one thing, I forgot how she likes to tell everyone my business," I said, as a preemptive strike. I took a bite of perfectly spiced savory chicken. With a hint of sweetness from the waffle, it was heaven.

"Like the time we got caught stealing our moms' driver's licenses?" Lauralee asked.

"They thought we snuck into town to buy beer."

"When we only wanted to go see the *Titanic* movie revival."

"They cut out all the good parts on TV," I said, forking a portion of grits.

"I don't know what made us think we could pass for our forty-something mothers, other than fifteen years of being told we looked like them," Lauralee drawled.

"At least your mom was discreet about it. My mom told everybody in town. She even tried signing me up for drawing lessons, like I was a young Leonardo DeCaprio. I mean, really. I would have been on the door, like Rose. I would have even made room for Leo."

Lauralee snorted.

But I was serious. "Has she always been this crazy?"

"Yes, hon." She planted a reassuring hand on my arm. "And she loves you to pieces."

Big Tom walked over with a plate and a drink for Lauralee, and she accepted it with an exaggerated air kiss. "Just be glad your mom has stopped talking about the time you stood flipping off cars on the side of Route 4," she said, popping a straw into her sweet tea and taking a sip.

"Oh, come on. I was six, and I saw how it made people laugh on TV. I didn't know what it meant." I dug into my grits, which were perfectly creamy. "Mom also thinks she's going to help solve the mystery of the dead girl in the time capsule."

Lauralee stopped mid-sip. "Well, she was best friends with Ashley Starling."

"Poor Ellis was trying to keep that quiet."

"This is Sugarland," Lauralee said, digging into her grits. "Besides, Ashley was legendary for running off in that red prom dress. While I was selling food yesterday, more than a few people from your mom's class asked if I'd seen Ashley yet. Lots of people were curious where she'd ended up."

True. "Well, even as we speak, I have no doubt Mom is zipping around the festival, asking questions about the night Ashley disappeared. I warned her not to, but she won't listen."

"She's in her fifties," Lauralee pointed out, picking the chicken off her waffle. "She's a grown woman. You don't have to babysit her."

"You say that, yet you know what she's like."

Lauralee took a bite and chewed. "Hmm…impulsive, brave. Thinks she can talk to anyone. Sounds like someone else I know."

"Stop being a smart-ass," I teased. "This food is amazing, by the way."

"Thanks." She beamed.

Lauralee truly had a talent. Right now, she worked at the diner and on any catering jobs she could scrounge up in addition to working festivals with the food trailer, but I had no doubt she was going places.

"Now stop sulking and listen to me," Lauralee prodded, brandishing the waffle part of her waffle slider.

"I'm not sulking," I said, ashamed to hear the pout in my voice as I rounded up the rest of my grits.

"Your mom is concerned about her friend, and she's asking questions exactly like you would be," she continued, as if I hadn't spoken at all. "I mean, truly—what can go wrong? It's Sugarland homecoming."

"You saw the dead body, right?" I asked dryly.

She shrugged a shoulder and nibbled on her waffle.

I rested my tea on my empty plate. "It's just that I was so looking forward to seeing Mom again, and I love her, but it's not going the way I'd like." Even without the tragedy from yesterday. Maybe it wasn't her. Maybe it was me. "What's wrong with me?"

"Absolutely nothing," Lauralee decreed. "You care about people, and that's a good thing. Now you simply need to extend that to your mother and accept her for who she is."

There was no *simple* about it. "She's not subtle," I said, digging my straw into my cup.

"And you are?" Lauralee jested.

"She's courting trouble."

"Yeah, you like to avoid that," Lauralee mused.

I shot her a look, and she held up her hands. "I'm only saying you never know. Tilly Roan could be the perfect person to help figure out what happened to poor Ashley Starling."

"That's what I'm afraid of."

Chapter Ten

I didn't see my mom again until it was almost time to light the bonfire on the soccer field behind the high school. The Dad's Club led the charge, and I swore every year it got bigger. The enthusiastic fathers had almost finished stacking the last of the wood onto the huge pyre when I finally tracked Mom down.

It hadn't been hard to guess where she'd be. Pretty much everyone had migrated to the bonfire by that point.

"Mom," I said, shivering in the cold. Now that the sun had started to set, I really wished I'd brought a jacket.

"There you are," she said, as if she'd been talking to me five minutes ago. "Do you remember Alistair?" she asked as a tall guy with glasses held out his hand to me.

I shook it, trying to place him. He looked familiar in a tall, dark, and geekily handsome kind of way. Then I remembered. "I think I've seen you at the library."

Alistair grinned. "I spend a lot of time there. I'm an engineer. The library keeps all the original building specs for downtown and pretty much anything constructed around here. And your sister puts aside all the new D&D expansion sets for me."

"She must like you," I teased. He seemed nice. Smart. This could be someone for Melody.

Just when I'd warmed to the thought, Mom added, "Alistair used to live next door to Ashley. He knew her best, next to me."

"Oh, wow." He appeared a lot younger than that.

"Class of '86," he said, as if he understood my unspoken assumption.

"He looked about twelve back then," Mom teased.

"Now I look like a prematurely gray thirty-year-old," he said, joining in on the joke.

"You look great," I said, shivering again as a gust of wind blew through me. In the weak light, I couldn't even tell he was going gray.

"Take my jacket," he insisted, slipping off his brown leather bomber and placing it over my shoulders before I could protest.

The heavy warmth was immediate. And wonderful. Still, I felt obliged to protest. "I can't take this."

"Alistair has always been a gentleman," Mom said. "Even if he's too nice for his own good," she added as I snuggled into the coat. "You might not remember, but after your dad died, Alistair was our on-call tech guru when you got your first computer. I drove him half-crazy with calls, not that he'd ever admit it."

I remembered the assistance, but not who'd given it. A lot of the people in Sugarland had pitched in during those first few years without Dad. "You saved my sixth-grade argumentative essay," I said, thankful to live in a community where people helped each other.

"'Do You Know What Your Pet Dog is Thinking?'" he asked wryly, amused at my choice of topic.

"I should have made it a skunk," I teased back.

"Alistair and I were just talking about Ashley," Mom said. "They were super close."

He nodded and edged a bit closer to the pyre as the dads coordinated the lighting with their handheld fire starters. "My mom babysat her after school when we were growing up," he said, wrapping his arms around his chest. "She was like my sister."

"Let's get closer," I suggested, weaving us through the crowd toward the fire that climbed up the rectangular pyre.

"Ashley told me how you'd get mad when your D&D friends tried to cast love spells on her elf warrior," Mom said, trailing behind, not in as much of a hurry thanks to the quilted jacket she'd tied around her waist this morning.

"Ashley trusted people too much, kind of like you," Alistair said to my mom. "Somebody had to watch out for her," he added, parking himself in front of the growing fire with a sigh. "I only wish I'd done a better job of it." He shook his head. "I expected her to strut back into town this weekend, telling stories about how she and her guy fell in with a yacht captain and sailed around the world, or how she happened to make best friends with some exotic sheik." He clearly enjoyed the memory; then his face fell.

"I'm sorry," I said, knowing there was no way I could make it better.

Mom drew close and gathered us in, lowering her voice. "Alistair was telling me earlier about an incident I'd forgotten with Mr. Norwood." She glanced up at her friend. "About a week before homecoming, Ashley stayed late to decorate Mr. Norwood's classroom door, and he took her for an ice-cream float afterward."

"Technically that's not out of line," Alistair said, not even appearing to convince himself.

He could be objective all he wanted, but... "I heard how Mr. Norwood was around pretty female students," I said.

"And after the ghost graffiti you saw on the desk," Mom was quick to add.

My mouth dropped open.

"Don't worry," Mom said, "we can trust Alistair."

"Great." That wasn't the point. I thought we had agreed to keep our ghost-hunting details private. Alistair was going to think I was as crazy as a catnip fit.

"Hey, I'm a troll king, so nothing is weird in my world," he offered. He adjusted his glasses and politely focused his attention back on Mom. "The thing is, Tilly, I know you've told plenty of people that story about the graffiti…"

"Truly, Mom?" I asked.

"Well, I—" she said, flustered.

"And I realize you think it makes your case against Mr. Norwood," Alistair continued.

"I can't imagine how any of this will get back to Mr. Norwood," I mused.

Or all over town for that matter.

"But maybe keep things more between us," Alistair suggested. "We want to gather information, not necessarily volunteer it."

"I got excited," Mom said helplessly. "I really think we're onto something."

Yes, but Alistair was right. She had to be craftier about it if she wanted to get information without scaring off suspects.

I tried to put it plainly. "Even if I wanted everyone and their brother to know what I do on a ghost hunt, it's still a bad idea to broadcast every fact about your investigation to anyone who will listen."

"How else am I supposed to put everything together?" Mom asked, stepping away from the fire as the smoke began blowing our way.

"You have me," I said, stepping away with her. This was why I never wanted her to investigate in the first place. The information we collected could be dangerous, and she was an open book. "You realize Ashley's killer is most likely still in town," I added, trying to reason with her.

"That's true. Very few people leave Sugarland," Alistair said.

"Except for me," she countered.

I was still trying to figure that one out.

"Well, you had it planned from the start," Alistair remarked.

This was news.

He cocked his head at my mom. "This one could recite all the state capitals and vowed to visit each of the fifty states by the time she was twenty-one. As I recall, you only had Tennessee and North Carolina under your belt when we were in school."

"And only because Mom and Dad took me to the beach every summer to visit Dad's cousin." She nodded. "But then I got married, and life took over. And…"

She was making up for lost time now.

"All the same, seeing as most people stay right here in Sugarland," I said, getting back to Alistair's point, "that means the guilty person is probably here at homecoming."

Mom shivered, and I didn't think it was because of the cold.

Alistair's expression went dark. "My money's on Jake Everett," he said, referring to Ashley's ex-boyfriend, the football jock I'd seen with that rowdy bunch in his convertible.

"He's a person of interest," Mom agreed, gathering us back into a small circle as the band started up. "But Jake didn't leave the dance with her the night she disappeared. In fact, Ashley left *him* on the dance floor."

"Exactly," Alistair said. "You think Jake is the type to stand for that? I watched her go. And you can bet he followed. My friends and I were hanging out by the doors when he stormed right through us like we weren't even there."

"Well, you did wear black a lot," Mom mused. "It might have been hard to see you in the dark."

Alistair gritted his jaw. "We weren't invisible, except to jerks like him."

The crowd flowed around us as people pressed past to get a look at the cheerleaders parading in.

"So Jake followed her." This changed everything.

Apparently, Mom wasn't the last one to see Ashley alive.

"I should have at least watched to see who she left with," Mom fretted.

"Jake had a mean streak," Alistair insisted. "Still does. This is the guy who went ballistic in German class when I borrowed the pen off his desk. He didn't like anything that didn't go his way."

This was bad. "You're sure he followed Ashley out of that dance?"

"I don't know where else he'd be going in such a hurry," Alistair said cryptically.

I turned to Mom. "Maybe the key isn't who she was going to meet," I said, "but who was upset about it."

"I should have tried to follow them," Alistair said, running a hand down his face. "This is my fault. She had a psycho after her, and I just let her go."

"You can't blame yourself," I urged, noticing Mom had gone stark and silent as well. "You can't either," I reminded her.

We scooted back as cheerleaders whirled and frolicked around the bonfire. This was usually one of my favorite parts of the pep rally. The girls positively glowed as they danced to the tune of "Hot, Hot, Hot."

"Jake can definitely go hot and cold," Mom said, clearly recalling her experience this afternoon.

"He could switch from zero to a hundred on a dime," her friend insisted. "Do you remember when he didn't get his big college scholarship? He trashed his locker right in front of everybody."

"I do remember," Mom said, deflating even more. "I also recall thinking the guidance counselor should have waited until the end of the school day to tell him."

"He would have been a jerk either way," Alistair insisted. "He was a selfish bully. You remember when he tried to make me do his homework?"

Mom cringed. "I thought he asked because you were friends with Ashley."

Alistair snorted. "Oh, I was on his radar because of Ashley, but he didn't ask. He demanded it because he was an entitled jerk."

"What did you do?" I asked, hating to think that this guy had endured that kind of pain.

"What else could I do? I did his homework," Alistair said simply. "But I did it wrong."

I gasped. "Did he come after you?"

"I don't think he was smart enough to notice," Alistair said. "Until he got a D in English, and by then it was too late."

"Served him right," Mom said.

Microphone feedback echoed over the crowd. "Welcome to the 106th Annual Sugarland Homecoming!" The crowd cheered as the band started playing "Eye of the Tiger."

Our little pod gathered closer to hear each other above the noise, and I saw other groups of old friends doing the same. "It doesn't seem like you knew Jake or his motives very well," I said to Mom.

"We didn't hang out at all until he started dating Ashley. Even then, he was always at football practice or with Ashley or off somewhere else."

"Plotting ways to torture the rest of us," Alistair added.

"His group had a hard edge." Mom shrugged helplessly. "I always preferred my friends on the cheer squad or your dad and his baseball buddies."

Alistair nodded. "And I had my group in almost all my honors classes. Jake Everett wasn't in any of those," he added, mollified. "Maybe I'm being too hard on him. I mean, it was high school."

Cliques died hard, even after all these years. "Well, we need to talk to Jake," I said, straightening as a guy in an old Sugarland

Biscuits jersey over a red hoodie sweatshirt clipped the back of my foot with a wheelie cooler full of beer.

They weren't even trying to hide the booze anymore.

"I'm not looking forward to it," Mom said. "Honestly, I have no clue what Ashley saw in him," she added to Alistair.

"Do the ex-football players hang out anywhere in particular?" I asked, trying to get a bead on him. From the sheer number of old football jerseys I saw in the crowd, he had to be here.

"Unfortunately, I can take you right to them," Alistair said, leading the way.

Tilly Garber Long Roan might as well have been a homecoming queen from the way she waved to friends and acquaintances alike as she made her way through the crowd. Although if you really knew her, you could see the brittle edges of her smile.

"When we were seniors, Ashley was the center of everything," she said to me, waving brightly at a pair of ladies several yards away. "I know she's gone, but I can't help looking for her everywhere."

"It'll get better with time," I promised.

"I wonder if any of these people are even thinking about her," she said as the crowd pressed in.

"I'm sure some of them are," I said. "Lauralee told me how people were looking for her yesterday."

That seemed to lift Mom's spirits.

Pretty soon we were up front, making our way past the band and the cheerleaders.

They did a triple lift right in front of me, and I couldn't help but cheer. What talent. What balance!

"Keep going," Alistair said to my mom and me.

I tried my best, until a few seconds later when I spotted a ghostly conductor standing on a real-world portable amplifier.

That was one way to keep from being touched in such tight quarters. He waved his baton as his hips boogied to the beat.

"I see a ghost," I said, stopping in my tracks.

The urn in my purse rattled. "Who is it?" Frankie demanded.

I couldn't tell. "He's conducting the band, and he has his back turned to me."

Frankie let out an audible sigh. "Just keep an eye out for you-know-who."

He didn't have to tell me twice.

"This way," Alistair said.

We cut right, toward a group of graying men wearing Sugarland Biscuits jerseys. Honestly, though, you couldn't throw a rock without hitting someone in an old uniform.

"Is Carl here?" I asked Mom.

"He's still working on the float," she said over her shoulder, dodging a family of four. "His old buddies are probably over by the woodpile. They helped break down the boards for the Dad's Club."

"Well, that's nice." I loved how so many people pitched in for homecoming.

"Yeah." She skirted around a group of teen boys with their faces painted red and white. "I didn't know the shop guys very well in high school. They liked to smoke outside, and they always had a little grease on them or something bandaged. And I thought it was crazy how none of them ever dressed up."

"Does Carl dress up now?"

"No." She laughed. "But he likes that I do. He says I jazz him up."

It made sense Mom and Carl had been in different crowds in high school. I couldn't remember them talking about their shared school days much. But when Tilly became a new widow and started showing up at the hardware store by herself, Carl had been glad to help her out and fix things. And whatever had blossomed between them stuck.

The song ended, the cheerleaders did a final flip and pose, and the principal resumed his place out front with the microphone.

"Now I heard…there's a football team one town over…who thinks they can whup the Sugarland Biscuits tomorrow."

The crowd erupted in a long, joyful boo.

"That's what I said!" the principal announced. "The Jackson Cavers are going to *cave* tomorrow—" he announced, to the whoops and the hollers "—like they do every year because Sugarland High has the best football team and the best football fans in the county!"

A Jackson Cavers stuffed bear arced over the crowd and into the raging fire.

We reached the group of former players, who cheered and smacked each other on the shoulders like they were about to take the field against the Cavers themselves.

Alistair slowed. "They should be somewhere around here," he said, keeping an eye out.

"I see them." Mom led us past the football players and around to the edge of the crowd as the band led a chorus of "Go! Fight! Win!"

"There," she said, pointing to a group of guys off by the soccer goal, drinking.

Among them stood the graying hulk of a guy we'd seen outside the school this afternoon. He wore the red and white letterman's jacket we'd seen him in earlier as he high-fived a guy who proceeded to spike a beer can to the ground and dance around like he'd scored a touchdown.

"Charming as ever," Alistair mused.

I realized I still had his jacket as the cold of the night seeped over me, stinging my nose and ears.

If Mom felt the chill, she didn't let on. She strutted out onto the field. "Jake Everett, as I live and breathe!"

"Little Tilly Garber!" Jake announced, as if he hadn't seen her at all this afternoon. "You came home."

I followed her out while Alistair kept his distance.

Mom accepted a bear hug from Jake. And then one from the guy who'd snubbed her, and from another guy holding a beer. And a guy with a whiskey bottle. All in uniform and all smelling like a bar floor. "I couldn't stay away a minute longer," Mom teased, all smiles. "You know what that's like."

"Nope." Jake raised a beer. "I never went anywhere," he stated loudly, to the joy of his buddies. "And look at this mini-me," he said, turning his attention my way. "You're a pretty girl, Melody."

"Melody's my sister," I said, cheerful and polite. "I'm Verity."

"Ah." Jake drew back, as if I'd announced I had head lice, scabies, and a mild case of the plague all at once.

So he'd heard about me.

"You got a ghost in your pocket?" his friend with the whiskey jeered.

"In my purse, actually," I corrected, and I took great pleasure in watching them try to decide whether or not to laugh.

Mom broke the tension. "I was hoping to have a private word, Jake."

The men guffawed at that, their minds no doubt spinning into dirty scenarios prompted by my mom's sweet Southern drawl.

"I could never say no to the ladies," Jake said, scratching his stomach. He made a show of following Mom and me a short distance away, toward Alistair and the light of the pep rally.

"I can't stop thinking about Ashley Starling," Mom began, and Jake's affable expression iced over. "Can you believe she ended up in that…place?"

"Yeah, I didn't see that one coming," Jake said, taking a swig of Coke. At least he didn't appear intoxicated like his buddies.

"When was the last time you saw her?" Mom asked.

"When she ditched me at the dance." He glanced from Mom to me, as if he didn't like admitting it to someone new.

"Did she say why she was leaving? Or where she was going?" I asked.

"No." He glared at me, as if I had nerve to ask. "Unless you count the nasty breakup letter I found in my suit pants the next day. Seriously. Who does that?"

"Can we see it?" I pressed.

He rolled his eyes and went to take a swig of Coke, frowning and tossing the can into the soccer field when he realized it was empty. "I didn't save it."

"What did it say?" Mom asked.

"I don't remember, and I don't care anymore." He looked down at her, like she was something on the bottom of his shoe. "Ashley didn't like the way I was living my life, and she wanted better." He shoved his hands into his pockets. "She didn't do better, though, did she?"

I wasn't going to dignify that with an answer. Instead, I asked him what I really wanted to know. "What do *you* think happened?"

"I don't know, sweetheart," he taunted. "Since she ditched me, I haven't thought at all about Ashley Starling."

He returned to his side party while Mom and I walked back to the rally.

"Alistair is right," I said, glancing over my shoulder as the former football great caught a short pass from his buddy and opened a can of beer. "Jake needs to check his attitude."

"We've been saying that for forty years," Mom said, with no small measure of regret.

I wished there was someone else we could talk to.

And then it hit me. "I have an idea."

Chapter Eleven

W e slipped back into the crowd, and this time I led the
way. Mom and Alistair seemed more focused on
keeping their heads together, no doubt talking smack about
Ashley's rude ex.

The band launched into the "Sugarland High Fight Song."

We are the Biscuits
Proud from Sugarland
We will sop you up and win
Biscuits take a stand! Yay!

Go! Go! Sugarland! Beat 'em, Sugarland!
Go! Go! Sugarland! Beat 'em, Sugarland!

I weaved past chanting alumni, a young mom corralling a little
girl wearing a home-sewn Sugarland Biscuits cheerleading
uniform over a turtleneck and sweatpants, and a group of graduates brewing up hot toddies in a turkey fryer.

"There's a bookie behind the PTO hot chocolate stand,

taking bets on the game," an elderly man protested to his friend. "Where are the police?"

"Trying to solve a murder," I informed him as I passed.

I'd do my best to aid them in that.

"Where are we going?" Mom asked, trying to keep up.

"I think I know someone who can point us to Ashley." He might have even seen what happened at the flagpole on the night of the 1985 dance.

"I bet she means a ghost," Mom said to Alistair.

We reached the band as they wrapped up the fight song, and I was heartened to see the large, bearded ghost still at the helm. The band blasted a victorious final note as he flickered and spun on his box. Quite a trick until you considered that he hovered about an inch above it.

He flickered once more as he and the band took a short bow, and I realized his twinkling wasn't part of the performance. It was an energy issue, probably with the ghost in my purse.

"How you doing, Frankie?" I asked, running a hand over my bag.

"I don't even want to know what parts are missing," his voice sounded in my ear.

"I realize this day has been draining for you," I said, glancing over my shoulder as I worked my way closer to the conductor, making sure I still had my posse.

They'd fallen behind, but they were with me.

"I give and I give..." Frankie groused, still managing the snark.

That, at least, was a good sign.

"We should be out of here soon," I assured him. Once the football team finished parading out, we'd give a final cheer, and the part of the night that wasn't pure booze would be over.

"I'll keep the power going. You help me keep an eye out for the Cubans," the gangster managed. "Or Molly."

I didn't quite think they were in the same league. "I'll do my best," I promised as I reached the spirit of the band director.

The principal grabbed the microphone once more. "Now it's time to meet the starting lineup for homecoming 2021!"

He began announcing each boy on the Sugarland football team in a big, booming voice.

The entire crowd, including Mom and Alistair, turned to watch the players run out while I kept my focus on the bearded spirit.

"You all played great," I said, smiling up at him.

He grinned back and jumped down off his box. "Thanks. I live for pep rallies, halftime shows, and band competitions."

Not technically.

"I'm Verity Long," I said, by way of introduction.

"John O'Brien, class of '84. I play trombone," he said proudly. "You may remember our rendition of 'Thriller' with the zombie clarinets."

"That was before my time, but I would like to see it." I laughed. "You should do it again."

"I would," he said, brimming with enthusiasm, "but I swear sometimes these kids today don't listen to a word I say."

I could see where that would be a problem. "I'm looking for Ashley Starling. Class of '86. Do you know her?"

He nodded, fiddling with his beard. "I've seen her. She's hard to find most of the time, but she never misses homecoming."

"Do you know how she died?" I asked plainly.

"Sorry." He shook his head. "You can ask her. I know she'll be making an appearance soon. She always rides in the parade with the homecoming queens."

"That's tomorrow," I gasped, my hope surging. If we could find Ashley, actually talk to her, that would be huge.

"Oh, you have to be there," John enthused. "It's the best show in Sugarland. We're seventh in line. The band alumni are marching with us. It'll be a complete blowout."

"It's perfect." If I could talk to Ashley, we could blow this case wide open.

"Yep," John agreed. "You can graduate, but you never leave the band."

I'd take his word for it.

"Thank you," I said as my image of the ghost flickered again. "I'll definitely be watching for you." I admired a guy who loved what he did so much, he never wanted it to end. "If you see Ashley, can you tell her Tilly Garber is looking for her?"

"Will do," he promised. "Hopefully, you'll be able to tell her yourself."

I sure hoped so.

In the meantime, I rushed back to Mom. She stood passing out compliments like candy as the parents of this year's football greats, armed with cameras, struggled around her and the rest of the crowd.

"Ashley is going to be at the parade tomorrow," I announced.

"See?" She thwacked a startled Alistair on the arm. "I told you Verity would work magic if we left her alone."

"That's great," he said, although I wasn't quite sure if he believed either one of us.

It didn't matter.

"We *have* to go to the parade tomorrow," Mom stated.

"Like we would miss it," I agreed.

There was just one problem.

"I'm not going," Frankie announced the minute we returned to my ancestral property.

He emerged from my purse as a weak, stuttering flame and slugged through the car door as I shut the engine down.

Mom remained in the car, on the phone with Carl, telling

him about our adventure and checking on how the Roan's float was coming along.

I hustled out of the car after my ghost. Luckily, he wasn't hard to catch.

"Frankie, I can see you have an energy issue," I said, easily overtaking him as he hovered and dipped like a mosquito in a windstorm.

"Yeah, and it's your fault." He ripped his energy back so fast it made my head spin. I bent over, bracing my hands on my knees as a tingling surge whooshed out of my body.

"Now we're done," he added, zipping as fast as he could toward the shed. "I'm staying home."

"I need you at the parade tomorrow," I called after him.

"I'd rather get strung up by my ankles," he vowed. "And I have before, too. When I used Stevie Switchblade's favorite knife to cut up a watermelon."

"But you did great today," I pressed, working to catch up despite my left leg having fallen asleep from the sudden energy jolt.

We'd been able to get a bead on Ashley. We'd questioned two suspects. We couldn't let up now.

"You almost got me nipped by El Gato!"

Well, there was that.

He flickered on ahead of me like a demented firefly. "Or maybe you mean how great it was to have my own urn passing through my body every time you jiggled when you walked, which—newsflash—is *all the time*." His flame dipped down into the earth and popped back up again. "Not to mention your keys and your gum, and who in God's name needs three kinds of lip gloss?"

"I can see your point." It couldn't have been comfortable even though I kept a fairly tidy purse, except for my receipts, which seemed to multiply like bunnies. "But you're the one who doesn't want to be trapped at home."

The ghost ground to a halt. "That doesn't mean you get to schlep me around for days and days on end with my urn clanging through me and my power seeping out my ears. Especially not to go to an overhyped parade."

"To see the 1985 homecoming queen," I corrected. "And the parade is always spectacular, a highlight of homecoming."

"Then I'm definitely skipping it." His flame flickered and then surged. "Besides, all I need is for Molly to find out I'm going to a parade without her."

He had a point. Not about homecoming, but about Molly. I glanced toward the darkened pond, thinking. "You know what? We should take Molly with us."

"No," he balked, as if I'd asked him to dance down Main Street naked.

"Or maybe you mean yes," I said, trying to tempt him.

My ghost made a fresh struggle toward the shed while I kept him company and explained my idea. "I'll talk to Ashley while you make things right with Molly." I didn't see the downside. "You'll be spending time with her at the parade of the year."

"What part of 'I don't like homecoming' don't you understand?"

"It's festive. Everyone's happy. She'll be happy. Besides, you get energy from your relationship when it's going well, so you'll feel better when she feels better."

"There could be Cubans on every corner," he said, as if my whole idea were ludicrous.

"You can hide among the crowd, get a good look at who is after you, and how many," I pointed out. He'd wanted to do that anyway. "You know how much Molly loves an adventure." Plus, I'd be keeping his urn safe.

"And you get exactly what you want," he snapped.

Well, that was merely a happy side effect. "I mean, be practical. You have to do *something* for Molly after standing her up today." She was a reasonable girl, but she had her limits. A festive day out, a side of danger… It would be a perfect way to smooth things over. "And think of it like this, if she's still hopping mad, she can't yell at you at a parade."

He ran a hand over his chin. I could tell he was tempted, by the risk factor if nothing else. "I don't know. It sounds fun and all, but it can get dicey fast."

I had a solution for that. "You can both hide out in my purse if you want," I said, waggling it at him to tempt him. "I'll even take out the extra lip glosses."

His flame grew stronger, and he began to sputter.

"Yay! Look at you!" I exclaimed. The mere thought of making up with Molly must be giving him strength.

"So your grand plan is for me to hide out in your purse," he said, low and dangerous, "a lady's purse—while I court my girl."

Oh goodness, he was angry.

Maybe that was what was making him stronger.

"We can make it romantic." I was all for true love. "I can sprinkle rose petals along the bottom," I suggested.

"I swear on all that is holy—" he began, threatening to erupt.

"You can be the dominant ghost," I added before he lost his cheese all together. "Remember when you were first courting her, and you turned an old outhouse into a love den? I'll take out all three of my lip glosses, plus the receipts, and you can whomp up my purse into whatever you'd like," I said brightly.

If that didn't work, maybe he could invite her inside his urn. She'd no doubt find it fascinating.

I was full of ideas tonight.

Frankie's light waned once more as he stopped in front of his darkened shed. "I can't fix things with Molly by taking her on a purse date. I can't keep dodging your keys and draining myself down to a nub while you traipse all over town. And I absolutely will not put myself in a position to be tortured or maimed by a Cuban cutthroat while you and the Sugarland marching band bebop to 'Everything is Awesome.'"

"How about I have Ellis add a basement under your shed? You know? For nefarious purposes?" I asked. When in doubt, go with a bribe. "As long as you go with me tomorrow."

He went silent.

"Are you thinking about it?" I asked. Technically, we could look at this as less of a bribe and more as a reward. "Ellis could make it real nice."

"Molly left her picnic basket," he said, his voice hollowing. "With a note."

"A love letter?" I hoped.

"It's over," he said dully.

My heart sank. "Oh, Frankie, I'm so sorry." I didn't understand it. I mean, yes, he'd been a jerk for standing her up. But only yesterday, she'd wanted to work things out. I'd seen those two together. Despite his crazy attitude lately, she was his world.

His flame flickered out.

I should have insisted he stay behind today. Or maybe I should never have invited her over without asking him.

"We can fix this," I promised.

"Stop. Fixing. Things!" his voice roared in my ear.

"Frankie—" I began, wishing I could think of something to say to comfort him. It wasn't only about solving the mystery behind Ashley's death—I wanted to do right for Frankie as well.

"I did my part today, and if you couldn't get the job done, that's on you."

"Let's simply—"

"I'm not man enough to keep my girl happy, and that's on me. Now leave me alone." The door of the shed rattled on its hinges, followed by silence. The chorus of frogs and toads in my pond overtook the night.

This was terrible. "Frankie?" I called, putting an ear to the door. "Frankie—" I raised a hand to knock, but slowly lowered it as it occurred to me that talking might not be the solution this time.

Frankie shouldn't be alone, but he didn't want me or Molly or anyone for company. He was in love with her. And she loved him. It should be simple.

I leaned my back against the door of the shed and stared out past the pond toward the lights from my mom's RV. I saw her moving around inside, still on the phone with Carl. At least one of us was smiling.

Frankie needed a reality check and a friend to help set things right. Only it didn't seem like he was going to listen to me. And he was actively avoiding Molly.

I needed to fix this somehow. Soon.

Even if he did tell me to stop fixing things.

I fished my keys from my purse and headed for the house. Lucy came running, her fur squished from sleep, as I let myself in the back door.

As we walked into the kitchen, I scooped her up and held her close. I stood for a moment, snuggling her little body still warm from her nap, as I tried to think of what to do.

"If I could somehow work something out with El Gato, Frankie could take Molly out proper tomorrow," I said to my skunk, who preened and arched her neck as I stroked her.

I walked her around the island. "We could tell Molly that Frankie's gaffe today was El Gato's fault, but that we took care of it. For her," I said, rocking my skunk gently. "Girls like it when you move heaven and earth…and mob complications to be with them."

She touched a wet nose to my hand. "You think I'm onto something?" I asked.

Lucy was both sweet and encouraging. I liked that about her.

"Maybe we can figure out something El Gato wants," I said as we strolled toward the parlor, flicking on lights as we went, "something he'd like more than torturing Frankie."

I fished Frankie's urn from my purse and placed it in the trash can with the rosebush that stood next to my mantel.

I understood the desire to teach Frankie a lesson, but El Gato was never going to change my snippy ghost, and there had to be something we could do to keep him from hurting Frankie. I deposited Lucy on the couch next to me and fired up my laptop.

"I mean, the Cuban cigar heist happened almost a hundred years ago," I reasoned as my skunk blinked her black button eyes at me.

I typed "Cuban cigar heist" into Google and expected to be amazed at Frankie's sheer audacity, if nothing else.

It looks like there aren't any matches for your search.

Strange.

I typed a few more combinations, but every time my search for the Cuban crime of the century came up with…nothing.

"Frankie isn't one for keeping things under wraps," I said to my skunk, who yawned and rested her head on my leg. "We'll learn more about this El Gato instead," I told her. I'd gotten a quick look at him today, but if he lost the zebra feather and the bamboo cane, I wasn't confident I'd be able to pick him out of a crowd.

My fingers clacked on the keyboard. It would be smart of me to get a real, clear picture of him in my mind so that I could keep a better eye out.

Or at least know whom I was speaking with if he tracked Frankie to my property.

But the notorious Cuban gangster didn't come up in my search, either.

I closed the laptop and set it aside. "And here I thought you could Google anything," I said to my skunk.

I dug in my pocket for my cell phone. My sister, Melody, was the real research expert. I had no doubt she could track the great Cuban cigar heist, El Gato, and the real contents of Al Capone's vault.

She answered on the second ring. "Hey there," I said, quickly telling her what I needed.

"I can look right now," she said. "I could use an excuse to step away from these artifacts."

Wait. "Are you at the library still?" It was nearing ten o'clock.

"It's really rather fascinating," she said, her boots echoing off the polished library floor. "We're making a list of every box, jar, and archival envelope from the time capsule, and then we're going to lock them all up—unopened—until it's time to unveil the contents."

"Who's we?" I asked. It sounded like a big job.

"Me and Jean, only she left to go to the bonfire."

"But you can't stop," I concluded, knowing my sister.

"It's so cool," she gushed. "Even the old tin boxes are cool. I can't believe I get to do this. And I get to supervise the opening ceremony. We'll do it as soon as the police give us the okay. People are dying to see what's in these things, and I have to admit I am, too."

Yes. I'd seen the gawkers at the flagpole today.

"Don't go too crazy," Melody had been known to spend the night at the library from time to time.

"I'll try to stop before midnight," she promised. "It'll give post-party traffic a chance to clear, anyway."

"You'd think the bonfire would be winding down by now," I said as Lucy pawed at her empty bowl.

"They doused the fire, but now there's an impromptu party in the square," Melody said as I went to warm some peas and squash I'd made for Lucy earlier. "A band of drunks have taken over the main stage. What they lack in skill, they make up for in volume."

"I'll bet I know where Ellis is." No doubt fit to be tied.

"Yeah, I'm looking out the window now. There's a conga line

going around the statue of Colonel Larimore," she said, and I could hear her typing. "You wouldn't know we were in the middle of another Sugarland murder mystery."

"Well, I suppose it's been a while since Ashley died," I reasoned, hitting the buttons on the microwave.

"I feel so bad for Mom," Melody said, echoing my thoughts earlier.

"You should make time for her." This wasn't exactly the homecoming Mom had expected. She'd appreciate seeing more of Melody.

"The time capsule has kept me really busy," Melody said, and I could hear her typing. "Plus...Mom tried to redecorate my apartment the last time she stopped by."

"She only wants to be involved in your life."

"And she tried to set me up with my cute neighbor," Melody added.

I'd forgotten about that. "Even so, you might not see her for a while after this," I reminded her. I didn't want Melody to have any regrets.

"Hold on..." she said, typing furiously on the other end. "I think I've found your El Gato."

"That was fast." Quicker than I'd been able to fix Lucy's dinner.

"Oh my." Her voice went hollow.

"What?"

"I'm sending it over."

"What's wrong?" I asked as the microwave beeped. "You know you can level with me."

"You're looking for El Gato, the Cuban gangster from Havana," she said clinically.

"Yes."

"I could be mistaken. I mean, I've never seen this exact photograph," she stammered. "I'm texting it over."

"You're freaking me out," I said.

The microwave beeped again while Lucy tried to climb my leg. I clicked over to my texts and opened the picture from Melody.

"You see it?" my sister's tinny voice demanded from the phone. "Is it him?"

I stared at the screen, at the photo of the legendary Cuban gangster, the words El Gato scrawled in hand along the bottom. And it didn't look anything like the squat ghost I'd seen this afternoon.

This was a black-and-white photo of a gangster with a pencil-thin moustache, wearing a white suit and a matching Panama hat. He held a stogie clenched between his teeth and a Tommy gun pointed at the camera. And he looked eerily familiar.

Too familiar.

"Oh my God, it is him."

I'd know him anywhere.

Chapter Twelve

"Melody, El Gato is Frankie."

Frankie stole the frame off the *Mona Lisa*. Frankie opened a dog racing track with puppies. Or nobody did, and he'd made it all up.

It took Melody a second to process it. "So he blamed all of his jerky moves on his alter ego?"

"Not all of them." Frankie had plenty of jerky moves on his own.

And he was absolutely terrible at disguises. Why did he always think a mustache would make him unrecognizable?

"Wait. I found an addendum. It says it right here: El Gato is an alias for small-time crook Frank Winkelmann."

Frankie would object to the small-time part. Not to mention being called Frank.

And did Frankie really seduce the wife of el presidente?

No. It was inconceivable. Impossible.

I objected to all of it. "I can't believe he'd lie to me like that."

"Because he's such an honest guy?"

"Well..."

"Like it or not, you have a screwy gangster at your house. You can't be surprised when he does screwy gangster things."

More like in my shed. And sometimes in my purse. "It's so huge of a lie I'm still trying to process it." I'd worried about him. I'd tried to protect him! I'd run from a shady guy by the flagpole.

No wonder the man hadn't chased us. He was probably enjoying the day with his live grandson.

"I can't believe Frankie lied to me! And he has the nerve to give a cocky little grin in his photo. As if El Gato is all that." Frankie had probably never even been to Cuba.

"But here's the thing," I continued. I was on a roll. "*Why* did he lie?"

"Because he's crazy and he wants you to suffer, too?" Melody supplied.

"You'd think, but no." Frankie never did anything that wasn't to his own benefit. "He was making himself miserable the whole time, too." I didn't get it.

"Wait," Melody broke in. "Oh, my God."

Oh, this was getting better and better. "What else did you find on him?" Another photo? Crime scene information? "Did he kidnap the Lindbergh baby? Is Lizzie Borden really Frankie in drag?" Melody had gone silent. "What?"

Her breath grew shallow.

"Melody, you're freaking me out."

"It's the artifacts," she stammered. "The ones I was cataloguing before you called."

Of course. "Yes. From the time capsule."

"The box from 1986. It's been disturbed."

"What do you mean?" How could she tell?

"The seal has been broken. It wasn't when I picked up the phone. Somebody's here in the building with me."

Oh my God. "Hang up with me and call the police right now."

The line went dead.

Heart racing, I dialed Ellis. Or at least I tried.

I let out a small cry as my hands shook and my fingers fumbled across the screen of my phone.

"Call Ellis," I voice commanded, only my voice warbled so much it didn't do anything. "Call Ellis," I pleaded.

The call went through, and he answered on the first ring. "You'll never guess what Tonya Jefferson's goat—"

"This is an emergency!" I cried, hoping he could hear me over the din of the crowd behind him. "Melody is in danger. There's an intruder in the library with her, and it might be our killer."

"I'm on it," he said, and the line went dead.

I bent over and tried to breathe. I should have told her to run, to hide, to grab a weapon, to do something besides call for help that might not come fast enough.

Somebody was in there with her, and they were messing with the box that our mom's dead friend had put into the time capsule, and I didn't think it was a coincidence at all.

I grabbed my keys off the counter, then slammed them down. I wouldn't make it in time. Ellis was already in the square. I had to trust him, and I did.

But waiting was hell.

I paced. I fretted.

I walked out the back door and down the stairs and halfway across the yard toward Mom's RV before I turned around. I refused to worry Mom.

Not yet.

She'd been through enough already.

I returned to the kitchen and tried to spoon Lucy's dinner into her bowl, only I dropped the bowl, and it shattered.

Lucy ran.

The phone rang, and I pounced on it.

"Melody is safe," Ellis said, with no preamble. "She's here at the library with me and Officer Duranja. We did a sweep, and the door at the back was wide open."

"But she's safe." That was all that mattered.

"Yes," he assured me. "Now we're looking to see if anything's missing."

"She said the seal had been broken on the Class of 1986 time-capsule box."

"It is," Ellis said, disappointment breaking through his tough-cop tone. "After I get off the phone with you, I'm going to figure out who was on the committee to put together that box."

"Ashley headed that committee."

"I know," he said softly. "But there's got to be others who helped. Hopefully, one of them has a list of the contents."

"What's going on?" I asked in vain. Whatever it was had touched too close to home.

"We don't know, but we'll figure it out," Ellis promised. "The most important thing is that your sister is all right. And kind of mad from the way she's snipping at Duranja."

"Yes, well, Duranja is easy to dislike." He was judgy, terse, and had accused me of murder once or twice.

"I'll touch base if I have any news for you," Ellis said.

We said our goodbyes, and I went boneless against the wall.

Melody was safe.

I slid down the wall and sat. With any luck, the thief had left a clue that would lead us to him or her—and possibly even to Ashley's killer.

That had to be enough for now.

I heard the pitter-patter of skunk paws and felt the warm weight of Lucy as she curled in my lap. She didn't know what was wrong, but she wanted to help. I stroked her, and honest to goodness, it did help. So much.

After a while, I stood her up and did the same myself. I

cleaned up her ruined dinner, heated her a new one, then looked out the window to the darkened shed in my yard.

It appeared so peaceful, so serene in the night. But it wouldn't stay that way for long. Now that my sister was in good hands, I had a bone to pick with El Gato.

Chapter Thirteen

I rapped my knuckles on the rough wooden door of Frankie's shed. "We need to talk."

To my surprise, his head popped out of the pond to my left. "What?"

His head glowed over the water, not making a ripple, the light reflecting off the water creating deep hollows under his cheekbones.

You could have knocked me over with a feather. "You're swimming?"

"Resting and recovering," he said, as if a dip in the pond were a solution for everybody. "Water helps me relax. You do not." He began sinking into the abyss. "So scram."

"No problem—*El Gato.*"

He halted with only his eyes showing above the waterline.

"That's right," I said, stalking the gangster in the pond. "I'm onto you. I know all about your lie, your deceit."

His brows slanted together. "You say it as if it's a bad thing."

It was a terrible thing, a violation. We were supposed to be friends. Or at least heading that way. I stopped at the water's edge. "And the worst thing is that I was actually worried about you."

"Worried enough to drag me downtown against my will," he shot back.

"You asked to go. Did you forget already?" It was yesterday. "I cared about you. I let you hide in my purse."

"In a mountain of old receipts and petrified restaurant mints."

"When all the time you were *lying!*" I glared down at him.

He popped out of the water up to his shoulders. "I've killed people, and you're worried about a little white lie that didn't hurt anybody."

"This is not a game of what is worse," I said, tossing my hands up.

"Now you sound like my brother, Lou." He rolled his eyes.

"Well, then Lou was right." And he wasn't listening. "Argh!" I spun in a frustrated circle. "You're lying, and you're scheming, and you destroyed my trust, and you don't even care. You know what? I don't care either because you don't matter. I don't matter. What matters is there's a dead girl from the Class of 1986 lying in the morgue. And now?" I said, pointing at him. "Someone is sneaking around the library while Melody is holed up in there by herself."

That got his attention.

"My sister could have been killed tonight. She barely avoided a run-in with an intruder because I had her checking up on *you* instead of keeping track of the artifacts."

"So I helped," he reasoned. "If she hadn't been checking up on me, she would have been there when the intruder showed up."

"That's not the point."

"I see where this is going," he snarled, gliding toward me. "You're gonna use this to try to guilt me into going to that stupid parade with you tomorrow." He stopped just short of the edge. I could see the whites of his eyes, his slightly crooked canine tooth. "Well, it won't work because I don't have a conscience."

He did. I'd seen it. But I didn't think he'd appreciate me bringing it up.

I sighed. I had to make him see reason, or I'd never get him to the parade tomorrow. And that was what we needed, despite Frankie's…issues. We had to get a lead on Ashley's killer, for her sake and for my sister's.

"Why did you do it, Frankie?" I still didn't get why he'd put himself—either of us—through it.

"It's complicated."

"Try me."

"El Gato is my alias," he said, rising out of the lake. He was missing his body from the mid-chest down.

"Yeah, I got that," I said, rubbing the ache in my temples.

"El Gato was there when I needed to blame somebody. He took the fall when things went wrong. El Gato forgot to put gas in the getaway car. El Gato stole the entire take from the convent heist."

I dropped my hand. "You stole from a convent?"

"Just the one." He shrugged. "But you see what I mean."

Not entirely. In fact, I wasn't sure I wanted to hop on the crazy train at all. But I needed to understand. "So El Gato didn't really steal the frame off the *Mona Lisa*."

"Who has time?" he asked.

"Or open a dog track that raced puppies."

"Oh, I did do that," Frankie said happily. "It was a dud as far as racing went. Turns out it's impossible to get all the puppies going in the same direction. Plus, I rescued mutts, and some of them had these floppy ears they kept tripping over."

"Frankie!" Not even puppies were safe.

"I have to admit it was adorable. And it worked out," he insisted. "El Gato took the fall for the lost investment, and I adopted the dogs out to the local shopkeepers El Gato was shaking down."

"Sure." Why not?

"Too bad they grew up to be good watchdogs," he mused.

"Frankie," I said, bracing my head in my hands, "why do you always have to make things difficult?"

He considered the question. "It keeps life interesting," he reasoned.

"So there was no revenge plot."

"I'm kind of bummed about that," he admitted.

"No blowing up El Gato and his henchmen into tiny pieces?"

"I'd like to see somebody try," he huffed.

And in typical Frankie fashion, he'd circled around the bigger issue. "Riddle me this. Why did you lie to *me* about El Gato?"

He ground his jaw, hesitating.

Oh, my goodness. "What was El Gato getting you out of this time?"

I saw the outline of a barely there hand caress his jaw. "Here's the thing…"

"Spill it," I ordered.

He dropped his hand. "Look. You saw my brother, Lou, and how great he is with his wife and how much she *likes* him." He said it as if the entire concept were a crazy, shocking surprise. "How am I supposed to handle that?"

"You should be thrilled for your brother." I was. "Lou and Chastity have earned their happiness. They've loved each other and trusted each other through true tragedy."

"Exactly." Frankie looked up at the sky. "How do I compete with that?"

"You don't."

He glided away, then back at me. "I can't ever have that with Molly. I can't be that guy. My brother sacrificed everything, and he didn't even get a guarantee that it would all work out. I mean, that's insane!"

"Yet he saved his family and the love of his life, and now they get to be happy for eternity," I pointed out. "I mean, there are no guarantees in love, but if you don't go for it, you're guaranteed to be lonely, wondering what you might have missed."

"That's a lot of pressure," he countered. "Molly loves my brother's story," he choked out. "She said it herself. She wants love and marriage and me…" He trailed off. "I love her. We connect on this soul level that I never even knew existed till I met her." He winced as if he were in pain.

"You realize that's a good thing." I suspected that connection had something to do with why his energy was so closely tied to hers.

He groaned. "I want to be with her and only her, but I'm not ready for the whole enchilada right this second. The thought of it makes my throat tight and my head spin, and I don't know if I'll ever be ready," he said, going pale.

No, wait. He was disappearing entirely.

"Stop," I ordered, as if I could halt his energy drain. I wasn't even hooked up to him, and he was losing power. "You don't have to decide right now." Technically, he and Molly had all the time in the world. "You do have to treat her with respect. You do have to spend time with her. And you definitely have to apologize for standing her up today."

"Seriously?" He winced. He was so transparent I could see clear through him and across the yard. "Like I should send her flowers or something?"

It was going to take a lot more than that. "You have to show her you love her. If you don't, you're going to lose her."

He looked at the ground. "I already lost her."

"You can still fix it," I urged. "You can take her out tomorrow." He shot a hurt, angry glance up at me. "And not because I want your power and not because we're investigating a murder but because you need to show her right away that she means something to you."

He cringed. "I hate to admit this, but I'm not always that great with women."

Shocker. Still, he wasn't going to get any better unless he believed he could. "Hey, who seduced the wife of el presidente?" I asked, trying to build him up. "Or, wait. Was that a lie, too?"

"Oh, that really happened," he said, running a hand over his hair, "but that was El Gato, not me."

Seriously? "You *are* El Gato."

His shoulders drooped. "El Gato is braver, smoother. He's *alluring*," he said, thrusting a hand at me. "Ladies like that."

"You can be that too," I insisted. "You can take all the good parts of El Gato and make them your own."

He dropped his hand. "That is the dumbest thing I've ever heard."

"Is it?" I prodded.

He stared at me.

"I'm serious, Frank."

He worked his jaw. "Okay, so what if I succeed? Here's the stupid thing about homecoming in this town; if I take her to the parade, she'll want to go to the dance."

"Then take her to the dance." He couldn't possibly dislike homecoming so much that he'd wreck his relationship or his health over it.

"You don't get it," he said, shrinking down to a flame.

"Then explain it to me," I said.

He flickered in the night, silent.

"I mean, who else can you tell?" He knew me. He trusted me. I was his only sounding board.

After a moment's hesitation, he cleared his throat. "Everyone knows—you take a girl to the homecoming dance, the next thing you do is you walk her down the aisle."

"Oh, Frankie, that's not how it works anymore." I wasn't sure if it ever worked that way.

He grew back into himself, or at least his head. "She'll be expecting it. The fancy kids who went to high school used to get engaged at homecoming, married the summer after graduation. I escaped all that. I was living free. Until I met you," he added, as if it were my fault he had a girlfriend and a respectable social life. "Now I'm getting sucked in, too. I mean, who am I to fight tradition? Especially in this town."

"So that's why you've been hiding?" Sure, our town took pride in its history and in homecoming, but it was meant to be fun, not a trap.

"I wasn't worried about any Cubans. I wanted you to keep an eye out for Molly," he grudgingly admitted.

It actually made sense, in a warped, Frankie kind of way. He'd lied about El Gato in order to hole himself up in his shed. He'd lied again in order to avoid her picnic lunch. He lent me his power because he'd known I'd greet her if I saw her downtown.

But lying and avoidance wouldn't fix this.

I looked at my sad, sorry ghost. "Take her to the parade tomorrow. Say you're sorry. Tell her your fears."

He wrinkled his nose. "You make it sound so easy."

Yes and no. "If she rejects you, at least she knows you care about her."

He sighed and shook his head. "Women are so complicated."

I rested a hand on my hip. "Yeah, and you've been real simple so far."

Frankie stared out over the pond, and I gave him a moment to think. Now that he was out of the water, the frogs had begun to chirp again. I swatted a mosquito that dipped near my cheek.

At last, the gangster spoke. "Can we go see her before I change my mind?"

"Gladly," I told him.

I fetched my purse and keys.

"Was there even a cigar heist?" I asked as he glided toward the car with me.

"Nah. Suds found a couple of cases of stogies in a cave outside Jackson. We figured it'd be cool to say we stole them."

"Well, you did steal them if you took them out of someone else's hiding spot," I reasoned.

"Hey." He brightened. "That's true."

We drove to the historical society that Molly haunted, and I waited in the car while Frankie glided up onto the white painted porch.

We'd rehearsed his apology on the way over, along with his invitation to the parade. I had a certain amount of confidence Frankie could pull this off, if only because Molly really did love him. God bless her soul.

He appeared in my passenger seat twenty minutes later.

"She's mad, but she's going," he said, out of breath, even though ghosts didn't need to breathe.

He'd also regained his entire form.

"This is good," I told him. We didn't have to fix it all in one night. "Did you tell her the truth about El Gato?"

"No," he said, drawing his hat low over his forehead. "I'm trying to make her less mad, not *more* mad."

It was too big a lie to let stand. "You really need to tell her. Soon," I said when he didn't appear to budge. "As in why don't you go tell her now?"

"Yeah, because you were real happy when you found out about El Gato," he groused. "Come on, let's go," he urged.

Despite my better judgement, I started the car.

Frankie settled back happily, as if he'd won. "Molly was real impressed with how I'm risking my life to take her to the parade tomorrow. It was the only reason she agreed to forgive me and come along."

"Because El Gato wants to kill you," I said flatly.

"Now you've got it," Frankie said, pleased as if I were a prized student.

"No, I don't," I said, hands braced on the wheel. "I don't get it at all."

He gave me the side-eye. "Do you want Molly at the parade tomorrow or not?"

"Fine." I *ker-chunked* the car into reverse. At least he'd made up with her.

Frankie turned to me, eyes wide. "I forgot to tell her what time," he said, disappearing again.

I turned the car off and sat alone in the dark, hopeful. Relieved. And I hated to admit it, but a little worried.

If Frankie did take my advice and confess... He was right. We might not have Molly at the parade tomorrow.

Telling her was the right thing to do. I knew that. And I didn't regret making it plain to him. Still.

As I sat pondering, a pair of headlights turned into the narrow drive that led both in and out of the Historical Society property. They stopped halfway down the drive. I couldn't determine the make or model, but I knew nobody living needed to be at the closed society this late on a weeknight.

My pulse sped up, and I reached for my phone.

"Frankie?" I called.

Maybe I could send the ghost ahead to see who it was.

Only Frankie didn't respond. And my heart sank when my phone wasn't in the pocket of my purse.

Did I leave it at home?

The car began a slow trek toward me.

Definitely weird.

Maybe I'd just misplaced my phone. I dug through my purse, past the keys and the wallet, and the nest of receipts and the three kinds of lip gloss and dang it! Frankie had been right about the state of my bag. I dumped the purse out as the car drew closer.

I couldn't leave. The other car blocked the entire way out.

Unless I drove over the lawn of the historical society.

I'd done it before while solving a different case. But I hadn't meant to do it that time.

This time, I'd have to drive over parking barricades. I started the car and revved the engine.

The other car sped up. It was coming straight for me.

I chugged my car into reverse, turned the wheel, and hit the gas. My land yacht flew backward as I spun into a U-turn, and right as I hit the gas to plow across the lawn, the other car lit up with spinning red and white lights and the shrill blip of a police siren.

Ellis slammed out of the driver's side and approached my car, his hands held out. "What are you doing?"

The adrenaline drained from me, and I went momentarily boneless. "Not driving across the lawn," I said weakly, running to meet him.

He caught me in a hug. "I tried to call you."

"My phone is at home," I said into his chest.

"Your mom said you were yelling at the pond about Molly."

"She's coming to the parade with us tomorrow," I said. "I hope," I added as Ellis stroked my hair.

"Sure," he said, as if I'd made perfect sense. "I wanted to tell you the library is clear. We locked it up."

"Thank you," I said into his shirt.

"Your sister refused to leave," he said, as if stupid bravery were a family trait. I raised my head to look at him in the moonlight. Dang, he was handsome. "Melody insisted on guarding the artifacts."

"You can't leave her there alone," I insisted.

"I didn't." He twisted his mouth wryly. "She's in there with Duranja. He's supposed to be off tonight, but he volunteered to watch over her."

"Poor Melody." She was sacrificing a lot.

"He's a good officer," Ellis reminded me. As if that made him less of a jerk. "Go home," Ellis added. "Get some sleep. It'll look better in the morning."

"Are you sure?" I asked.

"I don't know. I was talking to myself," he mused.

Just then, I saw Frankie glide out of the historical society building. Molly wasn't with him, but he appeared satisfied, nonetheless. When he saw me watching, he frowned and slipped into the car.

"Want to come home with me?" I suggested to Ellis. I hadn't seen much of him these past few days, and we could both use some cheering up.

He shot me his first real grin of the night. "Yes, ma'am," he said, bending down for a long-overdue kiss.

Chapter Fourteen

The next morning, I woke up alone. Ellis had to get down to the parade early to set up security. Between maintaining some kind of order at homecoming and investigating the death of Ashley Starling, Ellis could use more than twenty-four hours this homecoming Friday.

At least I could help him with the investigation.

I didn't like the boldness of the library intruder last night, and I shuddered to think what might have happened if Melody had gotten in the way.

I dressed in white jeans and a festive red V-neck sweater with faux pearl earrings. My red boots clomped as I walked out onto the back porch with a cup of coffee. Lucy dashed past me, down the steps, and out into the yard. I'd retied the red bow on her butt above her tail. She deserved to be festive, too.

Mom banged out of the RV, wearing red slacks and a white sweater with a Sugarland Biscuits patch sewn on over her heart.

"Hungry?" I leaned a hip against the porch rail. "I've got cinnamon rolls with cream cheese icing." I'd made them just in case and even heated the oven. "Ready in a jiff."

She stifled a yawn and held up her own mug of coffee, which

was a shame because I'd bought a special morning blend from the Happy Bean just for her. "I'd rather get going," she said apologetically. "I hardly slept at all last night thinking of Ashley and the parade."

I glanced down at my watch. It was only seven thirty in the morning. The parade didn't start until nine.

Mom stopped at the bottom of the porch steps, and I realized she already had her purse slung over her shoulder, ready to go. "Carl took off at dawn to hook up the Roan's float. They had to be in line an hour ago, and we need to get going if we want to get a good spot to do some investigating."

She was sure hopping this morning.

"Let me see if Frankie's ready," I said, heading down.

"Frankie will never be ready," the ghost's voice sounded in my ear.

"Great idea to bring in the mob," Mom said, gripping her mug with both hands. "Your gangster buddy can help you sniff out Ashley."

"I'm not a bloodhound," Frankie said, shimmering into focus next to her. "Tell this lady that's not what ghosts *do*."

I was still trying to figure out for myself what ghosts actually did.

Still, I was glad to see Frankie had regained all of his limbs. He looked like his old, grumpy self again. I'd have to thank Molly when I saw her.

"Think we can pick your girlfriend up a little early?" I asked him.

"I told her I'd meet her down there," he said, straightening his tie as Lucy came charging from behind the apple tree. She took one look at my ghost, let out a huffy grunt, and tossed grass with a kick of her back legs as she dashed straight under the porch.

"I don't think she likes your plan," I said to Frankie.

Or maybe it was that she didn't like the ghost in general.

"The gentlemanly thing to do is to pick your girlfriend up for a date," I chided. He should know that.

"That's how we always did it in my day," Mom agreed.

The ghost stiffened. "She suggested we meet out front of the feed store. I froze."

"Oh, well, then the gentlemanly thing to do would be to agree," I conceded.

Frankie ran a hand down his face. "I can't keep up with all these rules."

"You should send her flowers, like you talked about last night," I suggested as I backtracked to fetch my bag.

"I did," he said, while I made sure I had my cell phone. "I sent Suds to buy as many roses as he could find. I told him to fill her entire bedroom, El Gato style."

He really needed to tell Molly he was El Gato. I had a feeling it was going to blow up spectacularly on him if he didn't. But for the moment, I bit my tongue.

"You're making quite an effort," I said, trying to be supportive. Grand gestures weren't as good as truth and honesty, but Frankie was making positive changes, and I was happy for him.

Maybe he was finally on the right track.

We hit traffic even before we hit Main Street. Mom had been right. It seemed we were the only ones *not* downtown at seven thirty in the morning. We parked even farther down the street than we had on the first day of the festival, and by the time we made it to the corner of Main Street and Fifth, Mom had already seen a dozen people she knew.

And stopped to talk to all of them.

I played the dutiful daughter, helping to keep the conversation light and ushering her along. At last we made it to the old feed store, which was now the packed, popular breakfast spot Biscuits & Gravy. They'd taken advantage of their name, offering the Homecoming Biscuits Breakfast Special, and the line was out the door.

The parade-goers waiting for breakfast competed for space on the wide sidewalk with those who'd already set up lawn chairs along the parade route. My poor ghost had to work hard to dodge the living.

Frankie found a free spot uncomfortably close to the hostess stand out front while a girl in an old-fashioned red apron and frilly white shirt took down names and handed out buzzers to people waiting for tables.

"See what I put up with for love?" he grumbled.

"You're doing great," I said, giving him the thumbs-up. I couldn't wait to hear what Molly thought about her flowers.

Meanwhile, Mom crowded with Phyllis and Darcy, classmates from '86. Phyllis wore the same red and white scarf we'd seen her in two days ago, while Darcy had decorated her white straw hat with every Sugarland Biscuits souvenir known to man, from buttons and pins to a tiny stuffed goat. It seemed Vincent van Goat had a reputation.

I'd told Mom about the break-in at the library last night, and when I drew nearer, I realized she was busy retelling the story to her friends.

"Do you think that's a good idea, Mom?" I broke in right as she'd gotten to the part about the disturbed Class of '86 box.

If word spread that we'd noticed the broken seal in the library, it could tip off the killer. And put Melody in further danger.

"Oh, I heard it from Krissie Sue Klinger," Phyllis said, waving me off. "She was on the Class of '86 committee. Ellis called her last night."

It seemed Krissie was a talker, too. "Great," I said through clenched teeth.

"Does she always worry this much?" Phyllis asked Mom.

"She takes after her father," Mom assured her friend.

At least somebody in this family had the sense God gave a goose.

I needed to get out of there before I started lecturing my elders.

Not like it would do any good.

"I'm going to wander," I told them. I needed to see my sister, and if Melody had spent the night at the library, chances were good that she'd be there this morning as well. At least until Jean or someone else showed up to relieve her.

The more I thought about it, the more I didn't think it was such a hot idea for the science teacher's wife to be the one keeping an eye on the artifacts. It would have also been easy for her or her husband to sneak into the library. She had the keys.

"What about your ghost hunt?" Mom asked. Loudly. "Or are you going to wait until you see Ashley in the parade?"

Phyllis and Darcy turned to me with interest, along with a fair number of folks on the sidewalk.

"Mom!" I said, not quite believing she did that. Again.

I was going to have to stop telling her things. I'd hoped her visit to town would bring us closer, but it seemed like every little part of my life was now fodder for her storytelling.

"Why the face?" she asked, as if she were genuinely baffled at my distress. We both knew that wasn't the case. "Fine." She held up her hands. "I'll try to rein it in."

She wouldn't have to, because I was done.

Done telling her about my life.

Done sharing my secrets.

Done confiding in the one person I should be able to trust.

I walked down Main and crossed the street toward the town square. Police had blocked off Main Street since we'd arrived, so there was no more traffic to worry about. I was glad I'd listened to my mom about getting there early.

At least we could share that, the desire to arrive at places promptly.

I glanced back at her chatting away with her friends, as if nothing had changed.

Did this even bother her?

It should.

I mean, there I was last night, telling Melody to make time for Mom, when as soon as I let her into my life, she turned around and abused my trust. Every. Single. Time.

Sanitation workers crisscrossed the square, hard at work cleaning up the remainder of the party from last night.

Otherwise, the square lay quiet. Empty.

Even though Mom hadn't been around and I hadn't always counted on her, a deep down part of me had always felt like I could. But it seemed like her stories were more important than me. I sighed, aching at the loss.

I'd have to do this on my own.

The library stood dark. Closed.

As I drew closer, I spotted Officer Duranja standing in the doorway, arms crossed, wearing last night's rumpled uniform and a frown.

Exactly the man I didn't want to see.

I mean, I was grateful he'd stayed with my sister last night. The man obviously had one or two redeeming qualities. But still, it was ridiculous the number of times he'd called me crazy over the past two years. All because he didn't understand my relationship with Frankie.

For two years, Duranja had actively rooted against my relationship with Ellis, thinking he was somehow protecting my boyfriend. And don't get me started on all the times Ellis's overeager apprentice had assumed I was a killer.

Simply because I kept finding bodies.

"Happy homecoming," I said, taking the steps two at a time and facing the square-jawed, holier-than-thou, superhero wannabe. "Is Melody still here?"

"She is," he said, not even trying to hide his displeasure at seeing me.

It wasn't like I wanted to hang out with him, either.

"I'll just pop in and see her—"

He blocked me. "Nobody gets inside."

Oh, come on. "Look, I appreciate you protecting her last night. And…now," I added when he didn't budge. "But I was on the phone with her when the break-in occurred. She scared me to death last night, and I won't feel right until I see my sister with my own eyes."

"We have a crime scene inside this building," he drawled, as if I were an irresponsible junior detective eager to sneak inside and play Jenga with his artifacts.

"I need five minutes, tops. I won't touch anything from the time capsule." That wasn't why I stopped by at all. Melody wouldn't let me touch the artifacts any more than the police would, anyway. "I'm not your intruder. But I am going to hug my sister. So unless you want to piss her off as well as me—"

He stepped aside.

Well, all right. "See? That wasn't hard," I said, not quite sure why he'd given in, but not willing to question it.

I slipped past him and into the ornate arched lobby.

"Melody?" I called as the smell of old books enveloped me.

Footsteps echoed as she hurried down the steps from the second floor.

"Verity!" She enveloped me in a bear hug.

I pulled her tight, so grateful to have my sister alive and well. "You scared the pickles out of me."

"Now you sound like Grandma," she warbled, her voice not at all steady.

"Are you okay?"

"I was until you hugged me," she said, tearing up. "Sorry," she managed. "I think I'm fine, and then it hits me all over again."

"You did great. No 'sorrys' about it." Her skin had gone pale, her hair mussed. "It's okay to feel a little unsteady after what you've been through."

"That's what Alec keeps saying," she said, running her fingers through her hair. "He took really good care of me last night."

"Alec?"

Her cheeks flushed. "Alec Duranja."

I knew whom she was talking about. "So now you're on a first-name basis?"

I must have asked loudly because the door cracked, and Mr. First-name glared inside.

"We're fine," Melody insisted, taking my hand and dragging me into the main reading room. "It's nothing." She turned to face me. "The important thing is we don't know who broke in last night. It looks like Jean left the back door unlocked when she left."

"Of course." And I knew what her excuse would be: This was Sugarland.

"The intruder didn't leave any clues," she added, wringing her hands.

"Hold that thought," I said, spotting a trio of Civil War ghosts sitting on the floor near the lobby. We'd walked right past them. In all fairness, I'd been more concerned with my sister. "I see some old friends."

"The boys from the 142nd Infantry?" Melody asked, staying behind.

One and the same.

The library had been used as a field hospital back in the day, and some of the men had never left. I'd met this particular group before. They liked to hang out and play poker and, luckily, they liked me.

Unfortunately, these particular ghosts also tended to let days, months, and even years pass without noticing. Still, I hoped if someone had walked in through the front door last night, and if the boys of the 142nd had been in their usual spot, there was a chance they could at least describe the person, or people.

"Good morning, Stoutmeyer," I said to the dealer, a skinny young man with a bruised cheekbone and a chest full of gauze wrap.

"Is it?" he asked, focused on the cards as he dealt a new hand. He'd never been much of a talker. Good thing I was.

"Sorry to interrupt, but I have a question, and it's really important." They gave no reaction, but I pressed on. "Did you see *anyone* come into the library after dark last night?"

He scrunched his face. "Were we here last night?" he asked the curly-haired soldier to his left. Gauze shrouded half of the teen's face, including his left eye.

The guy looked to the ceiling with his one good eye, trying to recall. "Is it night right now?"

"She said it was morning," the dealer said, shrugging a shoulder at me.

The younger man's gaze settled on me, and he seemed to register my presence for the first time. "Oh, hi, Verity."

"There was a break-in last night," I explained, hoping to add some urgency to my request. "We think someone snuck in the back door. I'm wondering if you saw anything at all."

The third man, a corporal, tilted his head. "Why would we be watching a door?" he asked, as if it were the silliest thing he'd ever heard.

"The way you play, it doesn't look like you're watching your cards." Stoutmeyer laughed, eyeing his hand as he rearranged it.

The other soldiers laughed.

"Sorry," the curly-haired soldier added when he realized I didn't see the humor.

"If Frankie's around, tell him we can use a fourth," Stoutmeyer instructed.

"I'll let him know," I said, disappointed. I hadn't really expected much from these particular ghosts, but I'd been hoping all the same.

I left them to their game, and they didn't even notice my departure.

"Well, that was a bust," I said, glancing over my shoulder as I returned to Melody. It would be really nice if the men of the 142nd could see beyond their own little world. Maybe, after the violence they'd experienced, they didn't want to think of anything at all.

"You tried." Melody sighed. "I appreciate it." She leaned against a heavy wooden research table. "I'm racking my brain to think of what else I can do. Ellis told you the seal was broken on the Class of 1986 box, right? Well, I talked to Krissie Sue Klinger from the Class of '86 committee, and she gave me a list of the contents. We checked to see if anything was missing."

"And?"

"Everything's there. At least as far as we can tell."

I didn't understand it. "Why would someone break in if they weren't going to take anything?"

"Exactly," Melody said, breaking away to pace between the rows of polished wood tables. "Whoever broke in had enough time to take something," she said, turning back to me. "Why didn't they?"

I rested a hand on a chair back, deep in thought. "Could they have altered something?"

"Maybe," she said. "Although it's hard to alter homeroom pictures, sixty-eight student essays on Life in 1985, and a felted, stuffed, signed Sugarland Biscuit."

I could see her point. But… "There could be something hidden inside that Biscuit."

That had to be it!

"Duranja already checked."

"Well?" I prodded.

She sighed. "I know you don't like him, but he is an excellent cop."

I'd give her that. "Okay, well, Mom told me that Ashley put something special into the box."

Melody froze. "What was it? Because I didn't find anything in there that wasn't on the official list."

"Well, don't get your hopes up," I said, stomach knotting. "She never told Mom what it was."

"Who else knew about it?" Duranja's voice echoed from the foyer.

Him again. "Aren't you supposed to be outside standing guard?" I asked.

"And weren't you supposed to just duck in for five minutes and hug your sister?" he countered.

I snuck a conspiratorial glance at Melody. "You deserve a medal for hanging out all night with that guy."

"He's not so bad," she said, flicking her gaze at him.

Which was weird on about twelve different levels.

Duranja walked into the main reading room as if he owned it, his work boots echoing off the marble. "Who else was aware that Ashley added something to the time capsule?"

Melody dug a hand through her hair. "Knowing Mom, everybody." She sighed. "Why did I leave those artifacts alone?"

"Because you couldn't imagine someone would be lurking in the library," I said.

"I'm still so creeped out," she admitted as Duranja joined us. "I don't know what I would have done without you."

"It's okay," Duranja and I said at the same time.

He glared at me, and I gave it right back at him.

"Darla died in the library when she got in someone's way," Melody said, recalling an earlier case.

"Nobody's going to hurt you," Duranja vowed.

"I personally think one of you should be with the artifacts at all times until we get to the bottom of this," I said.

Melody nodded. "We already decided that."

Well… "Good." At least one positive thing had come out of this weird bond between them.

Melody was no doubt scared and grabbing onto any life raft that floated by. Once we solved this, she'd be rid of Duranja. One more reason to crack this case as soon as possible.

"I have it on good authority that Ashley is going to be at the parade today," I told them. "I'm going to ask her what happened."

"Ashley, the ghost." Duranja snorted.

"Stop it. I told you she's the real thing," Melody chided him. "Be careful," she said to me, giving me another hug.

I squeezed her tight and hoped we both knew what we were doing. "You too."

Chapter Fifteen

B y the time I made it out of the square, I could hear the band warming up. Drumbeats and horns echoed from the tree-lined street north of Main.

The crowd had also gotten antsy. Left and right, kids broke from their parents to run into the empty street and see if the parade had started yet. As frustrated parents ushered them back, I slipped past the barriers and jogged across Main to the stretch of sidewalk where I'd seen my mom last.

Frankie no longer stood outside Biscuits and Gravy. I hoped that meant he'd reunited with his lady love.

As for my mom? Well, I didn't see her, either. And she didn't have an excuse.

"Verity!" My friend Lauralee called from down the sidewalk. She'd staked out a spot right in front with her husband and kids. Ambrose wriggled in her arms while Tommy Junior stood on a big red Igloo cooler, wielding binoculars. Seven-year-old Hiram teamed up with his dad to try to keep George from falling over the barrier.

I rushed up and gave her a hug.

"Watch the parade with us," she beckoned, her cheeks reddened with the chill of the morning.

The first notes of the lead band drifted down the street, playing the brassy intro to "Stars and Stripes Forever."

"I will, but have you seen my mom? She was supposed to wait for me outside Biscuits & Gravy."

"I'm sure she's around here somewhere," Lauralee said breezily.

Yes, well, after all that had happened in the past two days, I couldn't be too careful. I tried to catch sight of Mom in the crowd, but there were too many people. And I couldn't see over half of them.

Tommy Junior had a smart idea going with that Igloo lookout point.

The flag line from the VFW marched past in perfect formation, leading the small, but powerful VFW band. Their fellow veterans of foreign wars strode proudly behind them, wearing service hats with pins. Some had even donned their old uniforms.

"I suppose I could stay for a little while," I told Lauralee.

"Good," she said, urging me up next to her right by the barriers. "Because this is my favorite part of homecoming."

Lauralee and I had been watching parades together since elementary school.

"Do you remember when the former homecoming queens go by?" I asked, wishing I'd paid better attention in past years.

"More toward the end, I think," Lauralee mused, handing me a Sugarland Biscuits flag on a stick. She busied herself passing flags out to the entire family. "The past queens should come right before this year's court and the football team."

"Okay, good." Ashley would arrive in due time. I just had to keep an eye out for her.

And figure out how to approach a dead homecoming queen during a parade without getting noticed.

I gripped my flag tighter.

Next up was the mayor driving his tan pickup truck, followed by the Sugarland High senior class float pulled on a flatbed trailer behind a dad on a tractor. They'd made a giant can of corn that said, "Cream the Cavers."

I thought it looked pretty clever. The seniors walked on the sides and behind, dressed in red and white everything—including face paint—and handed out red and white balloons to the kids.

Tommy Junior managed to snag two. He handed me his flag so he could focus on his balloons. The kid had priorities.

Just then, I thought I caught my mom out of the corner of my eye. But when I turned, I realized it was a different woman wearing red slacks and a white sweater.

Maybe I was being paranoid, wondering where she'd gone. She might have simply let her friends drag her somewhere. Hadn't I just been guilty of the same thing?

But she'd also been standing right outside a busy restaurant, discussing details about the library break-in. And she hadn't exactly been hiding the fact that she was hunting a killer.

I pulled out my cell phone and dialed her up.

It went straight to voicemail.

"You worry too much," Lauralee assured me.

Too bad Frankie hadn't died with a cell phone, or I'd try him, too.

The rest of the class floats paraded past, followed by a monster truck dragging a fishing boat with the girls' swim team tucked inside, waving.

There was a break in the parade as the ghostly class of 1921 paraded past, the men wearing striped jackets and the women in white dresses.

A dozen high school horse club members followed a safe distance behind, smiling and waving, their mounts rearing their heads any time a rider tried to close the gap on the ghosts.

Animals knew.

After a brief appearance by the broom and bucket squad, the high school band arrived, with John O'Brien out front.

"The poor horses are surrounded," I joked.

"What?" Lauralee asked as she helped Hiram keep a firm grip on his balloon.

"Never mind." The ghostly band leader danced some fancy steps, his baton held high.

"Go, John!" I cheered, waving a Sugarland flag in each hand.

He grinned, and I could have sworn he gave me a wink.

The Roan's Hardware float came next, a double-decker masterpiece that recreated the storefront to a tee. My stepdad waved from one of the upper windows. It was easy to spot his bald head and wiry torso. He caught sight of the kids and tossed a handful of candy out to them.

George yelled with joy, raising both hands as Tootsie Rolls rained down.

Hiram took a more pragmatic approach and whipped a plastic shopping bag out of his pocket.

The first of the beauty queens followed, waving from a convertible sponsored by Buck Neely Chevrolet.

I saw the Miss Teen Corn Queen, the Junior Miss Starlight, the Mid-Tennessee Miss World—full of smiles and waves. I strained to see what followed, wishing Tommy Junior had extra room on his cooler.

Then a hand closed on my shoulder.

Thank goodness. "Mom—"

I turned to find a thin, overly tanned brunette with white plastic hoop earrings and a death look in her eye. "We need to talk," she stated.

I think it was her entitled attitude that made me defy her. That and the fact that I couldn't afford to miss Ashley's float. "I'm watching the parade."

"You're also talking smack about my husband, and I'm sick

of it," she drawled, drawing concern from Lauralee and her husband.

"Hey, now," Big Tom stepped in.

"It's fine," I assured him. "We'll take a step back," I said, retreating with the brunette toward the Sews Life embroidery shop window. I glanced back at the parade. The various beauty queens were still passing by.

Luckily, that could take a while.

"Who's your husband?" I asked, pretty sure I hadn't talked smack about anybody.

She planted a hand on her hip. "You know damned well I've been married to Jake Everett since high school." It was more of a demand than a statement.

"I don't keep track of everybody," I said, in truth. Especially my mom's generation, whom I didn't see socially since she'd left town. "What's your name?" I asked brightly, trying to turn the tone of the conversation.

"Kiki Taylor Everett," she snipped, as if I should have known. She wore a *Class of '86 Cheerleading* button on her formfitting white nylon top.

"Well, Kiki," I said, maintaining my friendly demeanor, "my mom and I are trying to understand more about the night Ashley died."

"Tilly's in rare form this morning." Kiki frowned, the lines around her mouth deepening even more. "She asked me flat out if my husband killed Ashley Starling."

"Do you think he did?"

She reared back. "No. And I should slap you for suggesting it."

I went cold at the threat. "You touch me, and you'll be sorry."

"On account of you dating the police?" she taunted.

"On account that I'm real nice until I'm not," I informed her.

Her lip curled, as if she were weighing the odds.

"Try me," I challenged. Kiki was the type of person who

would walk all over me if I let her. Besides, too many folks confused kindness with weakness, and I wouldn't stand here and be insulted on the sidewalk.

"Yeah, well," she said, backing off as if she respected me for being plain with her. "You might not realize it, but your mom's friend Ashley was a real piece of work."

Sure. Blame the dead girl. "You must realize I've never met her."

Yet.

I glanced toward the parade. The Sugarland Players theater troupe rolled past on a flatbed, singing an off-key song from their upcoming original musical: *Showboat Sails to Sugarland*.

"Yeah, well, Ashley was head cheerleader," Kiki said grudgingly. "And she sure acted like little miss perfect. She dated Jake because he was the quarterback, captain of the football team, and the best-looking guy in school. She never really cared about him as a person."

"And you did?" I asked, realizing I could be talking to a prime suspect.

"Always," she insisted. "He had a tough go of it. He needed a friend, someone like me who understood."

"Sure," I said, watching the Sugarland High Bass Fishing Club parade past, wearing matching utility vests and carrying their poles like rifles. "Star quarterbacks always have it rough in high school," I added, baiting her, eager to learn more.

"Did you really just say that?" she demanded, swinging around to get between me and the parade. "Jake's mom was disabled, and his dad ran off. He had a lot more on his mind than football."

Poor kid. "I had no idea," I admitted.

She cocked her chin up. "It was only the two of them. Jake worked landscaping every day he wasn't at school or football practice. His mom's disability paid rent and that was it. Jake bought groceries and everything else. He worked until dark, and then he had to go home and cook for his mom. But he couldn't work as much once school started. I used to give him my babysitting money for the electric bill, but it still wasn't enough."

That was a lot for two kids to handle—too much, in fact. "Did his teachers know?" They would have stepped in and helped, or at least found him and his mom the resources they needed.

"Some people don't like advertising their problems," Kiki said, stiffening her back. "Jake was proud. Still is." She flipped her hair. "If Ashley would have stopped by after school like I did, she'd have seen. Instead, she accused him of not caring about her because he had to work instead of going to every homecoming court thing." She rolled her eyes. "He didn't even want to be in the court. He just wanted to play football and get a scholarship so he could make something of himself and send money back to his mom."

"I'm not sure that's how scholarships work," I hedged. Maybe for athletes.

"Well, he didn't get the chance to find out," she thundered, "because no electricity means no light to do homework after regular work, not to mention football practices. You try writing an English paper with a flashlight."

"Nobody knew that," I said, feeling bad for the child Jake had been. "You can bet my mom wasn't aware, or it'd be all over town," I added under my breath.

"You can't blame him for not wanting the whole town to know his business." She crossed her arms over her chest.

"Come to think of it, I actually can't," I admitted. I knew firsthand how it felt to be judged for things you can't control.

"And he did ask for help with school," Kiki insisted. "He figured if he could get that in line, and keep food on the table, he could live with the rest. But Ashley's friend only pretended to help him with his final English paper. He got a D and lost his scholarship over it."

"Oh my goodness." Alistair had gotten back at his bully, maybe a little too effectively.

Horns honked as Abe Ryther and a group of motorcycle riders drove past, balloons trailing from their bikes.

Kiki turned to watch. "I was glad when Ashley left town. Jake didn't need that brand of poison. He needed a girl who would be there for him. Me."

I hated to remind her, but... "Ashley didn't leave town. She died."

She turned back to me with an eerily cold expression. "All we knew was she disappeared and never came back. I sure didn't miss her. She was a bad person, Verity."

"Are you saying she deserved it?" Because that sounded like a murder motive.

She shrugged a thin shoulder. "I'm only saying I wasn't sorry. And I don't get why she's suddenly a saint, just for dying."

"I understand that maybe Ashley could have treated Jake better," I began. "She didn't need to break up with him with a note at the homecoming dance."

Her gaze iced over. "I saw it. I picked it up off the floor."

"You're kidding. What did it say?" I pressed.

She rolled her eyes. "It said she was running off with some guy. She obviously didn't get too far."

I ignored Kiki's callousness and focused on her words. "It specified she was meeting a boy? Did she say who?"

"Her secret love," Kiki said, with a bitter, exaggerated flourish. "So basically, the whole time, she was cheating on Jake. At least then he saw her for who she was and dumped her."

But he hadn't had the chance to dump her.

Unless he'd followed her out of the dance, like Alistair claimed.

And after that?

I was still trying to put it together.

"Well, I'm glad it happened because I gave him a good life," Kiki concluded. "Jake has his own landscaping business now. He doesn't even drink much anymore except when people like you push his buttons. He's the responsible one of the group. He does that for me. His mom moved in with us, and *I* took care of her until she passed. He never needed college. He just needed a good woman."

"Sure," I said. She was a regular ray of sunshine.

A chill radiated up my left side. I turned to see a petite Victorian ghost smiling at me. Molly.

Frankie snuck up behind Kiki and touched her right between the shoulder blades. She startled at the chill and slapped her back.

"Problem?" I asked innocently.

She quickly looked behind her, then back to me with a startled sneer. "People are right. Talking to you is creepy," she said before she turned and walked away.

I saw her dig for what it was, a hurt woman's attempt to hurt back. It still stung a little.

"Nice trick," I told my ghost buddies. "It's good to see you again," I added to Molly.

"You looked like you needed help," she said primly.

"I was fine letting you dangle," Frankie informed me. But he appeared happier, jolly almost. He also had all of his limbs.

He could give me all the attitude he wanted. It was obvious something good had happened between those two. I couldn't help but smile. Praise heaven my ghost wasn't entirely helpless.

The Shriners roared through the street in their red minicars. They zoomed in figure eights around each other, the black tassels on their red fez hats trailing in the wind.

"Who are these amazing daredevils?" Frankie asked, gliding closer to the street.

I took the opportunity to coax Molly to a quiet spot near the doorway of the closed embroidery shop.

"I'm so glad you and Frankie made up," I said. Truly, taking Molly to this parade was such a good idea.

She positively glowed. "I'm having fun. And I have an admirer," she teased.

She had more than that. "Frankie cares about you so much—"

"It's El Gato," she confessed in a rush, her cheeks flushing and her eyes bright. "He sent me a whole room full of flowers today."

"Wait, what?" I screeched, my mind racing. "Frankie is…" *An idiot?* "Frankie told me he was the one sending you flowers," I insisted, settling on the truth as I was allowed to tell it.

"The card said El Gato," she singsonged, clasping her hands under her chin. "He went on and on about my beauty and my charm." She sighed happily. "But Frankie is nice, too," she insisted, almost as an afterthought. "And I figure if El Gato tries to hurt Frankie today, I can protect him." She must have seen my look of horror because she quickly added, "I'll save Frankie without him even realizing—I mean, Frankie doesn't need to know about El Gato's mad crush on me. Or the fact that El Gato said he'd do *anything* to make me smile. It feels so scandalous," she added, with pure delight.

Curse Molly and her love of bad boys. "So Frankie is safe at the parade today because of your relationship with El Gato," I said dryly.

"Exactly," she said, glancing over her shoulder as Frankie approached. "But don't worry. I won't be seduced by a legendary ladies' man," she added in a whisper, even though she didn't appear too upset at the idea.

"Be careful," I said, glaring at the ghost approaching. "Because El Gato is so smooth."

"You don't have to tell me," Molly beamed, as if she'd been

around the block instead of cooped up at the Heritage Society house for the last century. "Did you know El Gato once seduced a girl named Zorina just so he could make it all the way through the alphabet?" Molly clucked, touching a hand to her lace collar. "He took her to Paris."

"That was the name of a nightclub on the North Side of Chicago," Frankie said, gliding up.

"Will you excuse us?" I asked Molly. "I have to ask Frankie about an issue I'm having with the 142nd infantry poker game in the library."

"Sure," Molly said, drawing a ghostly rose out of her purse and giving it a happy sniff as we left her.

"Is Stoutmeyer ignoring you again?" Frankie asked, trailing me as I led him up a few storefronts. "I told you to learn poker if you want to get his attention. And you gotta get better at bluffing."

I whipped around to face my ghost. "You'd better take credit for your roses," I said in a rush, keeping my voice low. "They came with a card that said they were from El Gato."

"Oh." Frankie winced. "I told Suds to send my regards El Gato *style*, not *from* El Gato." He ran a hand over his chin. "I'll fix it."

"You'll tell her," I insisted. "She thinks she needs to protect you from El Gato."

"Oh, I could take El Gato," Frankie countered.

"You *are* El Gato!" I hissed.

"Stop getting caught up in the technicalities," he said, waving me off. Then his face lit up. "I've got a better idea," he announced. "I'll do an even grander gesture."

"No, you won't." Wrong direction.

"This time, I'll make sure she knows it's from me." He clapped his hands together. "I'm going to out-romance Mr. Romance!"

"Do you hear yourself?" This was not the time to double

down on a bad idea. "You need to jump off this crazy train before it hits another station."

"You'll see," he insisted.

"That's what I'm afraid of." I absolutely did not want to see where this was headed. The more he deceived her, the worse this was going to be. "Helping you with your love life is like watching a slow-motion car wreck."

"Or is it the greatest love story of all time?" he countered. "You might be surprised."

I'd had enough surprises lately.

"Verity," Lauralee called from the street front, "I see your mom!" She pointed up the street a ways.

"Don't wait up for me," Frankie said, leaving to rejoin his love.

"No problem with that." He'd have to leave downtown as soon as I took his urn home.

The Sugarland High Show Choir paraded past, singing "Walking on Sunshine," and it brought me back to the reason I was there. I hurried up the street and spotted Mom with Phyllis, ten feet down by the barricade in front of the New For You resale shop.

A truck paraded past, pulling a trailer with a red monster truck on it. Drivers waved from the windows of both vehicles.

"Looks like Harvey couldn't get El Diablo started this morning," Mom said as I joined them.

"You were supposed to wait for me," I reminded her.

"We stayed close," Phyllis said.

"But we had to find a spot up front," Mom agreed. "Plus," she added as an aside to me, "I know you were a little upset with me back there. I thought I'd give you some space if you needed it."

That was all well and good, but… "What I needed was your discretion." The simple act of thinking of me before she spoke. "I want to be able to share with you, without you carrying on or making a scene."

"I know." She closed her eyes. "I just..." She opened them and looked at me plain. "Sometimes I talk before I think. I'm trying real hard," she promised. "I want to be as good a mom to you as your grandma was to me."

"You are a good mom," I assured her. She'd always loved me, and if anything, she supported me and my dreams too much. "Let's move past this, okay?"

"Okay," she said, giving my arm a little squeeze. "We saved you a spot right up front."

"If either of you decides to stop talking and actually start watching the parade," Darcy said, turning from her place next to the barricade. I hadn't even spotted her until she spoke, not even with the crazy white hat.

"Get on up there," Phillis added, making way for us. "Just beware of Vincent van Goat."

My elbows had barely hit the barricade when I got a fuzzy nose on the arm from Tonya Jefferson's goat, who wore a Sugarland Biscuits letterman's jacket and a wreath of flowers around his neck.

Tonya held back her long hair, done in cornrows with matching flowers, and wore her husband's vintage Biscuits football jersey, altered to skim her figure.

"I swear I've taught him manners," she said, apologizing for her goat. "He just gets carried away."

"I think he's darling," I said, stroking the cowlick of hair sticking up from his head. He couldn't be cuter if he tried.

"Look! It's MayBelle," Mom said. She rode the Park Manor senior housing luau float with about twenty of her fellow residents. A group at the front threw leis to the crowd. MayBelle and the rest of the ladies did the hula while a motley band of men backed them up on ukuleles.

I glanced up at Frankie floating above the crowd with his girl, glad to see from the surprised, proud expression on his face that he'd also spotted his niece hamming it up. On anyone else, the coconut bra might have been a bit too much. But MayBelle pulled it off, even while wearing it over her Hawaiian dress and matching jacket.

Speaking of Sugarland personalities...

"You'll never guess who cornered me," I said to Mom, and told her the story I'd heard about Jake.

Naturally, Phyllis and Darcy listened in as well. Phyllis dismissed what I had to say outright. Darcy rolled her eyes. And Mom simply asked, "What if she's lying?"

"What if she's not?" I countered.

"The truth is, Kiki always liked Jake and would have done anything to sink Ashley," Phyllis insisted.

"Yep." Darcy nodded knowingly. "Remember how she asked him to the turnabout dance, and he told her he only wanted to be friends?"

"I heard the reason they married after high school was because he got her pregnant," Mom added.

I felt like I was sitting back at a high school lunch table. And I couldn't believe they'd so easily dismiss the information I'd gathered. "What if there's some truth to the fact that Jake had a rough life and that Kiki took it upon herself to save him?" Whether that meant murder, or helping Jake cover up a murder, I didn't know.

"Are you saying Kiki might have killed Ashley?" Mom murmured.

At least she kept her voice down.

"I still think Jake is capable of murder," Phyllis concluded.

Yes, but so were a lot of other people. I mean, what if Mr. Norwood had gone too far with his student and needed to protect his reputation and his job? What if Kiki had done it to keep Jake from making up with the girl who'd cheated on him and didn't "understand" him?

And I couldn't discount the fact that Mr. Norwood's wife,

Jean, would have known exactly when and how to steal from the Class of '86 box while Melody worked alone.

But I wasn't about to discuss it in the middle of a parade crowd.

"Look!" Mom said, pointing. "The queens are coming!"

This was it! On a flatbed trailer with a cardboard sign that read Sugarland Salutes Our Past Queens, I saw Larissa Washington, who'd left to go to Louisiana Tech. How nice she came back home! She wore a frothy orange dress and sat next to three older women in ballgowns and one who appeared to be wearing her original white 1950s gown.

But no Ashley.

My heart sank.

Had the band director been wrong about her riding in the parade?

I didn't know where else I'd find her if it wasn't here. Today.

"Aren't they gorgeous?" Phyllis asked as the trailer with the 2021 homecoming court drew up next.

The girls sat on hay bales in their fancy dresses and waved. The boys walked along the sides, wearing suits and ties. And there was a ghost among them.

She perched on a hay bale, wearing a familiar red silky formal dress with big poufy sleeves. As she drew near, I could see her outrageous '80s hairdo and the same face I'd seen in the photo from the library table.

Ashley.

Chapter Sixteen

I t was Ashley for sure. I needed to talk to her. Now, while I
had her in my sights.

But she was in the parade, on a float. In front of the whole
town.

To think, I'd just given my mom a talk about making a scene.

I gripped the wooden barrier. Ashley deserved to tell us
what had happened on the night she died, whom she'd left the
dance to go see, who had killed her.

And how I could prove it.

But I really, really didn't want an audience. There had to be
some way to do this quietly—in the middle of a parade.

Maybe I could.

I ducked under the barrier as Ashley passed by, waving.

I needed to know what she'd placed in the Class of 1986 box,
and if her trusted science teacher had taken things a step
too far.

This was the first time I'd actually seen the murder victim I
was investigating, and as the float continued down the street, I
couldn't let her get far.

"Why are you in the street?" Darcy asked, no doubt seeing the crazed look in my eye.

I could think of no good answer.

"She sees Ashley's ghost!" Mom gasped. Quietly. At least she'd learned.

Darn it all. I needed a reason to be on the wrong side of the barriers, and I needed a diversion.

Fast.

I turned to Tonya Jefferson. "Can I borrow your goat?"

"Please," she said, exasperated.

Maybe people would think I was a 4-H member who had fallen behind. Maybe they'd be too busy looking at Vincent to notice what I was about to do.

Tonya handed off the goat's lead, and I'd scarcely grabbed hold before Vincent seized the opportunity and made a run for it.

We launched into the street, Vincent prancing with delight as we chased after the homecoming float.

"The Goat Club went by a while ago!" Lee Treadwell hollered from the other side of the street.

Yeah, well, we'd never catch up.

Vincent van Goat capered gleefully next to me while I hurried to catch up to the murdered homecoming queen.

She smiled and blew kisses, as if this were her big day.

It was, I realized. Just not for the reason she might think.

"Ashley," I said, catching up to her, dodging a boy in a too-large suit.

Ashley wasn't paying attention to me at all. She merely smiled and waved to the crowd.

The live girl sitting next to her, hair stacked up to heaven, smoothed her pink dress and avoided making eye contact with me and crazy Vincent jogging next to the float. "Um...my name is Penelope."

"Not you! Ashley Starling," I tried again as Vincent van Goat about yanked my arm out of the socket in order to dance a circle in the street.

The ghost startled and peered down at me. At last.

"I'm Tilly Garber's daughter, Verity," I said quickly, by way of introduction. At that point I was a little breathless and very aware of the crowd lining both sides of the street.

I gave them a little wave and tried to look like I was having fun.

Give me a haunted mansion or even a spooky forest. I'd never felt so exposed while ghost hunting.

Ashley returned her attention to the crowd. "Tilly doesn't have any kids, silly."

"I meant to say I'm her cousin," I fibbed, not willing to take the time to explain to the ghost.

There was no time. No space to do this properly.

"Are you having a mental break?" Penelope asked. She turned to the girl next to her. "My mom said Verity Long is crazy. Looks like she's right."

I ignored her. "Accept my apologies," I said, focused on the ghost. "I realize it's a bit...quick...to drop this on you." Normally, I'd chat a bit. "But I need to know how you died."

Ashley dropped her waving hand. "That's rude."

"Oh, crud. She's talking to a ghost," Penelope said and quickly scooted away.

"Do you remember who hurt you?" I asked, trying a different tack as I kept up with Ashley.

Her eyes filled with tears. "I don't know!"

I hated to corner her like this. I knew it was traumatic, and I wasn't handling it as sensitively as I could if we'd had more time or privacy or—

Vincent van Goat leapt onto the parade float. A collective *oooh* erupted from behind the barriers as homecoming ladies shrieked and scattered.

"Who did you leave the dance to meet?" I pressed, keeping

my focus on Ashley as the goat tried to make friends but only succeeded in instigating a courtly stampede to the other side of the trailer.

The float lurched.

"I didn't leave to meet anyone!" Ashley balked. "I'm not that kind of girl."

Maybe so, maybe not. I understood why she wouldn't spill her deep, dark secret to the stranger chasing her parade float, but now was not the time to be coy. The float rocked again as I jumped on it to keep Vincent from strangling himself.

"Okay, then tell me one thing," I said, plopping down on her hay bale.

"You're making a scene," Ashley protested.

"Please don't remind me." Perhaps I was my mother's daughter after all. "Don't worry, they can't see you." Only me.

No doubt I was going to relive this moment in my nightmares, but I couldn't let that stop me. This was too important.

I might never get a chance to talk with Ashley again.

A girl in a green dress shrieked as Vincent began munching on her hem. She obviously didn't grow up on a farm. While the other girls hurried to her rescue, I focused on Ashley.

"I want to help you," I said to the ghost, low and urgent. "We need to learn what happened to you, right?" I added. "You want that, I know you do."

"Yes," she said quietly, her eyes shining with tears.

Okay. Progress. "Then tell me. What did you add to the Class of 1986 box for the time capsule?"

Her eyes widened as she stared at me. "How did you know about that?"

"Tilly tells me everything," I assured her as Vincent van Goat pranced past us with a corsage in his mouth.

"Tilly needs to learn to keep things private," Ashley admonished.

From her mouth to God's ears. "Tell me and I'll leave you alone," I promised. For now, at least. "Please," I added.

"You're ruining homecoming." Her lower lip trembled, and she began to disappear. "This is my chance to run away, and you're ruining it."

"You left something in the '86 box for Jake, didn't you?" I said, grabbing at straws.

She faded even more.

"Wait. I meant it's for Mr. Norwood," I tried again, desperate. "Or about Mr. Norwood."

Her mouth formed a shocked O. "Don't you dare tell anyone about him," she said, and then she disappeared.

Chapter Seventeen

"At least Tonya got her goat back," Mom said later as we gathered around my kitchen table.

"But not before Vincent van Goat ate three corsages, Detective Marshall's badge, and the flowers out of Loyola Anderson's hair." I cringed, accepting a glass of sweet tea from Carl, who'd taken over my kitchen.

"It's not all bad. Vincent also won the Sugarland spirit award," my stepdad said, placing the pitcher on the table.

Mom stirred more sugar into her tea. "I think that was to keep Tonya from sending him to the butcher."

"She'd never," I said. "That goat is like a son to her."

"A delinquent son," Carl added, delivering a plate of lemons.

"I really can do that," I said, guilt propelling me out of my chair. "You don't need to wait on me."

"Sit," Carl said, placing a hand on my shoulder. "You've had a rough enough afternoon."

"He's a modern Southern gentleman," Mom said, eyeing him lovingly while sipping her tea.

He snuck up behind her and gave her a kiss on the top of the head. "You mind if I cook those cream cheese cinnamon rolls from the fridge?" he asked.

"Be my guest." We could all use a sugar-laden pick-me-up.

Turned out he'd already heated the oven.

I was glad Mom had someone like Carl to take care of her. And I didn't mind including myself in that equation at the moment. But all the pleasantries in the world wouldn't make me feel better about my run-in with Ashley that afternoon.

"Why did Ashley say I was ruining her chance to run away?" I asked, leaning back in my chair.

We'd been over my talk with Ashley a dozen times—in the moments after I'd been kicked off the homecoming court float, on the walk to the car, on the way into the house…I still didn't get it.

"She didn't have anything to run away from," Mom insisted. "I mean, yes, her boyfriend could be a jerk sometimes, and she hated how he ignored her."

"Jake might be easy to blame," I countered, "but now that I know more about him, I wonder if he should still be our primary suspect." Teenage Jake had had other things on his plate, bigger things than his girlfriend or a dance.

"Kiki is no treat," Mom added. "I don't believe a word of what she told you."

"True," I said, taking a sip of tea. I could see her feeling justified in hurting Ashley. But murder?

"Kiki grew up rough," Carl said, leaning against my kitchen island, towel over his shoulder. "She and her mom used to sell eggs to pay for extras, like her cheerleading and such. Only sometimes, they had more to sell than their hens could have laid."

That was interesting. "So you think they were stealing from their neighbors?"

"Stealing from somebody," Carl said. "Her dad plays chess down at the hardware store, and he's all but confirmed it, seeing as his wife's dead now and he's gone around the bend, mentally that is."

Mom made a face. "Stealing from your neighbors is terrible. Especially when a lot of people don't have extra to spare."

"But it's a far cry from murder," Carl pointed out.

I nodded, running my fingertips up and down my glass. "On the other hand, Ashley got real squirrely when I asked about Mr. Norwood."

"But you said she was agitated anyway," Mom said.

"She was," I admitted. I hadn't been quite as pleasant and open as I usually was when meeting a ghost for the first time. Our encounter had been a little stressful to say the least. But I'd still left with something to chew on. "A science teacher should never figure so prominently in a student's personal life. If he did get involved with her, it could end his teaching career if anyone found out."

"That's a definite motive for murder," Carl agreed.

"Did you see anything strange between Ashley and her teacher?" I asked him.

Carl shook his head. "I was two classes above. I knew who Ashley was, but I didn't have classes with her."

Mom pursed her lips disapprovingly. "I would have known if she'd gotten involved with her teacher."

"She was definitely hiding something," I insisted. "She told me not to say anything about Mr. Norwood."

"He could have made her promise to keep their relationship a secret," Carl said, going to investigate a scratching on the outside of my back door.

"Even then," Mom insisted "there are some things you don't keep from your best friend."

"I think Lucy smells the sweet rolls," I said as Carl opened the door, and my skunk dashed in like she needed to catch a train.

"Well, hey, short stuff," Carl said, scooping her up. "You'll have to wait like everybody else."

She huffed like a little diva and struggled to escape.

Mom had dressed the skunk in her Sugarland Biscuits cheerleading outfit. Again.

I glanced at Mom, and she shrugged. "I needed a pick-me-up."

"You mean she wandered too close to the car when we got back." Carl whipped off his orange and black *Roan's Hardware* sweatshirt to reveal a *Roan's Hardware* T-shirt underneath.

Mom leaned her elbows on the table. "Let's say Mr. Norwood had started something untoward with Ashley and she didn't tell me," Mom said, fiddling with her teaspoon as she thought it through. "Why would Ashley leave the dance to go see a teacher?"

"Because they didn't want to get caught talking, or…" Carl said gently, as if he hated to break the news.

"But why run off with a teacher?" Mom protested. "It would never work. A teacher is never going to run off with a student."

"Yes, but she didn't run off. She was killed," I pointed out. "Maybe Ashley threatened to tell people Mr. Norwood was coming on to her."

"Or maybe she told him she'd added something about him in the 1986 box," Carl added. "Although at that point, I wonder why he didn't just take it," he said, letting Lucy down to investigate the kitchen. "The time capsule was obviously still open when Ashley died."

"Maybe someone interrupted them," I suggested.

Carl considered that. "I asked around the hardware store crowd, and Abe Ryther was the one responsible for sealing the time capsule. They loaded it in a big ceremony on the final night of homecoming, before the dance. He said everything looked fine when he put planks down and poured concrete over it early the next morning."

"He should have looked harder," Mom concluded.

"Maybe," Carl admitted. "He feels real bad about that. But Abe says he told the police the same thing he told me. He said he had no reason to think anybody would tamper with a time capsule."

"I can think of plenty of people who might want to dig out Darcy Johnson's secret apple pie recipe," I mused.

I tried to think if anyone had made a suspiciously stunning apple pie in the last thirty-five years.

"But think about it," Carl added, "surely any hypothetical treasure hunters would have reported seeing a body."

"It depends on how passionate they are about pie," Mom said, only half joking.

"No, Carl's right," I said. "You couldn't keep a secret like that in Sugarland."

"They definitely locked it at the 1985 ceremony," Mom said. "We all saw them do it."

"I remember," Carl said, frustrated.

My skunk concluded her investigation of the kitchen and curled up at my feet. "Ashley's last words to me were that I'd better not dare talk about Mr. Norwood," I said, folding my hands on the table. "That has to mean something."

"Mr. Norwood made me uncomfortable when I had him," Carl said, washing his hands at the sink. "It was the way he treated women. I never liked how friendly he was with the girls in my class."

There it was again. And Carl was two years older than Mom.

"I still don't believe he hurt her," Mom said, growing agitated. "She would have told me if she felt threatened by him or anybody." She took an unhappy sip of tea.

"Think of it this way," I said, "if Ashley left something in the 1986 box for or about Mr. Norwood, then he or his wife could very well be our library intruder."

"Maybe both of them," Carl agreed.

"So we need to account for both Mr. Norwood and his wife during the library break-in," Mom concluded. She glanced at me. "We can do that, can't we?"

"I can ask the guys from Roan's," Carl offered.

I wasn't sure the men who played chess at the hardware store hung in the same crowd as the science teacher and his wife, but it couldn't hurt to see.

"I'll ask Melody," I said.

"Between me, Phyllis, and Darcy, we've got the rest of the town covered," Mom joked.

The football game tonight would be the perfect opportunity to ask questions. Everyone would be there, and it would be easy to track people down in the stands.

"Just...try not to be too obvious about it," I cautioned them.

"Oh, don't worry about that," Mom said, "I'll be as subtle as I can!"

That was what I was afraid of.

"I've learned," she added, with the same enthusiasm.

I hoped so. Now I had to be on top of my game as well.

I walked out onto the back porch shortly before we all left, just to clear my head, and I saw Frankie sitting under the apple tree by the pond. The corner of his mouth turned up when he saw me.

"Well, look who's had a good day," I said by way of greeting.

He drew a lazy arm over his head. "That parade schtick was perfect. Molly ate it up."

"So you leveled with her and told her that you were not in danger at all from El Gato and you only said that because you crave her love and respect."

"Not in a million years. I'm doing one better," he said,

popping to his feet. He rummaged in his coat pocket and drew out his cigarette case. "I'm rescuing a puppy for her."

I inhaled so fast I choked. "You can't give her a live animal."

"It's a ghost puppy," he said, drawing a cigarette out from behind his ear. "A maltipoo," he added, lighting up. "The little rascal needs a home, and Molly has always wanted a pet."

"This is not how you romance a girl," I warned. "It's not even how you take care of a dog. It's—"

"It's beautiful," he said, drawing on the cigarette and blowing out the smoke. "I'm taking inspiration from El Gato and doing one better," he smirked. "El Gato got her flowers that die. I'm getting her a puppy that will live forever!" he announced, spreading his hands wide. "Unless it goes to the light," he added.

"Giving a pet a forever home is a huge responsibility," I explained while he smoked happily. "There's more to it than sending Suds out to sign adoption papers."

"I know. That's why I need you to drive me there so I can do it and take the credit." He drew on his smoke. "We'll leave at sunset. I'm going to present her with the puppy while Suds stands behind me with sparklers, and those look better at night."

Then we had another problem. "I'm leaving for the football game as soon as I can get my parents into my car."

He stared at me.

"The homecoming game," I reminded him. "It's tonight."

"Then cancel." Ash fell from the end of his cigarette as he brought his hands to his head. "You did the parade today. You were *in* the parade. How much homecoming do you need?"

"All of it," I told him without hesitation.

"This is my love life," he protested.

"This is my murder investigation," I insisted.

"And I suppose you want my power," he said, taking a hard drag.

I already had it. He'd forgotten to turn it off.

"Listen, I'll take you to Molly's place any day. Any time. Just not tonight. And not with a puppy."

"If I don't adopt Trixie, somebody else will," he warned.

"Good. Hopefully, it will be someone who has thought it through."

He gave me a dirty look. "So what am I supposed to do tonight?"

I would have suggested he go with me, but I knew better. "Cool your heels. Think about telling Molly who you really are."

"Like that ever works," he griped, taking another drag.

"It has and it will again," I reminded him.

His image began to fade. "Fine. Take my power. Leave me stranded."

"Frankie—"

"Use me to talk to other ghosts."

"You know it's not like that." Surely, he understood.

"I'll just float around for the rest of whenever."

"We'll fix this with Molly. Soon," I promised. Just not at this very moment. And Lord willing, with the truth this time.

I arrived at the game with Mom and Carl in time to see the band march across the field, playing the fight song. Cheers rose into the night sky as they finished the pregame rally.

Fans packed the bleachers on both the home and away sides, and those who didn't fit stood along the track and in the grass beyond. I couldn't even see the Dad's Club Snack Shack on the other side.

"The Cavers made a good showing," Mom commented, and I noticed the way their cheerleading squad of at least two dozen pretty much took up the track between the visiting team's bench and the bleachers. They spun and danced in their black and gold uniforms, doing some kind of dance about melting the sugar off our biscuits.

I'd like to see them try.

The Jackson Cavers came from the next town over and were our rivals in everything. If their football plays were as bad as their cheerleaders' taunts, Sugarland should do well, indeed.

"Let's find a spot," Mom said, ushering us along. Carl had already stopped at the entrance to talk to his friend taking tickets. "Keep an eye out for Darcy and Phyllis," she urged. "They can help us learn where Mr. Norwood and Jean were during the library break-in."

"No, Mom," I said, stopping to get her attention as she waved to one of our old neighbors in the stands. "We can't advertise the fact that we're investigating."

This had *mistake* written all over it. "Listen," I said, stopping her. "If Jean or Mr. Norwood were involved in Ashley's death, they won't take kindly to us asking questions. And if they're somehow innocent, we'd be doing damage."

"I understand." Mom nodded solemnly. "I'm glad you trusted me with this. I was afraid after I got carried away this morning, you'd stop telling me things."

I'd come close.

"I won't let you down," she pledged. "You'll see." She glanced past me. "Oh, look. There's a spot by Sheri Barker," she added, pointing to the top of the stands. "She lives next door to the Norwoods, and she has those kind of curtains where you can see out real easy, but nobody can see in."

"What a gem," I said dryly.

"I learn things. This is my superpower," she assured me.

It took me a moment to see where Mom indicated, and when I did, I realized why the space next to Sheri Barker remained open.

A pair of ghosts occupied the seats. They glowed in shades of gray. The man wore a wooly coat and a fedora, and he waved a pennant on a stick. His date, in a chic headscarf and fitted coat, couldn't stop clapping. She was the happiest ghost I'd seen in a long time.

They must be big fans.

Not that I blamed them.

"Let's get up there before somebody takes that spot," Mom urged.

"Um," I said, not eager at all to begin the climb up the metal bleachers. "I think I'll stay down here."

No wonder nobody wanted those seats. The living could sense the dead, even if they didn't realize it fully, and tended to keep a wide berth.

As for my mom, well, she might very well be the type to squeeze in next to a ghost despite the chill in the air and the prickle of unease tickling down her spine. She was bullheaded that way.

But there wasn't room for both of us. Touching those ghosts would give me the willies on a good day. And when I had Frankie's power, it would be downright shocking to physically encounter anything from the other side.

It would be no picnic for the dead couple, either.

"You go ahead," I urged. She might come up with some good intel, and it wasn't like I could stop her.

As for me? I'd spotted Mr. Norwood.

Alone.

He stood all the way at the end of the field, on the track behind the Sugarland Biscuits' end zone.

"If you're sure," Mom said, and I sensed her hesitation was only for show. Chantilly Garber Long Roan had her target in her sights and was already starting to climb.

I silently wished her—and the ghosts—good luck.

It heartened me to see that the ghostly images next to Sheri Barker appeared crisp and in focus. In fact... I looked for the band on the other edge of the field and spotted John O'Brien talking excitedly to a pair of ghostly trombone players. The three of them glowed brightly as well.

Thank goodness and hallelujah. Frankie's power seemed to be on overdrive tonight, even if the ghost himself was less than thrilled with the situation.

Well, once I got through tonight, I'd be glad to help him try to sort things out with Molly.

Maybe El Gato could fall overboard while hijacking the *Queen Mary*.

I stuck around until Mom was halfway up the bleachers then returned to the track and made my way toward the science teacher.

To my left, the Sugarland bleacher crowd did the wave. It was short and sweet, but full of enthusiasm.

Frankie should be here to see this. Maybe then he'd understand the joy of homecoming.

I passed a group of laughing high school students and sighed. It didn't feel that long since I'd been one of them. I still felt the pull of the Friday night lights. I wouldn't be surprised if Ashley did, too. Especially if she liked to relive homecoming, as the lunch lady had suggested. Despite our failed encounter earlier, there was a good chance she'd be at tonight's game—if only to stand with the court.

Hopefully, my strong, steady ghost vision would come in handy at tonight's game. If Ashley showed up, I wanted another chance to talk with her.

I did a quick scan, and while I saw a few more groups of ghosts scattered in the stands, I didn't see Ashley.

Yet.

Mr. Norwood began walking back toward me and the Biscuits' grandstand as the live team concluded their pregame practice. Beside them, gathered closer to the goal post, Sugarland football players in old-fashioned uniforms continued warming up, practicing their passing, joking around, excited for another big game. They cheered as the present-day team jogged past me on my left, heading for the bench.

The handsome science teacher would have walked right past me as well, if I hadn't gotten in his way.

"Hi, Mr. Norwood," I said brightly, not unlike one of his flirty students, I realized too late.

"Verity." He nodded, dodging me, as if he could merely continue on his way.

His greeting was a far cry from his earlier, jovial attitude. Perhaps he'd heard about my investigation.

I fell into step next to him. "So…" I began, wishing I'd had the good sense to plan out a line of questioning on the walk over. Unfortunately, I wasn't a planner. "Where's Jean tonight?"

"At home," he said absently, waving to one of the players who passed us to grab a cup from the water table. "Jean isn't feeling like herself tonight."

Murderous guilt, perhaps?

Or maybe she wanted something else from the library. I hoped Duranja had kept his guard up.

I studied Mr. Norwood's strong profile and overall pleasant features and tried to muster up the urge to flirt. It would be the best way to connect with the ladies' man, to coax him to let down his guard. Yet… I couldn't do it.

For one thing, he was married. For another, I usually related to people and ghosts because I cared about them, or wanted to understand them. But deep down in my soul I wanted nothing to do with the smarmy science teacher.

The silence stretched between us.

I had to say *something*.

This was my chance.

"So… What did you and Jean get up to last night?" I asked in a creepy-casual way, trying not to cringe because, really, I was usually so much smoother than that.

He gave me a strange look, which I'd totally earned.

"We hit the party like everyone else," he said, as if reluctant to keep the conversation going.

I'd have to do better. Maybe tell him that he looked like a fun guy, or that I wished I'd seen him at the party, but I couldn't make myself say the words or bat my eyes or even smile.

What I really wanted to ask was if anyone could verify his whereabouts.

We were coming to a break in the fence. He quickened his pace.

He was going to bolt.

That was what I would do if I were him.

"So…last night," I began, jogging a little to keep up. "Did you see anybody I know?" I asked, feeling my body warm.

Real smooth, Verity.

Considering I knew half the town.

"No," he said before turning and walking toward the bleachers and away from me.

I knew how he felt. I didn't even want to be around me at the moment.

"I talked to Ashley Starling's ghost today," I said to his back.

He hesitated.

"She talked about you," I said plainly. "She said your name outright."

He turned, his expression hard and uncomprehending. "What?"

That was one way to get his attention. "Why is a dead girl's ghost so interested in you?" I asked, giving up on any subtleties as he walked slowly toward me.

His expression grew cold, calculating.

I found that interesting. Perhaps the congenial, flirty science teacher had a dark side.

Or maybe I was just pushing his buttons.

But he couldn't hurt me. Not in front of all these fans.

"I don't know anything about Ashley Starling," he said

slowly, deliberately, as if weighing each word. "I barely remember *you*."

"No need to get personal," I said, with a hollow smile.

"Oh, this is very, very personal," he said, drawing close, well into my personal space, as if daring me to step back.

I held my ground.

"I don't know what I ever did to you," he hissed, "but I don't appreciate you painting me to be some kind of predator. I take my job and my students seriously. And I would never, ever hurt a child."

"Then why did Ashley say your name?" I pressed.

"I don't think she did," he ground out. "None of this is real. Ghosts, boogeymen!" he added, as if the whole idea were absurd. "You need professional help."

He could fling all the accusations he wanted. I knew the truth. I also knew how to lie when I had to. I'd learned that from Frankie.

"Ashley told me what she left in the time capsule," I said, taking a gamble, watching for his reaction.

He stared at me for a long second before his anger boiled over. "Stop this insanity," he commanded. "Now. This is my career you're messing with."

Because he'd been so responsible. "I think you did enough damage when you hit on your students."

He took my arm. Hard. It hurt as he dragged me closer to the empty Sugarland bench. The team had gathered on the far side, huddling before the start of the game.

"I never hit on you or any of your friends," he ground out, shaking me a little as he did.

Glaring at him, I yanked my arm back. "You did it in my mom's day. You gave extra credit to girls in short skirts."

He pulled back and ran a hand through his thick, salt-and-pepper hair. "That was a long time ago. I can't help it if some of the girls in my class got the wrong impression when I was nice to them."

Nice, indeed. "What happened between you and Ashley Starling?"

He glanced around us. "Absolutely nothing."

"Try again," I ordered. "This doesn't end until I figure it out."

"Look, we were close," he said, growing uncomfortable. "She was a good kid. Restless and eager to leave Sugarland and make something of herself. I thought she ran away. We all did."

If he was lying, I'd find out. "I'm going to ask her myself."

"You do that," he said, clearly not believing I could. "In the meantime, you'd better watch yourself."

"In what way?" I asked, my spine stiffening.

He treated me to a cold stare. "Nosy girls like you can get into trouble real fast."

I felt his words down to my bones. "Is that a threat?"

His mouth turned up into a ghost of a grin, as if he enjoyed making me nervous. "It's a warning. You're going down a bad path," he said, sickly sweet, with an edge of steel. "I worry about you."

I notched my chin up. "Worry how?" I asked, nervous even with the crowd all around us.

He held out his hands. "Like a former teacher, of course."

I didn't believe that for a second.

Chapter Eighteen

❦

Finally, the game started. As Sugarland took the field against the Cavers, I kept an eye out for Ashley Starling. She had to be here somewhere.

This was the second-to-last night of homecoming, the only time of the year Ashley made an appearance at all. She couldn't miss the big game.

It was important that I talk to her again. I wanted to apologize for scaring her this afternoon, but that was only part of it.

It had to have been a shock to see me dash from the crowd with a goat. And then to hitch a ride on her float during her big day? It hadn't been my finest moment.

Still. We needed to talk about her relationship with Mr. Norwood and, more importantly, learn more about the night she died.

As the teams lined up for the kickoff, the ghostly Sugarland team lined up directly behind their live counterparts. It warmed my heart.

The ghostly fans went wild.

Ellis stood almost directly across from me, in uniform, next to the visitors' bleachers. I headed that way as the Biscuits kicker launched the ball at the Cavers. My run-in with Mr. Norwood had been disturbing, and I could use a port in the storm. I'd questioned more than my share of dodgy characters, and his chilling insistence that the teenage girls in his class misunderstood his intentions was right up there with the "nice guy" who'd tried to bury me alive, or the upstanding gentleman whose wives had run into bad luck time and time again.

The crowd roared as Sugarland tackled the Caver receiver at the thirty-five-yard line. The player hit the dirt with a grunt, taken down by two of our current high school players, plus one ghost.

I wasn't sure how much I wanted to tell Ellis about my run-in with Mr. Norwood. Ellis already knew I suspected him, and he wouldn't be thrilled to hear I'd started investigating on my own. Besides, it wasn't like I had any evidence—yet.

The last thing I wanted Ellis to do was confront the science teacher about his threat. If anything, Mr. Norwood needed to know that I was strong, a formidable force. That I didn't send my boyfriend to fight my battles for me. That he'd best deal with me or suffer the consequences.

A ghostly Sugarland cheerleading squad breezed past me, giving off an otherworldly chill. They wore big pom-poms on their saddle shoes, which didn't quite touch the ground. Their laughter echoed in my ears.

I loved how people stayed in Sugarland.

I reached Ellis as the crowd went crazy again for something on the field I didn't see.

"What's up, handsome?" I could never get enough of him in that fitted tan and black uniform.

"The usual pandemonium," he said, cocking a grin at the sight of me. "All four high school math teachers had their houses TP'ed during last night's bonfire. They wrapped Mrs. Jorgen's mailbox so tight in industrial toilet paper that we had to cut it off."

"At least it didn't rain last night." Wet toilet paper was tough to get out of tall trees.

"We caught the perpetrators on a neighbor's doorbell cam. It was the English teachers." He shook his head in disbelief. "And they blamed us! Said we should have had more patrols out."

He'd been doing his job and then some. You couldn't account for English teachers gone wild. Besides, Ellis had done the most important job of all. "Thanks again for keeping Melody safe last night."

"I didn't do it alone," he said. "Duranja was right there as well."

"Don't ruin my mood." I leaned against him, and he snaked an arm around my back.

"Watch yourself. The library intruder left no evidence behind, and I don't think they're finished causing trouble."

"How so?" I asked, looking up at him.

He ground his jaw, clearly debating how much to tell me. "This way," he said, ushering me away from the crowd.

"Where are we going?" I asked, taking the hand he offered, intrigued, as he led me into a deserted area under the stands.

It wasn't like Ellis to be so sneaky.

"You know this is where kids make out," I teased.

"Don't tempt me," he answered as we stood in the grass together.

It was wild to hear the echo of the fans in the bleachers above us, yet know we were totally alone.

"I'm going to show you something," he said, pulling out his cell phone. He opened up his photos and showed me a shot of a lock on a steel table. A numbered plastic bag lay nearby. "Notice anything unusual?"

It was a regular combination lock with a navy blue face. The rounded bar at the top had been sliced through. "This looks like the one I used on my locker in high school." Except for the color. Mine had been pink.

"Exactly," Ellis said, closing the app and tucking his phone back into his pocket. "Only that's the lock they cut off the time capsule. Why did they use a cheap combination lock instead of a padlock? A combination lock has more moving parts that can jam."

"Plus, the combination is easy to lose or forget." I'd forgotten combinations more than once.

He smiled at that. "Also, think about it. More than one person would be able to open the combination lock at any time if that code got out."

Wow. I mean, I wouldn't put it past the committee to just grab a lock, but still… "I think you may be onto something."

He ground his jaw, and I could sense his frustration. "Detective Marshall doesn't agree. But yeah, something tells me that's not right." He gave me a long look. "There's no record of the lock the committee used, and no one on the original committee can recall."

"Trust your instincts, Ellis." He was a great officer and one of the smartest people I knew. "You'll figure it out."

He smiled down at me. "Thanks, Verity," he said, playing with the hair on my shoulder. "You make me think I can do just about anything," he added. Then he cupped my chin in his hands and kissed me. He did it so well that I started imagining what it would be like if we could live under the bleachers for a while.

The crowd cheered and stomped above us, shaking down dried mud, dust, and a few pieces of spilled popcorn.

Ellis pulled away with a laugh. "And here I thought we could get out of here with no evidence," he said, brushing a piece of popcorn from my hair.

"You're worth it," I said, taking the opportunity to free a little dirt from his broad shoulders. He enjoyed every second of it.

"How's it going with your mother this weekend?" he asked.

I leaned back to look at him. "You know how to kill the mood."

The corner of his mouth lifted. "I never said I was smooth."

And I'd never accused him of it. "Mom's a force of nature. Carl is good for her."

He seemed happy to hear it. "You know, I teased my mom for going to a spa this weekend, but I'm kind of glad I don't have to worry about her."

I couldn't argue that. Virginia thrived on drama, and we had plenty here this weekend without her.

"At least we're not paying for a mud bath, like she is," Ellis said, nudging me.

"I can just see you with cucumbers on your eyes," I teased.

"And caviar between my toes," he added.

"Ick." I playfully pushed him away. "That's not what they do at spas."

He shot me a cat-eating grin. "I'll be happy if I never know what they do at those places," he vowed. "Just give me a beer and a pizza and a boss who does his job right."

Cheers to that. "We'll figure this out." We would.

Somehow.

"I know," he said, taking my hands in his. "Tell me, what did the ghost Ashley have to say?"

"So you saw me crash the parade this morning." He would have been one of the only ones who understood.

He huffed. "I heard all about it," he said with a half-smile. "I was at the station, arguing with my boss about padlocks, dusting the one we had for prints."

"And?"

"Only the mayor's." He shrugged. It made sense, seeing as he'd opened the door a few nights ago.

I told Ellis about the theories I'd discussed with Mom and Carl. None of it surprised him. Ellis was usually one step ahead when it came to putting together a mystery.

"Just...try to keep your mom out of it," he said, being diplomatic.

"I am," I promised. "For the most part."

He cringed. "Try harder. In fact, how about you focus on Ashley and I'll keep after our live investigation?"

"Yay for teamwork," I said, trailing my hands up his chest. No sense letting a private spot under the bleachers go to waste.

Ellis wasn't one to ignore a hint, and just like I'd hoped, he kissed me again. And again. And I was having a great time of it when Duranja's voice pierced the haze.

"Hello?" He stood several feet away. It still felt like he'd invaded our personal space.

Ellis cursed under his breath.

"At last," Duranja said when he'd gotten our attention. "For a second, I thought I was going to have to go get a bucket of water."

"Which is probably why you don't have a girlfriend," I said.

Duranja made it a point to ignore me. "You might want to get back up there, Ellis," he said. "The Cavers mascot fell off the top of the Snack Shack. Some say he was pushed. I had to keep the Biscuits mascot from climbing up to do a victory lap, and we're good so far, but I think the rest of the fans are starting to get ideas."

"When is homecoming over again?" Ellis asked aloud.

In about twenty-four hours. I had to get back to investigating.

Wait. "Why is Duranja here at the game and not guarding the library?" I asked.

Duranja shot me a look like I was pestering *him*.

Ellis brushed the remaining dust out of his hair while heading out. "The chief put Officer Ryan on it. Duranja is better at crowd control."

"As long as somebody's there," I said, although I suspected the intruder might already have what they wanted.

"Don't worry," Ellis said, coming back for a quick kiss.

"Stop getting distracted," Duranja groused. "It's like she has this mojo power over you."

It was called love, and Duranja had no idea.

"Be safe," Ellis said quietly to me.

"You too," I said, letting him go.

When I emerged from under the stands—a few minutes after Ellis in order to avoid any scandal—I realized we'd been chatting and kissing for the entire first half of the game.

Time flies when you're having a good time.

The scoreboard read: *Sugarland 35, Visitors 7*

It was a homecoming miracle! The Cavers had been state champions last year, but our Biscuits were ahead anyway.

Although come to think of it, we'd beaten them last year as well—their only loss of the season. Not even the Cavers could topple Sugarland spirit.

The players lined up with only ten seconds left on the clock. The hometown Biscuits had pushed the Cavers almost all the way to their end zone, and I was thrilled to see I might get to see our team score again.

I stood by a couple drinking hot chocolate.

"Sugarland is cheating!" the woman complained.

"They do it every year," her date agreed, exasperated.

I was about to turn and correct them when the center snapped the ball, and our quarterback passed it to...one of the Cavers! The Cavers player intercepted the ball and took off running toward our end zone.

Our players chased him, but they couldn't catch him. One by one they dove and fell a hair short of the sprinting Caver.

But then—ohmygoodness. I saw it clear as day. A half-dozen ghostly Sugarland defensive lineman appeared out of thin air and tackled the Cavers player.

That had to hurt!

The ghostly Biscuits passed straight through the live player, of course, but the Caver stumbled and dropped the ball.

Our live players were on it in a second, taking the ball to the ground and stopping the big run.

The Cavers player stumbled a few more steps, batting at the air, no doubt feeling the prickling of the ghosts or at least a sudden, shocking cold spot.

The home team went crazy and emptied the bench in an uproarious early halftime celebration.

"Why didn't we make that touchdown?" the man next to me exclaimed.

"One of the Sugarland players must have grabbed his foot and tripped him," his partner insisted.

Not exactly. It was a fair tackle. Sugarland had simply fielded an extra team.

I wasn't sure how to fix that.

The scoreboard now read: *Sugarland 42, Visitors 7*

Which now felt like a big, fat lie.

Was that why we always won homecoming? I'd always assumed we'd been propelled to victory by good old-fashioned Biscuit pride.

I hurried back to our side. Maybe I could have a word with the ghosts who couldn't seem to stop playing for Sugarland.

Only now they floated above the field, hamming it up for the deceased crowd in the hometown bleachers. Our ghosts stomped and cheered while the spectral fans on the other side booed and tossed popcorn.

"Okay, what's going on?" Kelli Kaiser asked, sidling up next to me.

"You wouldn't believe it if I told you." She'd seen me work enough times to know I wasn't focused on the present-day game.

Kelli had assisted me on a case at the Heritage Society last year, and she had her ear to the ground when it came to the happenings in Sugarland. She wore a red faux fur coat that instantly tickled my nose as she drew closer. "Your mom's been asking all kinds of questions about where the Norwoods were last night."

"Please tell me she's being subtle."

Kelli smoothed a lock of hair behind her ear. "I don't like to lie."

My heart sank. Perhaps it was a mistake to trust her. A break in the case wasn't worth my mom's safety. Or her life.

"She's trying," Kelli added, as if that would help boost my mood.

It didn't. What I'd said to Ellis under the bleachers rang true —we were running out of time, at least on the ghostly side of the investigation.

We had until tomorrow night to fix this before Ashley disappeared again for another year. If we didn't make it, well, we had to hope the police would discover something to tie the killer to the scene.

Melody hurried from the crowd that had gathered by the snack bar, carrying a box overloaded with popped corn. "Did you see what Alec did over there? He was magnificent."

"Who?" Kelli asked.

"Officer Duranja," I said, pleased when Kelli made a face.

"He talked the rock climbers club out of scaling the snack bar," Melody said with pride.

"It's not like it would be a challenge for them." I could probably climb to the top of the cinderblock structure if I tried.

"Alec also told me about you kissing your boyfriend under the bleachers," Melody said, flipping a bite of popcorn into her mouth. "Way to get into that high school spirit."

"I'm going to kill Duranja," I grumbled, taking a handful of popcorn.

"I think it's cute," Kelli said as Melody offered a snack to her.

"Ellis has been the voice of reason all weekend, and now he gets to act like a crazy teenager."

Duranja needed to stop talking to my sister. At least he wasn't the type to tell the town.

The homecoming court had begun to line up on the far side by the band. Excited, I looked for any ghosts among them. I didn't want to miss Ashley if she hopefully—please heaven—decided to join.

The teams had cleared the field, and that included the ghostly Biscuits.

The band struck up the "Coronation March," and Kelli began to clap and cheer as the ROTC kids marched out in uniform and made a sword arch. "Third one from the front is my cousin, Randall," she exclaimed.

"Go, Randall," I enthused, and then I spotted Ashley in her poufy-sleeved dress. "I've got to go," I said, scrambling away from my sister and my friend.

Ashley stood in line with the rest of the court. They hadn't marched onto the field yet, which was a definite plus.

Ashley preened like the excited teen she was, while I dodged a family of three and nearly ran smack into a ghost carrying a megaphone. I passed straight through his arm. He shrieked like I'd tried to cut it off, and I felt the cold, stinging zap of the supernatural.

"Sorry!" I called. Stumbling, I recovered. It could have been worse. If the ghost had been at full strength, I could have gotten knocked on my rear.

And then I noticed Ashley hadn't taken full form, either.

That...wasn't good.

Either these ghosts had gotten together and decided to go filmy—very unlikely—or more worrisome, Frankie's power was evaporating.

I doubled my pace, not even caring that I was running.

"Verity!" Melody called, coming up behind me.

"Wait!" Kellie huffed out. "My boots have heels!"

I ignored my posse and instead looked to the ghosts in the stands. And I didn't like what I saw.

They were all fading.

Correction: Frankie's power was fading.

I felt it seep out of me like a slow, cold drip. I couldn't imagine what would rob him of his energy like this.

"Frankie!" I called, as if he could hear me.

He wasn't taking his energy back willingly. I knew what that felt like.

I watched as Ashley dwindled to a shadow of her former self.

If I kept losing power like this, soon I'd have none at all.

I ran past the band. John O'Brien had lost his entire torso. Or at least I couldn't see it. He didn't seem bothered in the least.

I made it to Ashley, who startled when she saw me.

No doubt I was a sight—eyes wide, hair flying in every direction.

"Ashley," I said, out of breath, trying for my usual charm. Thank heaven I'd made it to her in time. "You might remember me from—"

"Why are you following me?" She stepped back, looking for help. Only she was surrounded by a living, breathing home-coming court, and they were staring at me instead of her.

But I couldn't worry about them right now. I could barely see Ashley. And of course she probably thought I was a nut, and... "Well, I—"

"Excuse me, ladies," said a very alive teacher with a clip-board. She appeared startled to see me, as well as my friends, who had just caught up. "If you're not part of the homecoming court, you need to step away."

"Verity is hunting a ghost," Kelli said proudly.

First my mother, now her.

"It's important," Melody insisted, spilling popcorn out of the box as she halted next to me.

"It'll only take a minute to—" I turned back to my mom's old friend, but she was nowhere in sight. "Ashley?" I asked. "Ashley Starling, where did you go?"

The teacher touched me on the arm. "Dear," she said in a tone reserved for the slow and the crazy, "Ashley Starling died thirty-six years ago."

Oh, for Pete's sake. "She was here," I insisted.

Only now, she was not.

And as I scanned the stadium, I no longer saw the ghosts in the stands or the former Biscuits hovering above the field.

They'd all vanished, along with my power.

Chapter Nineteen

✦❀✦

I spent the rest of halftime, and into the start of the game,
hoping Frankie could fix whatever glitch he had and my
power would come back. Ashley had been right in front of me…
until she wasn't.

"I don't understand it," I said to Melody. We'd squeezed into
the end of Kelli's row while some of her other friends were off
chatting. "Frankie's energy has never faded like this before." I
mean, sure, he'd lost his power at times, mostly back in the pre-
Molly days, but it had been sudden and always for a reason I
could pinpoint. "I hope he's all right. Something's different this
time." In a very bad way.

"Maybe you're thinking about it too hard," Melody said,
offering me the last bit from her nearly empty popcorn box.

"Believe me, the ghosts usually pop up without me thinking."
Or sometimes even wanting them around. "What could have
possibly gone so wrong in Frankie's life that he'd cut me off
completely?"

Surely this wasn't because I'd refused to get him a puppy.

"I could run back and check," I said as Melody downed the

rest of her popcorn, "although I parked so far away, I'll miss the rest of the game."

"You can take my car if you want," Melody offered. "I can always catch a ride home with Kelli."

"Or Alec," Kelli suggested, offering me one of her nachos.

"No," I said, and not to the bright yellow cheese on chips. "Melody needs to stay away from Duranja."

"I think he's nice," my sister said noncommittally.

I had to believe Frankie was okay. It wasn't like El Gato could pop up and snag him. And he'd been fine on his own for nearly a century. "I need to stay," I vowed, and not only because I wanted to keep Duranja from sniffing around my sister. This could be a temporary power glitch. It would be irresponsible to leave the game if there was a chance I could still see Ashley.

I wished I could call my ghost.

Not that he had a phone or knew how to use one.

I waited, and I kept the faith, but I never did regain my ability to see ghosts.

The game ended with a score of *Sugarland 56, Visitors 7.* Afterward, Mom and Carl wanted to linger among the groups of people socializing. I left them my car and accepted a ride home from Melody.

"I'm sure Frankie's fine," she said as she navigated her Ford Focus through the small neighborhood that butted up against my property.

I hoped so. It wasn't like him to lose power like that. And I was pretty sure he hadn't cut me off intentionally. This time felt different from all the times he'd simply snapped the line.

In the beginning of our somewhat unorthodox association, he would have left me in the dust with glee. But now? We'd been through too much for him to sabotage me like that.

"Slow down," I said to my sister as I caught sight of a glowing area of grass among the rows of peach saplings I'd planted in my front yard. Generations ago, my family had grown peaches, and I was trying to revive the tradition. "There," I said, catching sight of a silver flicker among the tallish grass. "Let me out here," I said, opening the door as the car rolled to a stop.

"Are you sure?" Melody called.

"Very sure," I said, making out a white Panama hat and heading straight for it. "You go on home. Thanks for the ride!"

"My life is so weird," I heard her mumble as she ran around to close my door.

But I was focused on the gangster ghost splayed out on my grass with his hat askew and his suit rumpled, his gaze trained on the sky.

As I heard my sister pull away, I followed his gaze to the carpet of stars glowing in the chilly night.

"This had better not be about the puppy," I said, making my way across the yard.

"I'm a loser, and nobody's ever going to love me," Frankie declared.

I sat down in the cool grass next to him. "What happened?"

He stared up at the sky. "Molly came by. She said she thinks I'm the one. Me," he added, as if she'd accused him of being Jack the Ripper.

"Well," I hated to break it to him, but, "that means she loves you."

His Adam's apple bobbed as he gulped. "She did until I told her I didn't think she was the one for me."

"What?" I demanded, louder than I'd intended. The gangster flinched. "That is…" I tried to be understanding. "That is one way to approach it," I ventured. "I mean, if she's not the one for you, you owe it to her to be honest."

It hurt to even think that way, because I'd always imagined them together. But if he didn't really love Molly, he had to let her go.

He sat up on his elbows. "She is the one. She's my best

friend." He popped up to his feet. "But I'm going to mess it up, and she deserves more."

"You can't know that," I began.

He gave me a long look.

Okay. He was right. "We all mess up from time to time."

"Yeah, but love in life is 'till death do us part.' Love in death is…forever. How does a guy manage that?"

Geez. "I don't know." I hadn't really thought about it.

He dragged his hands through his hair and began to pace. "Sure, I was Mr. Romantic when we first started dating, but I can't keep that up until the end of time. And I can't seem to stop disappointing her." He turned to me. "Always. I mean constantly. I'm a freak of nature when it comes to idiot moves with women. Look at you." He thrust a hand out. "You're not even arguing. You've seen it. You know it's true."

"I—" Well, he wasn't a dolt all the time, just a lot lately.

"It's time to call it quits now," he declared, "before I take her down with me."

"There's only one problem with that," I said, stopping him cold. "You'd be miserable and so would she."

"She'll get over me." He shrugged, his nostrils flaring and his jaw tight. "She told me she's going to move on from me, to someone who appreciates her. She's going to date El Gato. Like he's so great."

"You are El Gato," I reminded him.

"She doesn't know that!" he said, tossing his hands up. He lowered them slowly. "Hey, maybe I can dress up as El Gato and date her that way."

"Frankie—"

"It'd be like a whole 'nother chance," he said, warming to the idea.

"No. Absolutely not. You owe her the truth."

"Where has that ever gotten me?" he demanded. "I don't deserve her anyway." He slumped.

"You absolutely do." He had to give himself some credit. "Ellis and I don't have smooth sailing, and I deserve him."

He chewed on that for a second. "Maybe you don't," he concluded.

"This isn't about me," I informed him.

"No, seriously. You're always dragging him into haunted houses and on ghost hunts, and you snore something terrible."

"I do not snore," I declared. "But I do have other faults." Small ones. "And I still think I deserve love and happiness."

Frankie shoved his hands into his pockets and looked at the ground. "Then I'm the only nutball. I'm okay with that."

"Look, Ellis and I have a lot of fun times together, but it's not always perfect. That's life. Or…the afterlife in your case."

"Don't patronize me," he grumbled.

I walked up to him and faced him so he had to look at me or the ground. He chose the dirt. "Look, I don't expect Ellis to be perfect or to woo me constantly, and Molly doesn't expect that from you, either. It's not natural. It's not *life*. In fact, some of the best times I've had with Ellis are when it's been the two of us simply being ourselves."

His gaze flicked up from the ground. "That kind of relationship doesn't just happen to a guy like me. I have to earn it," he insisted.

"Maybe in the mob," I conceded, "but love doesn't work that way."

"It doesn't work at all," he grumbled.

I wasn't letting him off the hook that easy. "You accept love. You give love. It's that simple. And that's where you're screwing up. You're so worried about being enough that you're forgetting to simply love her, be with her." He started to speak, and I shut him down. "If you can't accept yourself—" I searched for the words "—that's something you can work on for the future. But there's one thing you can do now to rebuild what you almost had with Molly. You can accept *her*."

He ground his hands into his pockets. "She wanted me to take her to the homecoming dance in the town square tomorrow."

"Then take her. It's a fun thing to do."

He eyed me skeptically. "That's what she said. Did she tell you to say that?"

"I know Molly," I assured him. "She cares about you because of the day-to-day, real Frankie."

He fiddled with his tie. "She likes bad boys."

"And you are that." I didn't know anybody else who'd locked his business associates in trunks as a means of negotiation. "But you're also loyal," I assured him. "You do the right thing by your friends, and you care deeply about her." Molly had grown up poor and overlooked. I knew for a fact she'd never had any kind of love or attention from a man until him. "She's waited more than a hundred years for you."

The corner of his mouth turned up at that. "One hundred years is a long time to wait for a guy who keeps screwing up," he reminded me.

"Only if you don't learn," I insisted. "It's not our mistakes that define us, it's our love and our willingness to do better."

He rolled his eyes. "You get that off a bubblegum wrapper?"

I didn't dignify that with an answer.

I merely waited as he contemplated the dirt at his feet, his brows furrowed, his hands clenched in his pockets.

"Stop staring at me. I'm thinking."

"Okay," I said, waiting.

"You're pushy."

"I know," I admitted.

"Seriously." He glanced up at me. "Can you leave and let me be?"

"Sure," I said, hoping I'd given him something to think about.

I fished in my purse and realized I'd given my parents my

keys. No matter. I'd left the back door open. This was Sugarland, after all.

With one last glance at the brooding gangster, I made my way down the gravel side driveway, toward the back of the house. I liked to leave that door open, much to Ellis's dismay.

Yet he still loved me.

I hoped I'd helped Frankie understand at least part of what I was saying tonight. Teaching love and acceptance to a gangster was a tall order on any day, much less when his romance hung in the balance.

It must have been the sudden breakup with Molly that had cut off his power to me tonight, her declaration that it was over for good.

I hoped Molly would give him yet another chance.

Mom and Carl's RV stood dark in my yard, as did the back entrance to my house. I must have forgotten to turn on my porch light. The still pond appeared like black ice.

"Lucy!" I called to my skunk. It was a nice enough day, so I'd left her outside. "Lucy, I'm home!" I hoped she'd enjoyed her afternoon of freedom. Soon, it would be too chilly for her to frolic in the yard as she pleased.

My boots crunched on the gravel as I passed my grandmother's rose garden. "Are you under the porch?" I asked, trying to see under the latticework, but it was impossible at night. Especially with the lights off.

Lucy always greeted me. I felt her absence in the pit of my stomach.

I walked to the porch steps. Ellis had installed lights on a sensor. I stood at the bottom and clapped my hands.

"Luuuuucy!" My call turned into a scream as the sensor lights illuminated my back porch. A skunk dangled from the railing, tied at the neck with a thick rope. She wore her cheerleading uniform and a bow on her tail.

Chapter Twenty

I grasped the motionless little body, which was too light and spongey soft in my hands. It took me a second to realize it wasn't a real skunk at all.

It was a child's plush toy.

I sat back on my heels, still holding the stuffed skunk. Who would do this? It was sick. Awful. And where was my little girl?

Claws clattered against wood as my darling skunk dashed up the stairs and straight into my arms. "Ohmygod, sweetie." I hugged her trembling body. Mud smeared her head and leaves tangled in her fur, but she was alive and breathing. "Who did this?" I demanded, holding her tight. "Were they loud and mean?"

I dialed Ellis, and he promised to come over right away. In the meantime, I carried Lucy to the couch in the parlor, picking leaves out of her coat as we went. She looked fine. I held her close, never so glad to be holding my warm ball of fluff.

Not even five minutes passed before Ellis burst in the back door. "You really need to lock this," he said, striding over to where I sat with Lucy. "You said she's okay? Do you want me to call the vet?"

"She's fine," I promised. But then a terrible thought hit me. "You know, the house was unlocked the entire time I was at the game."

Ellis opened his mouth to say something, then slammed it shut. "Come with me," he ordered. "I'm not letting either one of you out of my sight," he muttered to himself as he locked my back door and checked the front door.

"Hey, that one's locked," I said, counting it as a win.

I didn't get a yay from him. Not that I expected one.

Relieved and thankful, I followed him all over my house as he looked behind doors, in closets, and under my futon for intruders. We didn't see a soul except for Frankie out on the lawn, wrapped up in his own problems. I caught a glimpse of him through one of my windows.

So much for the gangster guarding my property. Although Frankie had never even pretended to be that kind of guy.

Ellis secured the scene and checked the front door one last time before squishing me—Lucy included—into a big hug. "You've got to stop scaring me."

"How do you think I felt?" I asked, still shaky from my discovery on the porch. "Talk about a sick joke."

"More like a warning," Ellis said, taking my hand and leading me down the hallway into the kitchen. A note sat on my counter. It read, *Next time, it won't be a toy.*

Oh, sweet heaven.

"I found this tied to the rope," Ellis said, all business. "Have you received any other threats?"

Not to my poor, darling skunk. Who would do such a thing?

"Verity?" Ellis pressed.

I tried to think while my head swam and my stomach hurt, and all I wanted to do was hug my skunk.

"There was Mr. Norwood tonight," I managed. "He wasn't very happy with me." I leaned against the kitchen island and told Ellis about my encounter with Mr. Norwood at the football game.

His jaw tightened. "Next time, you tell me if someone threatens you."

Well, in that case... "Kiki Everett was none too happy with me at the parade today." I told him about that, too—while I kept stroking Lucy, touching Lucy, making sure she was safe in my arms.

"Did you see either one of them during the second half of the game tonight?" Ellis pressed, sneaking in a pet for Lucy. "I talked to Officer Ryan on the way over here, and he did a drive-by earlier, around the end of the first half of the game. Everything looked fine then."

"Wait." I held my skunk closer. "You've had the police patrolling my house?"

He didn't bother to sugarcoat it. "Homecoming is crazy. And your mom hasn't exactly been subtle with her questions about Ashley's death. I wanted to make sure you were safe." When I didn't respond right away, he added, "And your mom and Carl. They're the ones sleeping out back."

"Sure." Ellis had been thinking all about Mom and Carl. My sweet, yet bullheaded boyfriend could sometimes be too overprotective for my own good, and consequently *his* own good. But this time, I was glad he'd taken extra precautions. "You know, Mr. Norwood's wife, Jean, wasn't at the game at all. He said she was sick."

"Good to know," he said, filing it away in his mind. "I'm going to go take some pictures and file a report. Why don't you clean Lucy up and relax?"

"Because bathing my skunk is so relaxing," I said, dislodging a clump of mud from under her ear.

He huffed out a laugh. "Then simply hold her and love her, and I'll help you when I'm done," he said, giving me a kiss on the top of the head.

I'd thought it was cute when Carl had done the same to my mom. Now I knew exactly what it was—a little *I love you* after a very long day.

Ten minutes later, Mom and Carl burst in the back door. "We heard what happened!" Mom exclaimed, rushing to where I'd curled up on the couch with Lucy. I stood and hugged her, and she used the opportunity to give me a thorough once-over. "The whole town is talking!"

"How?" I asked, extricating myself from her grip.

"It went out over the police scanner," Carl said, as if that was a normal way to get the news. "Ellis reported it in."

"We were on our way to have coffee and dessert with Darcy and Phyllis and that boy Darcy likes from Roan's," Mom added.

"That 'boy' is in his fifties," Carl chided.

"Either way." Mom waved him off. Her focus stayed on me. "I have to say I'm shocked. I'm so glad you're okay."

"I am," I promised her.

This time.

"I didn't think it would get this serious," Mom said to Carl.

"Really? What *were* you expecting?" I asked. "We're going after a killer. Whoever murdered Ashley probably thought they'd gotten away with it. Nobody was supposed to discover the body for a hundred years. The killer is probably desperate. They may have left loose ends, thinking time was on their side. Now we've dug everything up. We're asking questions. We're trying to put them in jail. Basically end their life as they know it."

She shook her head. "I'm too overwhelmed to think. We have to stop asking questions! I don't see any other way to keep you safe."

Hardly. "I think that's exactly the message someone was

trying to send. Stop investigating. Stop asking questions. As far as I'm concerned, that means we're close."

"But at what cost?" Mom protested.

"I don't know," I said, hugging my skunk tighter. "Certainly not Lucy's health or happiness." She struggled a bit, and I realized I was holding her too tight. "Sorry, sweetie." I tried to let her down, but she clung to my embrace. "Look, I'm not going to let them win just because they're horrible enough to threaten my skunk."

"They could have hurt you or your sister," Mom said, as if it hit her for the first time.

"Or you," I pointed out. "They already killed your friend."

She gasped, and I felt kind of bad for saying those things, but nothing I'd said so far had made her understand. "Of course it's ten kinds of dangerous to mess with a murderer. That's why I've been cautioning you to be careful asking questions. It still doesn't change the fact that whoever it is has to be stopped."

It chilled me to think a person like that could live in Sugarland, hidden among us for so many years.

"Well, Tilly, I don't want you asking any more questions," Carl said, wrapping a protective arm around Mom. "And I'm going to be on you like a tick at the dance tomorrow."

"You should do the same," she said to me. "Stick close to Ellis, and as much as I hate to say it—leave the past in the past."

She had to be kidding. "If I did that, I wouldn't catch any killers. I don't see how that makes any of us safer."

"At least then they won't be after you," Mom said, breaking away from Carl and pacing over to the mantel, as if she simply had to move. "Tell her, Carl."

My stepdad chewed on that. "It seems to me that Ellis has already expressed the same opinion and gotten nowhere." Carl looked at me, as if he expected me to save him from Mom.

"Well, maybe Ellis is right," Mom said, turning her back to the mantel. "You tell me about how he's overprotective and he frets about you, and now I see exactly what he worries about. You have to admit it. Ghost hunting is dangerous."

She'd been gung-ho about it not two hours ago. "You can't let one incident throw you off like this."

And technically, I didn't need her help. If anything, Mom made things harder.

She tossed up her hands. "You have a rosebush in your parlor and a terrified skunk in your arms, and you don't see a problem at all."

"That's where you're wrong," I said simply. "Lucy's mental health is very much my concern."

Mom pointed her finger up into the air, which meant she was about to start a lecture. Carl saw it, too. "Come on, Tilly," he said, taking her hand gently and placing it in his.

That was one way to keep her from pointing.

"Let's all take a break," he added, practical to the core. "Nobody's convincing anyone, and we've all had a long night."

"Verity's not safe," my mom said, rooted to the spot.

"Ellis said he's staying tonight, and she has us right outside," he coaxed, moving her along. "Let's sleep on it. It'll look better in the morning," he promised us both.

I breathed a sigh of relief when the door closed behind them. How could Mom be serious about breaking off our investigation? We only had one night left before Ashley would be gone for another year.

Who knew how cold the trail would get in that time?

Worse, I wasn't sure I'd get Frankie's power back in time to investigate anything more on the ghostly side.

I saw police lights out my kitchen window and sighed. That would really get Mom going.

If it was Duranja out there, he was probably telling her how I took too many chances and went too many places where I didn't belong.

Peeking past the curtain, I saw the tall, thin form of Officer

Ryan. Good. I didn't even feel like going outside to argue. I already knew I was doing the right thing.

Soon after, the lights cut out and the kitchen door cracked open. Ellis slipped in, looking a lot more tired than he had earlier.

"Officer Ryan is taking the evidence in, although I can't say I found anything that would give us a clue who did this." He walked over to me, his work shoes echoing off my linoleum. "How is she?" he asked, taking a peek at my skunk.

"She's calm. Warm." My sweet escape artist had turned into a cuddle bug.

He stroked her head.

"She's sleeping with me tonight," I vowed.

"She sleeps with you every night," Ellis pointed out.

He smiled as he stroked her head.

"What?" I asked.

He tilted his head as he gently drew a burr from behind her ear. "If I didn't know better, I'd think she was trying to get out of a bath."

My phone rang.

Ellis held his hands out. "I've got her," he said as I gently handed Lucy off before answering.

"Verity?" Melody's voice sounded in my ear. "Oh, my God. How are you? How's Lucy?"

"She's fine," I said, watching Ellis walk her over to the couch and sit. "We're fine."

"Good." Melody sighed. "Mom called me. She's fixing to throw a duck fit."

"I know," I said, looking out my kitchen window to the back-yard, where the RV sat lit up like a Christmas tree. "How are you doing? Maybe you should come over here tonight, just in case."

"Oh, I'm fine," she said quickly.

She didn't sound fine. "Did something bad happen to you too?" I could tell by her tone she was holding something back.

"I'm great," she insisted. "Perfect."

Now I knew something was up.

I rested a hand on the counter. "I can keep asking, or you can simply tell me," I informed her.

"Fine, but...do *not* lecture me," she said slowly. The last part came out in a rush. "Alec came by when he heard about Lucy, and he offered to stay over. On my couch," she was careful to clarify.

I cocked my head back. "Great. So now Duranja is using Lucy to get to my sister," I laid it out plain.

"Ellis's friend and fellow officer is making sure I'm safe," she said primly.

Yeah, right. I dragged a hand down my face. "That's not all there is to it."

"He also brought over a first-edition signed copy of *The ABC Murders* by Agatha Christie, and he's in the kitchen making me dinner."

I dropped my hand. Lovely. He was bonding with my sister over a serial killer story. "Are you dating my nemesis?" I asked her plainly.

She paused way too long. "No...I'm getting to know him."

Either way, I smelled a rat.

A big one named Alec Duranja.

But clearly, my sister had to discover for herself what a jerk he could be.

"Stay safe," I instructed her. At least Duranja was good for that.

"You too," she told me before signing off.

The whole world had gone crazy, and nobody noticed but me.

A snore sounded from the parlor. I went to the doorway and found Ellis stretched over the length of the couch, with Lucy passed out in the crook of his arm. She snurfled loudly in her sleep.

"I think Duranja is after Melody," I said.

"He's liked her for years," Ellis said casually.

"And you don't see a problem with this?" It was one thing for me to deal with family issues when dating Ellis. I didn't wish it on Melody. Because I certainly didn't approve, and neither would my mom once she realized how Duranja treated people.

"Not my business," Ellis said simply.

"I'll have a talk with her later," I vowed. I'd figure out what to say to rescue her. As for my mom? I had no idea what to think about my run-in with her. "Can you believe the nerve of my mother? Telling *me* to be careful?"

Ellis gave me a long look. "Yes."

"And she's the one who has been so reckless." I'd been warning her this whole time.

"Apple, meet tree," Ellis drawled, stroking my skunk as Lucy stirred and raised her head.

He was no help.

And I was in no mood to relax. "I'm going to go talk to Frankie." I hadn't thought to ask him if he'd seen anything unusual at the house tonight. You'd think he would have told me, but then again—this was Frankie.

Lucy gave a low, yowling yawn and resettled herself in Ellis's arms as I walked past them toward the front of the house. At least one of us could forget our worries.

I peered out the window of the front room and saw Frankie still sitting in the grass, in roughly the same place I'd found him earlier. I unlocked the front door and walked out to join him.

"Hey," he said, his knees bent, his arms wrapped around them.

"Did you see any cars drive past before I arrived home tonight?" I asked, plopping down next to him.

He shot me a sidelong look. "I was kind of busy torpedoing my love life."

"So the answer is?"

"No," he snapped.

"Well, while you were beating yourself up, someone drove onto my property and hung a fake skunk from my porch rail."

Frankie gaped at me. "How's the real Lucy? If they did anything to that skunk, I'm assembling a hit squad, and there's nothing you can do to stop me," he vowed.

"She's fine. They didn't touch her," I assured him.

"Man," he said, shaking his head, "I've got to keep more of an eye out for that little skunk."

Never mind me. And unlike Lucy, I actually liked him. Well, most of the time.

I shifted to face him. "Whoever we're after is getting dangerous." And desperate. "We must be getting close."

"What did you do to break the case?" Frankie asked, as if he expected me to list it.

But that was the trick. "I've said a lot of things to a lot of people. So has Mom. We've questioned everyone from Ashley's old boyfriend to her science teacher to the dead cafeteria lady. It looks like one of us got something right."

"Well, see? That's a positive," he mused. "Look at me. I'm helping you now."

Not unless he could describe the car or person who'd trespassed on my property tonight.

"So Molly came by and saw me," he said, clearly bored with my topic. "She felt bad for tossing one of El Gato's roses at my head."

"Your rose."

"Right." He shrugged. "She's still set on dating that fancy boy Cuban. I need to make El Gato disappear."

"That shouldn't be hard," I mused.

He shot me an appraising look. "Yeah, well, first, I need to know what he has that I don't."

Seriously? "He has a mustache." A bad one. "That's it. That's the only thing he has that you're not walking around with right now."

"No," he stated sharply. "It's got to be something else, because she doesn't want me. She wants him."

"Of course she wants you." He was the only show in town. "There is literally no competition."

He narrowed his eyes. "Next time, it might not even be El Gato. It might be some other guy with something enticing that I'll never have." He stood and began to pace. "I need to know what's going to happen before I trust her with *everything*."

"El Gato doesn't exist. This fake other guy doesn't exist," I pointed out. But he didn't appear to be buying a silly thing like logic. I got up to join him. "Please don't do this to yourself." Or her. He needed to trust, not test.

He stood grinding his jaw for a moment.

"I have a plan," he announced. "And it's better than a puppy."

"That wouldn't be hard."

He turned to face me, serious as a heart attack. "El Gato will take Molly to the dance tomorrow night."

Oh no. "How about you take Molly to the dance tomorrow?"

"That's ridiculous. No." He held up a finger. "El Gato will send her a string quartet and an invitation she can't refuse," he ground out. "El Gato is going to romance her. He's going to use his charm and his mad dancing skills. He's going to *try* to seduce her. And we'll see who she likes better."

"You or you?" I asked dryly.

"Exactly!" he announced, as if it were all falling into place.

I hated to break it to him, but… "This is dishonest on about ten different levels."

"You're surprised I'm dishonest?" he asked. "I don't know if that's cute or sad."

"Okay, wise guy, answer me this. How are you going to be El Gato without her recognizing you?"

Frankie huffed. "El Gato has a pencil-thin moustache," he explained, as if I were daft.

That wouldn't fool anyone. Rather than argue that, I pointed out the obvious. "If you didn't die with it, it'll disappear after a few minutes."

"All taken care of," he said smugly. "Suds will be standing by with a fresh moustache every time El Gato gets called away to direct rum shipments or give orders on where to stack the money."

Unbelievable. "Which is?"

"About every half hour."

Geez.

But I could see by the set of his jaw and the glint in his eye that there was no talking him out of it.

I sighed. The only question I had left was exactly when this would blow up on him. And while I cared about his love life, I also had a job to do at the dance. "I need you at your best tomorrow night," I reminded him.

"You are pretty needy," Frankie agreed.

"I'm serious. I need strong, steady power from you if I have any hope of finding Ashley and talking to her, much less any other ghosts who might have seen her."

"Trust me, I'll have power to spare when El Gato makes Molly swoon," he said, digging into his coat pocket for a cigarette.

"Are you sure that will make you happy?" I asked. "Not jealous?"

He withdrew the case and tapped one out. "Maybe I'll just stay El Gato." He ignored my huff of exasperation and lit up his smoke. "It's better than being a sad sack who mopes around in your front yard. Who likes that guy?"

"I do," I reminded him.

"Then my life is complete," he said, doing a little wag with his cigarette hand. "Listen, don't worry about me. I'm done being pathetic." He took a drag. "I get that my power zapped out on you tonight. I felt myself let go of you like a balloon." He blew smoke out his nose. "In my defense, I felt like my life was over."

It kind of was, with him being dead and all.

"Don't say it," he warned.

I stood quietly with him as he took a long inhale.

"Anyhow, that's over now," he declared.

"Well, I hope you work something out with Molly tomorrow night."

He nodded. "I hope you don't need me to solve your mystery for you."

"I'm fine on my own," I promised. Although I would call in the cavalry if needed. "The dance is my last shot," I told him. "Do you have any words of wisdom for me?"

"Yeah," he said, snuffing out his smoke. "Find Ashley."

Chapter Twenty-One

The next night, I curled my hair into soft waves and tried not to think too much about the challenge ahead. Or the fact that this would be my last chance to set things right. On top of it, the police had discovered nothing about who had threatened Lucy last night, and it worried me.

The killer was desperate, and they could spot me coming.

As for me? I still had no idea whom I needed to watch out for.

I rested the curling iron on the top of the toilet tank—I'd emptied my entire makeup bag all over the small pedestal sink —and fluffed my hair.

My mom's face appeared in the mirror behind me. She was ready to go—early—in a classy red sheath dress with a matching jacket. The dance didn't start for a half hour.

"You look great," I told her. She'd done up her hair in a twist, making her look sophisticated and youthful at the same time.

She smiled and smoothed her dress. "I bought this for the New England cruise we took last year. I barely fit into it by the end. Too many buffets."

She was being too modest. "It looks like you picked it out special for homecoming."

Pearl ball earrings swung from her lobes, and she wore the gold pendant necklace Ashley had given her in high school. "I'd still feel better if you'd drive with Carl and me tonight."

"I'll be with Ellis," I assured her. He was far less distractable than my social butterfly mom and stepdad.

She didn't appear convinced. "Well, if he has to do something police-y, find me and Carl," she insisted.

"The dance will be crowded," I reminded her. "There will be plenty of people around. I'm sure I'll be perfectly safe."

Although to find a ghost, I could have to wander into the shadows.

She fidgeted with the gold pendant at her neck. She had something on her mind.

"I would have figured you'd wear pearls," I said, fiddling with my mascara again.

"I haven't wanted to take this off since…" Her voice choked. "Well, since we found Ashley. She bought us matching necklaces for Christmas 1985. See?" she asked, holding it out to me. "It has my initials and a starling, because that's her last name."

It was pretty, with a scripted monogram and a bird taking flight.

"Hers had a shamrock under the initials to remind her of me. It's an inside joke." She gave me a small smile as she held her hand over the pretty pendant. "We wore our necklaces every day, and we developed this code to use in class." She flipped the pendant on her necklace to the back. "This meant 'I'm about to pass you a note, so pay attention.' I'd gotten sent to the principal's office more than once before we came up with our system. You used to get into trouble for note passing in class. It wasn't like we could text."

"I'm familiar with note passing," I said, using a makeup brush to highlight my cheekbones. "I'm not that young."

"I'm young, so you're young," Mom declared.

And I knew better than to argue the point.

Mom hesitated. "Is there anything I can do to convince you to leave your ghost at home?"

"Frankie needs to be there," I said, separating my lashes. The second coat of mascara had gone on all clumpy. "His love life hangs in the balance, and if he doesn't get it back on track tonight, I won't be seeing any ghosts, much less Ashley."

"Well, I'm not investigating anymore," Mom vowed. "And I'm going to tell everybody how I'm not talking about it."

"Please. *Don't*," I said, slamming down the mascara a little harder than I'd intended. "And don't tell anyone what I'm doing, either."

She drew a sharp breath. "I'd be glad to tell them you backed off, if you would only realize what you're doing is stupid and dangerous!"

"You got me into this by blabbing our secrets all over town," I declared, fairly or not. "And I wouldn't even be investigating if you hadn't asked me!"

"So now this is my fault?" she reared back. "That's rich. All I do is support you and love you, and that's not enough? It's never enough. You don't even want me to live my life. And when I stop my life and come back to Sugarland, you complain about that, too!"

"You wouldn't even be here if you didn't have homecoming and Ashley and the whole works. You didn't come back for me." That much was obvious. "You skipped the last three Christmases. You forgot to call Melody on her birthday last year."

"I sent flowers!" she seethed.

That she probably preordered and forgot about. "You're not around. You're never around, and now you think you can lecture me on how to do my job."

"Because you want someone to hang your real skunk next time?" she demanded.

233

A chill shot through me, and I wasn't sure if it was because she'd said something so awful, or if it was because she'd hit too close to the truth.

"I'm done talking," I stated.

She hesitated. "All right. Then I am, too."

I listened to her heels clomping down the main stairs as I tossed the mascara tube into my bag, hard. My lashes were as good as they were going to get, and there was nothing I could do about my mom, either.

But it needed to be said. She couldn't traipse in and out of my life whenever she wanted and think there wouldn't be consequences. She couldn't choose to be enthralled with ghost hunting and then declare it terrible as soon as the novelty wore off. This was my life, not another one of her wild adventures.

And if she didn't want to be around for the tough part, well, fine.

I was used to it.

Turned out she'd also taken my spare keys and locked the door tightly behind her.

I only realized it when Ellis arrived a short time later and complimented me on the fact that both of my doors had been locked.

Being a polite Southern girl, I didn't even dwell on the strangeness of my date inspecting my home security. Instead, I welcomed him with a kiss and a smile while Lucy tried to climb his leg.

"For you," he said, presenting me with a bouquet of the most gorgeous red roses I'd ever seen. "And sweets for the sweet," he added, bending to give Lucy a blueberry-encrusted treat.

"Where'd you get that?" I asked as I went to put the flowers in water.

He cradled my skunk, following me. "Bree is thinking of starting a pet treat business. I'm her first customer."

"The way Lucy gobbled down that treat, you won't be the

last," I said, glad to hear my favorite pet rescue friend was trying a new venture.

We drove Lucy to Lauralee's house, where she'd spend the night safe with four kids who adored her, and a babysitter who might soon qualify for sainthood—considering the fact that the boys had been playing "marching band" with Lauralee's pots and pans when we'd arrived.

"You think Lucy will be okay?" Ellis hesitated as we made our way back to his police cruiser.

"She loves those kids." And the chaos. "I mean, they did make her the official band mascot."

"The Sugarland Skunks does have a certain ring to it," Ellis said as he opened the door for me.

The kids and the sitter waved at us through the living room window.

"Oh, and Tessa volunteers at the pet rescue with Bree," I added. "She knows Lucy pretty well."

"Lauralee knows how to pick her sitters," Ellis mused, sliding behind the wheel.

With four kids, she ought to.

Although if you asked me, Lauralee didn't get out enough.

I braced Frankie's urn between my feet like a hot casserole while Ellis backed out of the driveway.

"How are you doing, Frank?" I asked.

He didn't respond, not even to tell me not to call him Frank.

That was okay. I knew he was somewhere close. Possibly scheming up ways to win Molly back by being himself.

A girl could hope.

Ellis and I chatted as we made our way out of Lauralee's neighborhood in the older part of town and toward the town square.

"We'll be there soon," I said to Frankie's urn.

I tamped down a niggle of worry when I still got no reaction.

Usually, Frankie would be telling me to can it if he didn't want to talk.

"Oh, by the way, your mom gave me this," Ellis said, holding up an emergency whistle.

Sure. That would work better than the pistol he carried in his belt.

"She gave me this," I countered, digging around on the car floor next to my foot and coming up with a vial of pepper spray.

"That might actually come in handy," Ellis conceded. "If you keep it in your purse."

"It won't fit," I said, showing him how my lipstick and mascara and phone had taken up all the space in my formal clutch. "Besides, I've never needed pepper spray before."

"Find room. Do it for me," Ellis urged.

"But I'm going to be *with* you." And I wasn't really up to accepting help from my mother right now.

"We don't know what's going to happen tonight," Ellis said in his better-safe-than-sorry tone.

I hated that tone. And not just because it was inconvenient at the moment.

Then it hit me.

"Only for you," I said, giving him my sweetest smile while I stuffed the tube of pepper spray down the front of my dress. Ellis's eyes popped as I snuggled it in tight between my breasts. "There," I said brightly, pleased when he lost his lane for a moment.

"Now I'm going to be thinking about that all night," he said, gripping the wheel a little tighter.

"At least you'll know I have my pepper spray," I informed him.

"Come on," Frankie's voice rang out between us. "I'm glad El Gato doesn't know you, because I don't want to be around that all night."

"Oh, good," I said. We'd gotten his attention.

For a hardened gangster, Frankie could be a prude.

"For a second, I forgot you were here," I added, by way of apology.

"I can see why, after you tossed me on the floor," he said, appearing as a flickering flame on the seat back between Ellis and me.

"I meant no disrespect." Ellis parallel parked along Main Street, and I braced Frankie's urn between my feet extra tight.

He was probably just nervous about tonight.

"How's your power feeling?" I asked as Ellis opened his door to check how close we were to the curb.

"Fine," Frankie muttered. "It's my patience that's wearing thin."

Ellis barely shut the engine off before the flicker of light that was Frankie shot out from the front of Ellis's cruiser and darted low to the sidewalk.

"Well, that was interesting," I said, watching him go.

Ellis shut down the car. "As in?"

"He's not taking form, which usually means he's feeling weak or vulnerable. If I have to guess, I'd say it's the second."

"Well, we can at least get him off the floor," Ellis said, leaning over and plucking Frankie's urn from the passenger side.

"Umm..." I said. "That might not be the best idea. Frankie doesn't like strangers touching his urn," I added as my boyfriend got out and locked it into the trunk of his police cruiser.

"I'm not a stranger. Frankie and I bonded in the morgue at the old asylum." Ellis rejoined me, looking quite proud of himself. "I've got compartments back there, so it won't tip over," he assured me. "We'll know exactly where it is while we're at the dance. You won't have to carry it," he kept on. "Frankie's final resting place will be perfectly secure."

"I think Frankie is a little sensitive tonight. Even more so than usual, and he's definitely protective of his earthly remains, and—"

The rest was answered for me when Frankie's horrified face appeared about two inches from Ellis's. The ghost's lip quivered under his pasted-on pencil-thin mustache. "You locked me in the trunk?" he demanded, as if Ellis had commandeered his urn to use as a lemonade pitcher.

"The thing is, Frankie is usually the one to lock *other* people in trunks," I explained to my boyfriend.

"He won't mind," Ellis said cheerfully as the gangster wrapped both hands around my boyfriend's neck.

"Ahhhhh!" Frankie's face scrunched tight with the gut-deep pain that came with touching the living, yet he refused to let go of my boyfriend's neck.

Ellis froze. "Is it me, or is it colder out than we expected?" he asked me.

"It's you," I answered.

Before I could figure out how to keep my ghost from strangling my boyfriend—and getting even more mad that Ellis didn't notice—Molly took form across the street.

"Showtime, El Gato," I drawled.

Frankie gritted his teeth, torn between revenge against Ellis and keeping up appearances with his dance date.

He drew his hands back from Ellis's neck and clenched his fists. "And that's the last time you try to arrest me for laundering diamonds at the Missing Sock. Big jewels need big machines," he said loudly. "I'll kill you later," he added to Ellis.

"Want me to move your urn out of the trunk?" I asked while he faced the storefronts and frantically smoothed his mustache.

"No." He slumped his shoulders. "Stop making a big deal about it."

Sure. I was the one making a big deal about it. "All right," I said brightly, turning my attention to the Victorian ghost gliding across the street toward us. She had a lovely corsage pinned to her black gown. "Those peonies are gorgeous."

"El Gato sent this to me." Molly beamed, fingering the corsage. "It's from Mildred's Flower Heaven."

"Ah, yes." The mob cover-up operation. I knew it well.

"I hope this isn't awkward," she added, touching a hand to her hair, "me dating El Gato."

"You'll have to tell me," I said as Frankie spun to face her. He held a red rose and had pulled the Panama hat low over his forehead.

I supposed the ladies' man, man's man, man about town El Gato didn't have a big round bullet hole between his eyebrows.

"*Mi corazón*," he said, presenting her with the long-stemmed rose. "I'm afraid I must press charges against you for stealing my heart."

Molly tittered and accepted the bloom.

"How's it going?" Ellis whispered.

"Unbelievable." She had to know it was Frankie.

Instead, she merely simpered and took the arm he offered. "I can't believe you noticed me."

"Dear." El Gato leaned so close his lips brushed her ear. "I will take you to the stars."

And with that, they disappeared.

I turned to Ellis. "Did that actually work?" Frankie's plans never worked. "How did she not see through him?"

"I don't know." Ellis shrugged, taking my hand. "I can't see a thing."

We found a break in the traffic and walked across the street toward the square. "I mean, even if it did work, it's not going to work," I reasoned. "Frankie can't pretend he's El Gato for the rest of his afterlife." He couldn't have Suds standing by with moustaches day and night for eternity. And how was he going to explain El Gato living in a shed behind my house? Molly should have caught on to him from his association with me alone. Not to mention Ellis.

"Hey." Ellis nudged me. "You have your power?"

"Yes," I said as I stepped up on the sidewalk.

"Then let's dance."

Strings of lights lit up the town square, and the alumni danced under the stars. A live band played on a stage in front of the statue of the town's founder, and the dance floor spread out from there. White fencing hemmed the party in, with a single entrance on the far side nearest the mayor's office.

We passed through clustered round tables before reaching the dance floor. The good citizens of Sugarland—both alive and dead—packed the area and shimmied to the beat of Michael Jackson's "Smooth Criminal."

The ghosts had mostly commandeered the far-left part of the dance floor, and the live citizens instinctively avoided it. Probably because it was also right by the speakers.

I watched as El Gato whisked Molly across the floor in a tango. He dipped her unexpectedly, and she laughed.

"What are you smiling about?" Ellis asked, drawing an arm around me.

"Life," I mused. "Death," I corrected. I caught sight of Lauralee and Big Tom hamming it up. "Let's join them. If Ashley is reenacting her last homecoming, then she'll be on the dance floor."

Ellis took my hand and led me through the crowd.

As expected, the whole town had turned out. I even saw one of my favorite deceased couples, Matthew and Josephine, doing a fast waltz.

There was no sign of Ashley. Yet.

I saw Kelli and her husband and waved them over to dance with us.

"The Norwoods are here," she said, leaning close to me as they joined us. "And Kiki and Jake sat down right after you walked in." She pointed to a table right off the dance floor, where Jake joked with his buddies. Kiki sat next to him with a smile pasted on her face, and when I caught her eye, she gave me a dirty look.

I scanned the ghostly crowd for any sign of Ashley, but I didn't see her.

"Jean and Mark have been on the edge of the crowd all night," Kelli said, not even bothering to hide her search. "There," she added, spotting them.

I couldn't see past the crowded dance floor.

"They've been standing by the exit of all places," Kelli added.

Maybe they wanted to see who was coming and going. Come to think of it, Jake and Kiki had positioned themselves so that they could watch my movements.

They couldn't all be working together, could they?

"Have you seen my sister?" I asked Kelli.

She took a sudden interest in the lights strung overhead. "Umm..."

"Kelli," I pressed.

"She's dancing," my friend said evasively.

"With whom?" Instead of answering, Kelli fell into her husband's arms and kissed him on the cheek. Next to her, Lauralee only had eyes for Big Tom. Neither of them was going to answer my question.

"What's Duranja doing tonight?" I asked Ellis.

"How would I know?" he asked, drawing me into his arms as the band started up Garth Brooks's "Papa Loved Mama."

"Well, he should be guarding the library." Away from the crowds and my sister.

"We have Officer Ryan guarding the artifacts at the library tonight. Duranja is kind of like me," he said, pulling me closer, "off duty, but keeping an eye out."

Ellis buzzed a kiss on the top of my ear, and I sincerely hoped Duranja wasn't acting like him.

A ghostly couple whizzed past, doing the foxtrot.

They appeared clear and whole. At least my power was working.

For now, I added to myself as Molly glided swiftly away from the dance floor. It was only a matter of time before she uncovered Frankie's ruse.

"Excuse me," I said to Ellis as I moved to follow her.

Molly shrank into a gray wisp of a shadow as she retreated from the dance. Oh no. I knew she'd see through Frankie sooner or later.

I hurried to follow.

Why didn't he take my advice? Why couldn't he have been honest for once? I cared about the lug, but I also couldn't afford a power blackout like last night.

Molly crossed the sidewalk outside the dance and floated straight through the wall of the mayor's office.

Strange.

I rushed to follow, heartened to see the signs for the ladies' room available inside. At least I wouldn't have to break in to follow her.

A few groups of ladies milled in the foyer, and I turned left, toward the approximate place I'd seen Molly pass through.

I hurried down a hallway and into what turned out to be the ladies' powder room.

There the Victorian ghost stood, retwining a bit of hair into her updo.

"Hey," I said, trying to act casual. Truthfully, I was a bit out of breath. I hoped she didn't notice. "How's it going?"

I was relieved to see a small smile cross her features. "If I can crack this nut, he's going to be the love of my death."

Lord have mercy. She couldn't fall for El Gato. I mean, it was good news for my power, but awful news in every other way.

"Molly," I began. I wanted to tell her. She deserved to know.

But it wasn't my secret to tell, and the truth could end my ghost hunt and any chance I had to solve Ashley's murder.

"What's the matter?" she asked, concerned. "Why did you chase me?"

"Ah." I flushed with embarrassment. My first urge was to lie, but she had enough of that from Frankie. "So you saw that," I ventured.

She seemed amused at my surprise. "I appreciate the concern. I do. El Gato is a wild and dangerous man. A shocking and surprising man," she added with relish. "But we are grown adults. Older than you."

"Technically." When she put it that way, I was starting to feel silly for following her. "Look, I'm worried about Frankie," I admitted.

She gave me a cat-eating grin. "Don't. I won't string him along too much. I just enjoy role-playing."

Hold the phone. "So you know—" I was afraid to say it out loud.

"Frankie is El Gato," she finished the thought with a gleam in her eye and a radiant smile. "El Gato is Frankie. Of course I know. I know Frankie better than anyone. You think I'm going to be fooled by a silly moustache and an accent?"

"But he—"

"He's madly in love with me, or he wouldn't be acting this way," she said, turning back to the mirror. She began pinching her cheeks for color. "Now I have his undivided attention. Of course, he's going crazy because he thinks I'm smitten with El Gato. He deserves it for the way he's acted. And for lying to me," she added, touching up her bangs. "So I'll let him pursue me. And I won't let him dangle forever," she added. "I'm going to enjoy tonight, and then he and I will work out the rest tomorrow."

"Well, you go, girl," I said, joining her at the mirror to check my lipstick. "I suppose I shouldn't have been worried." Although she'd surprised me as much as Frankie ever had. "You know, Frankie's a handful, but he's worth it." He drove me crazy. A lot. But even I could see the good in him.

"Funny. He said the same thing about you once." She winked.

"Seriously?" Like I ever got into the kind of trouble he did.

"He told me what you're up to tonight," she said, securing her corsage.

He was as bad as my mother. Or maybe I was extra sensitive tonight, too. I sighed. "I just hope I can find the ghost of the 1985 homecoming queen. She died the night after she was crowned, and she's supposed to be at the dance."

Molly's ghostly reflection appeared next to me as she took one last look at her dress. "Then go to the high school dance and find her."

I stared at the ghost in the mirror. "She's not at the alumni dance?"

"Why would she be if she's still in high school?" Molly said simply.

Ashley haunted the high school. She'd ridden on the current queen's parade float yesterday. "She never left high school. Of course she didn't. Molly, you're a genius."

She beamed. "I like solving mysteries with you."

"Please keep putting up with Frankie," I said, dashing from the bathroom. I never wanted to do without her.

The sound of her laughter echoed after me as I hurried down the hall.

I made it back to the dance in record speed. Ellis was no longer on the dance floor, which made sense because they were playing a slow song.

"Lauralee," I said, rushing up to her and Big Tom, "have you seen Ellis?"

She turned to me. "What? Um, did you lose him?" She hadn't even realized I was gone.

I circled around the side of the dance and found Mom and Carl with Alistair by the door. "Have you seen Ellis?"

"He was talking to Melody and Alec a moment ago," she said, looking around as if he'd appear next to us.

"I think I know where Ashley is going to be," I told them. "If she still thinks she's a student at Sugarland High, she'll be at the dance in the gym. I'm going to go check it out."

"Melody will know where Ellis went," Carl said, leaving to ask her.

"We'll find Ellis and join you," Mom promised as Alistair looked at us like we were both crazy. "I don't care how it sounds; she needs me," Mom insisted to him while I took off across the town square.

"Go around the right way, down the street!" Mom called after me. "You're going to ruin your heels."

I didn't care if my heels sank in the grass. I didn't care if they flew off entirely. I wanted to see if Molly's theory panned out. I silently thanked her, even as my silver shoes plowed into the soft path between the square and the football field.

I burst out of the trees, ready to take off across the football field, when an unexpected sight stopped me cold.

A gray, glowing ghost sat at the top of the Home bleachers. She wore the prom dress I had come to recognize, with poufed-out sleeves and a hairdo teased out to Graceland.

I slowed and came to a stop below her. "Ashley?"

She frowned down at me, and I saw her clear as day. Ashley Starling. Now I just had to get her to talk to me.

Chapter Twenty-Two

T he ghost stood nervously as I rounded the bottom of the metal stands. "Go away," she called from the top. "I don't want you here."

She didn't have a choice, and at this point neither did I.

"I'm sorry, Ashley," I said, grabbing hold of the handrail and beginning the climb. "I didn't mean to scare you at the parade."

"You jumped on my float," she protested, glancing behind her for a way to retreat. Only she already perched on the very top row. "You're crazy. The entire homecoming court was talking about it."

How wonderful. I hadn't even needed my mother to make me look like a fool. "I'm not crazy. I'm just…concerned about you. Tilly's concerned about you, too. That's why she asked me to talk to you," I said, hoping to avoid our prior issue with her teenage friend having a daughter. "I'm her friend, Verity, remember?"

"Tilly never told me about you," she insisted, scooting farther down her row.

"Well, she told me about you," I said gently. "I especially like the story about the gold pendant you gave her and how you two sent each other secret messages."

Her mouth dropped open. "How did you know that?"

"From Tilly." I shrugged. "She says you're her best friend."

"I am," she agreed, watching every step I made. "Tilly talks too much."

"I couldn't agree more with you on that one."

The ghost didn't appear convinced, but at least she'd stopped retreating. "Go away. Tell Tilly I'm fine. She knows better than to mess this up."

"Mess what up?" I asked casually, continuing my climb.

"I have a…a secret admirer," she said, in a halting voice. "And he won't be so secret if you're here when he shows up."

"I won't tell," I promised.

"I don't even know you," she said, as if I were ready to plop down between them. "Besides, if I'm not alone when he comes, he might decide to leave altogether." She glanced toward the high school, fretting. "That would be a disaster."

"Why?" I asked, stopping in her row.

She smoothed her dress, flustered. "Because it has to be tonight. I set it up for tonight. Now, please!"

"My boyfriend and I dated in secret too," I told her. "Well, at first," I added when I saw a glimmer of interest. "His mother didn't approve of me at all."

She touched a hand to her halo of hair. "My mother would be shocked at my guy. She'd never understand."

"Mine dropped the phone when I told her about my guy," I confessed.

That made her laugh.

"My mom actually likes him now," I added.

"Well, you're lucky." She forgot about her hair and focused on me. "We're going to freak everybody out."

"Yeah," I said, risking a step toward her, then another. "There are still some people who don't understand why my boyfriend and I are together."

"Really?" She didn't retreat this time. "But you're so old. By this point in your life, why does anyone care?"

"Well..." I wasn't quite a teenager anymore, but I thought I looked pretty good. "It isn't anybody else's business, but you and I both know people in Sugarland still like to have their opinions. Still, Ellis and I worked it out."

She didn't appear convinced. "Did you run away together?"

"We hopped on a train," I said, skipping forward a bit in the story of our relationship.

Her eyes grew wide. "Is that why I haven't seen you around?"

"Among other things," I said, drawing within a few feet of her. "The important thing is that I've been where you are."

She plopped down onto the bleachers. "I'm not sure I know what I'm doing at all."

"It's fun to have a secret boyfriend," I said, gently taking the seat next to her. "Ellis and I used to sneak over to Jackson and go for Italian food."

She smothered a surprised huff. "Mark talked about taking me out for Mexican. But we never went."

"Mark Norwood? The science teacher?"

I shouldn't have been shocked. I wasn't. But hearing it from her made it different, real. I tried to hide my distaste. Still, a tinge of disapproval made it into my voice, and I saw the fear well up in her eyes.

"He treats me real nice," she insisted. "He's never done anything gross or weird or anything like that. We haven't been alone for more than five minutes ever."

"So how'd you fall in love?" Obviously, it wasn't over a plate of fajitas.

She let out a breath. "We fell in love through letters." A tear slipped down her cheek. "I can't believe he fell in love with *me*."

"That's...romantic," I admitted. "People did that in the old days." Although not usually with their science teachers.

She directed a wobbly smile my way. "You know, you remind me of Tilly. You listen and you don't judge." She looked out over the darkened football field. "But you have to leave now," she insisted. "He won't come if I'm with you, and I'm all ready to go."

"Where's your bag?" I asked.

"Don't need one." She waved me off. "He's buying me all new clothes and a new life and everything."

I hated to break it to the ghost, but Mark Norwood was never coming for her.

Last I saw him, he had been at the alumni fundraiser with his wife.

It seemed poor Ashley still didn't realize she was dead.

"Say, Ashley," I began as casually as I could, "what year is it?"

She looked at me like I'd asked her to fly. "Well, I'm a senior, Class of 1986. You do the math."

Right. "Did you go to class this week?"

Her brows furrowed. "No, it's homecoming weekend. I hung out and decorated Mark's classroom door. I rode in the parade with the homecoming court. I went to the game. I did all the important things."

And nothing else? "How long have you been doing these things?"

"What are you getting at?" She huffed like the teenager she was. "Those things are what I do," she said, matter-of-fact. But even as she said it, I saw her begin to doubt her words. "It's what I always do."

I braced my hands on the cold metal bench. "Have you done it more than once?" I wished I could wrap an arm around her.

She stared at the bleacher seat below us. "I...I don't know."

"I mean, if you and Mark don't run away happily ever after,

do you try another year?" I planted my feet on the bench in front of us. "And maybe another year?"

She chewed her lip.

"Like the movie *Groundhog Day?*" I pressed.

"What's that?" She squinched her nose.

"Scratch that," I said, waving her off. She didn't need to get the reference. But I had a feeling she might be going through something similar. Most ghosts I'd met had real afterlives. They did things with other ghosts; they pursued the things that made them happy when they were alive.

Ashley seemed stuck.

Although I could be wrong. "Do you have a big social life?" I asked. I mean, she was a popular teenager. "Like, did you see your friends last week?"

Her breath became shallow. "I don't remember last week," she said in a frightened whisper.

And she shouldn't even need to breathe.

"I think you're stuck," I said, not wanting to alarm her. Still, she deserved to know.

Here was a ghost with no close friends or passions on the other side. Nothing she could remember doing. She only appeared at homecoming and then disappeared until the next one.

She said she was waiting for her secret love, but I had a feeling she was also waiting for her real life to resume.

Only something terrible had happened on that night in 1985, and she'd never have that life again.

"Why are you looking at me like that?" She brought her hand to her chest and gave a little hiccup. "You're starting to freak me out."

Or she was beginning to realize that her life didn't make sense anymore.

She jerked to her feet. "I mean, I must have gone to school

last week, only I'm at homecoming, and then I'm at homecoming, and then I'm at homecoming…" She shrieked.

"Ashley—" I jumped up onto the seat in front of her and faced her. "Ashley, it's okay."

How do you break it to a girl that she's dead?

I'd tried to explain it once to a ghost trapped in a bank vault —Frankie's friend who died tunneling. He'd denied ever being dead. I didn't want the same thing to happen to Ashley.

"You're fine," I said over and over again until she calmed. "I mean it," I said as she gulped air. Or at least made the motions. "Nothing bad can happen to you." Not anymore.

"I'm so confused." She brought a hand to her head.

"Go ahead and sit," I urged.

She did it without thinking.

I had to help her realize what was happening, but I had to be gentle about it. If I could learn what had happened to her, maybe then we could discover who'd killed her and left her body in the time capsule. And also, if she understood she was dead, maybe she could move on. Or at least live her afterlife.

I sat down next to her. "Let's wait together," I said to her. "Waiting is good, right?"

She rubbed her hands over her dress. "I've done this before. I remember this. Oh, my God. What's going on?"

"Let's not get ahead of ourselves." We were only reliving the night she died. No worries. "Can you tell me, since you've done this before—what happens next?"

She looked out at the football field. "I don't know. You've never shown up before."

"Okay, well, if I hadn't shown up," I suggested. "You wait on the bleachers for Mark," I said, walking her through it. "Does he ever come?"

She scrunched her brow. "We're going to run away together," she said, doubt creeping into her voice. "He asked me to elope.

We'll be married, and there won't be anything my mom or his boss or anyone can do about it."

"What a lovely plan," I said through gritted teeth. "What happens when Mark gets here?"

Other than me punching him.

She blinked hard several times. "Well…" She dug her hands hard against the metal bench.

"I mean, he said he'd be here," I prodded.

"Yes," she said, her voice going up an octave.

She began breathing hard again.

I hated to press the point but, "Does he show up?"

She swallowed hard. "No. Not yet." She stood. "My friend shows up instead," she cried out.

"Not Tilly." Mom would have told me.

"No, no, no! Alistair!" she lashed out. "Why is Alistair always following me around?"

I ducked out of her way. "He was your friend," I reminded her gently. "Or at least I hope he was," considering I'd left him with Mom.

"Yes," she smirked. "But he always wanted more." The smile fell from her face. "He acted like you. He refused to leave me alone."

"What happened after Alistair showed up?"

She snorted. "He said he found a group of ladies cutting the lock off the time capsule. They wanted a pie recipe. Can you believe it? He startled them, and they scattered like mice. Left it wide open. He said he almost fell in." She smiled at the memory, looking for a moment like a carefree teenager.

"And then what?" I pressed.

She stepped up onto the top seat of the bleachers. "I told him to go away. I said I was meeting someone!"

"And then?" I pressed. "What happened after you told Alistair to leave you alone?"

"He wouldn't stop following me. He followed me all the way up!" She stood on the edge.

"Maybe it's time to come back down," I urged, wishing I could offer her a hand. But I didn't want to startle her. She was too close to the edge.

"I can't. He won't let me!" she shrieked, then gulped. "It happens every year whether I want it to or not. It happens too soon."

Dread pooled in the pit of my stomach. "What happens?"

Her body shook. "Stop, Alistair. Let go of me!" she cried, looking through me as if I weren't there. "I need to wait for Mark."

She took a step backward, but there was nowhere to go.

Shock bled over her features. "Oh!" she said faintly.

I reached for her as she pitched violently backward, off the back of the bleachers.

She landed hard on the ground, her neck twisted at an impossible angle, her lifeless eyes staring up at the night sky. It had happened so fast.

"Ashley!" I called. "Alistair pushed you, didn't he?" I asked to myself.

Her image began to fade.

"Wait!" I called. I had to get down there before she disappeared completely. I turned to run, and there, blocking the way, stood Alistair.

Chapter Twenty-Three

"Hi," I managed, hoping to sound casual. Friendly. I had to get out of there.

Alistair swallowed hard and appeared almost as if he were seeing me for the first time. "I didn't believe for a second you could see ghosts." He knit his brows, drawing closer. "When Tilly's right, she's right."

"Ha." I wished I could take a step back, but he had me trapped at the top of the bleachers. "I'm not out here speaking to ghosts," I said, as if the whole idea were ludicrous. "I'm—well, it got a little hot at the dance."

"The dance outside?" he countered.

He needed to stop staring at me.

"Right, well, crowds. But I'm fine now. I'm going to go back," I said, desperate for some way to get around him, to get down. Off.

Only he wasn't moving.

He tilted his head. "Why did you say I pushed her?"

I really regretted saying that. "You must have misheard." I smiled so hard my face hurt.

Should I go for the pepper spray in my bra? I couldn't exactly run. I'd be toast if he wanted to catch me.

I cleared my throat. "Now if you can step aside, I'd like to get down." God willing, he'd fall back on his Southern manners.

"What were you doing here? At this spot?" he pressed, studying it, studying me. His eyes narrowed. "There's only one way you would know to be in this exact place."

I'd rather not dwell on that.

He was way in my personal space, making it impossible to maneuver.

I drew a hand up, reached inside my bra. I didn't care how it looked as I located the vial of pepper spray and pulled it out.

In a flash, Alistair caught my hand and yanked the spray from me. "What is this?" he demanded, turning my first, last, and best defense over in his hand. "You think you need this?"

I did. Desperately. I didn't even want to question him. I just wanted to get away.

He tossed it past me and over the back of the bleachers. "I'd never hurt a girl."

After what I'd seen tonight, I wasn't sure I believed that.

I took a deep breath to calm the fluttering of my heart in my chest. "You're making me uncomfortable," I managed.

"You didn't answer me," he ground out. "What are you doing here?"

The last thing I wanted to do was make him angry. Or...*angrier*. "Well, you pose a good question," I managed, trying to stay bright, friendly. Downright chipper. "I mean, what are *you* doing here?"

The corner of his mouth curled, as if he was pleased he'd caught me. "You told your mom you were going to the high school dance to talk to Ashley. Tell it to me straight. How did you end up here?"

"You bring up a good point about my mom," I said, ignoring the question. "I promised I'd meet her over in the gym. I'd better get going," I said, scooting down so that maybe I could step around him.

Mom would be eager to meet me, but she was also the type to get talking and hardly notice the time passing. And looking for me would consist of stopping to have a chat with everyone along the way.

He blocked my path, reaching for me. "You did see Ashley, didn't you?" he pressed, almost hopeful.

"In a manner of speaking," I hedged. I had a feeling we weren't following the same playbook, and worse, he had my life and safety in his hands. But if I could keep him talking, and stay as far as I could from the edge of the bleachers, this might just work out.

A girl could hope.

"You'd better be careful," he said as I stood with my back to the open air. "It would be easy to fall."

I'd seen it firsthand. "Step back," I ordered. "You're making me nervous."

He leapt up onto the back of the bleachers with me. The metal shook like a tuning fork. "Do you see her now?" he asked, as if it were a matter of location.

"No," I said, attempting to jump down off the seat.

He caught me and kept me up there. "Look again," he urged.

"I really think she's gone," I said, staring down, way down at the spot where she'd broken her neck.

"It was her fault she died," he said, peering over the edge with me. "I never would have hurt her."

Sure. Blame the victim. "You tried to stop her from running away," I said, attempting to back up.

"What's the matter?" he asked, matching my motion, blocking me in tighter. "Are you afraid?"

"A little," I admitted.

He looked far, far down at the grass below. "I didn't stop her from trying to run away. I was the guy she was supposed to run away with."

Wait. "What?"

"You're just like your mom." A wistful smile crossed his features. "You jump to conclusions, and you don't listen."

"To be fair, you're kind of freaking me out," I told him.

"That's a terrible thing to say," he chastised. "Ashley was *my* girlfriend." He barked, startling me. "Mine," he added, jabbing a finger at his chest. "She fell for me through my letters. It was damned romantic. It was like a John Hughes movie."

I'd watched a few of those with my mom. "Like *Sixteen Candles?*"

"No," he snapped. "Our love story worked out right." He drew a hand down his face. "God, it was perfect. Of course I'd loved her all my life. Who wouldn't?"

She hadn't said a word about it to me. And she certainly hadn't been glad to see him tonight. "But she said…"

"So you did talk to her!" he said, getting in my face again. "Is she still here?" His gaze darted past me, around me. "Does she see me?"

"I'm sure she watches over you," I said automatically, reaching past him to grip the chilly metal rail with both hands. I had to get out of here before he got even more unhinged.

"What did Ashley say about me?" he demanded. "Did she say she missed me?"

"We actually didn't get to that." I cleared my throat. Maybe I should lie and appease him, but I also wanted to understand what was going on. And that meant asking more questions, drawing him out.

Ellis was bound to come looking for me soon. Or Mom. *Or anyone.*

Only they would look for me at the school. Ellis would make a thorough search of the gym and the rest of the building. Mom might lead him to the cafeteria and the second-floor science room.

She never would guess to look here. Ashley never told her she was going to the bleachers.

I looked to my mom's old friend. If he wanted to talk about this, we could at least go over the facts. "Ashley said she was writing to Mr. Norwood."

"The creepy science teacher." Alistair wrinkled his nose in disgust, and for once, I agreed with him. "Why would she think he liked her? He flirted with every girl, but he wasn't really into them. He just liked the attention." He shook his head. "I thought Ashley was smarter than that. Although she did stay with Jake for almost a year." He leaned against the rail, keeping a close eye on me. "Jake was so selfish he didn't know she existed half the time. But I showed her she was special. I started leaving her treats and notes in her locker, a secret-admirer thing. I figured she'd realize what a jerk Jake was and what I great guy I am."

"That is very thoughtful," I said, inching away. "She must have loved getting those letters." Maybe he'd talk long enough for somebody to find me up here.

"I had to let Ashley know how I felt, or I was going to implode," he gushed. "It worked," he added, as if that was proof he'd been right. "She started telling *me* about her admirer, how great he was and how he was the perfect guy for her. I almost spilled the beans right there, but then she said she wished she could write back."

"That's...romantic," I managed. I mean, it would have been if the feeling had been mutual.

He scooted down until he was right next to me again. "It was mind blowing," Alistair corrected. "I wrote and told her to leave me notes in this empty locker by Mr. Norwood's classroom. Hardly anyone used the lockers on the second floor."

"They're smaller."

"Right." He adjusted his glasses. "I put a lock on it, gave her the combination, and it was like our private mailbox."

"And she thought she was writing to Mr. Norwood," I said flatly.

"No, she was writing to *me*!" He slammed his hand so hard onto the metal railing that he sliced his palm on a support post. He gripped my shoulder with his bloody hand and cornered me up against the rail. "The locker combination was the same number as my Strength, Dexterity, and Charisma stats in D&D. She had to know it was me!"

"Of course," I said. He'd broken into a sweat, and he wasn't giving me an inch. "Um, you're bleeding," I said as the blood pooled onto my bare shoulder and dripped down.

He appeared shocked, as if he hadn't noticed.

He yanked a handkerchief from his back pocket and held it to his bleeding hand. "Ashley told me her deepest, darkest secrets, and I told her mine," he said, as if he couldn't quite believe it hadn't been enough. "We planned to run away together, to elope before anybody could stop us. She was mine, you understand?" He clenched the handkerchief so hard that blood bloomed across the white cloth. "She was going to model. I was going to start my own computer business. We were perfect together."

"But she wasn't waiting for you," I said quietly.

"No. She *was* waiting for me." He dabbed the sweat from the back of his neck with the handkerchief. "Only she didn't know it yet." He tilted his head. "I had to make her see. I knew I could make her see," he ground out. "But you know the rest, don't you?"

Maybe, maybe not. "I wasn't there," I said, gripping the rail as if my life depended on it.

It very well could.

He crowded me so close, I found myself leaning backward

over thin air. "She said we were *just friends*." He jerked back, and I gratefully moved away from the edge.

I scooted away as far as I dared, still gripping the rail as he opened up the handkerchief and studied the blood seeping from his palm. "Well, once she knew I was the one writing the letters, Ashley decided she didn't want to run away anymore," he said, picking at the wound. "She wanted to call the whole thing off. She wanted her old life back," he mocked. "Like I was supposed to pretend it never happened." The hurt shone in his eyes. "She wanted to apologize to that idiot Jake. Can you believe that?"

From a young girl? "Yes."

He fisted the top of my dress with his bloody hand. "No! It blew a hole in me," he cried, giving me a shake. "It killed me. She had to know it was me. It was my handwriting. *My* words. I was the one who knew her best. How could she not even notice?"

He was like Cyrano De Bergerac gone bad.

I knocked his hand away, and he gripped my shoulder.

"She always talked about kissing me in her letters," he said, pulling me toward him. "I figured if she'd kiss me, she'd feel it like I did." His breath tickled my cheek. "All I had to do was kiss her and she'd know." He gazed at me, and I wondered if he saw her in his mind. I flailed for the railing, but couldn't find it. "She wanted me. She was waiting for me. She just didn't know it."

"Did you kiss her? Or did you push her?" I demanded, shoving him away.

I caught him off guard, and he staggered back. He reached for me, but I'd already ducked around him. I leapt down onto the bench below, slid off, and banged my shoulder on the metal plank between seats.

I shoved myself up partway before he grabbed my arm and dragged me to my feet. "I didn't murder her; I loved her!" His grip was hard, bruising. "Once she kissed me, she'd know I was the right guy for her. But rather than see what it was like to kiss the guy she'd said over and over that she loved and adored and couldn't wait to marry, she twisted straight off the top of the bleachers and broke her neck."

"I saw that part." Or at least I'd witnessed the result.

"Is she still down there?" he asked, with the barest hint of guilt.

Alistair had helped me up, but he hadn't let me go.

"No," I said. "Her ghost disappeared shortly after she hit the ground."

Ashley had died so quickly, and it didn't seem like she'd come to terms with it this time around, either.

I expected she'd be back next year, still trying to meet her guy and make it right.

"How did her body wind up in the time capsule?" I asked.

His fingers dug into my arm so tightly that blood seeped between his fingers.

His blood, but still.

"Please let go of my arm," I added. "It really hurts."

He didn't notice.

"It was the crazy pie ladies," he chuffed. "I was walking across from the school parking lot to go meet Ashley, and I caught three old biddies digging up the secret to the perfect apple crumble. They scattered empty-handed when they heard me coming, left the thing wide open, and I needed a place to stash poor, clueless Ashley."

"It was close by," I managed.

"And it was getting buried in concrete come the morning," he said. "Nobody was supposed to open it for a hundred years."

"Well, half of that worked out." Abe had come along in the morning and poured six inches of concrete over poor Ashley in the time capsule.

Alistair appeared lost as he thought back on that night. "I closed the door. I put the boards back. I even padlocked it with our special lock."

"You didn't think anyone would ever find her."

"Why would they even look? She'd told Tilly she was running off," he said wistfully. "And, of course, Tilly told everybody."

Lights blazed from the high school up on the hill. Modern music *thwump-thwumped* from the gym, so loud that nobody at the school would hear me if I screamed. Sugarland High might as well have been a hundred miles away.

I looked back to Alistair. I wasn't sure if he wanted to kill me or not, but I wasn't dead at the bottom of the bleachers yet, so I guessed it could still go either way. Maybe I could keep him talking until he loosened his grip enough so that I could try to make another run for it.

"What did you say to Ashley to make her fall in love with you?" I asked.

He shook his head slightly. "I was myself. No magic to it."

It was sad in a way—that she'd liked him for who he was, only to reject him when she found out the truth. It wasn't justification for sexual assault or murder, but it was sad.

"Ashley kept every letter I sent her," he mused, loosening his grip a fraction.

Thank goodness—on both counts. "What happened to the letters?"

"I needed them back," he said. "Everyone wanted to know who she was going to meet on the night she disappeared. If anyone found the letters and figured out the handwriting was mine, they'd expect me to know where she was."

"You did know." He'd buried her.

He looked out toward the flagpole where he'd made her grave. "I volunteered to clean out her room in order to find them, but they weren't there. I cleaned out her locker. I tried everything. I never knew what happened to them."

Oh my. "Until my mom mentioned the secret addition Ashley made to the time capsule," I said, my heart sinking.

"Thank you for not hurting my sister," I added. I just wished I could get away.

If Melody had interrupted him—if she'd angered Alistair or kept him from taking what he wanted—I shuddered to think what might have happened.

"I'd never hurt Melody," he said, as if surprised I'd even think it. "I like her."

He'd also liked Ashley. He'd claimed to love her.

He took a seat, dragging me down too. "I found my letters. Every last one of them. Ashley even wrote a sweet note that she bound up in twine with them. She wanted to immortalize our letters as a tribute to our love." He shook his head fondly, still keeping a vise grip on me. "She wrote a poem at the bottom. It was really sweet. It reminded me all over again how much we loved each other."

"Okay," I managed as his fingers tightened, digging into muscle. I felt his grip down to my bones.

"She loved me," he said, rattling me by the arm. "I don't care what anyone else thinks. I don't even care if she was confused the night she died. I know it."

"Okay." I cringed. God, he was hurting me.

"I made our letters into an album so I can look and see anytime I want how much she cared for me."

If I could get to them—and Ashley's time-capsule note—I could prove Alistair broke into the library. I could also prove a motive for murder. And maybe then poor Ashley could find some closure as well.

Wherever she was.

"You know," he said, dragging me closer, "you're a lot like your mom. You're easy to talk to. She's a good friend," he added, almost as an afterthought.

"She'll understand about Ashley," I told him. "The whole town will. I mean, it was a terrible, heartbreaking accident." I hoped. "Let's just get down from here and end this. The letters can be part of the time-capsule display. We'll let the whole town know how much Ashley loved you."

His fingers dug so hard I cried out. Blood ran down my arm and dripped down onto the metal below. "I like you, but I'm not stupid." He glanced over my head toward the place where Ashley had gone over. "I don't want to hurt you, but I don't see any other way."

"Nobody would ever believe I jumped off the stands," I declared, becoming dead weight as he hefted me by the arm.

"And you might not die," he said, regarding me critically. "That would be a disaster. Your boyfriend would know if I finished the job. He catches everything."

I attempted to wriggle out of his grasp. "Which is why he'd understand you don't mean me harm if you *just let me go*."

He tightened his grip like a monster and began to drag me toward the stairs. "I'm going to need to console your mother. She's the one I'm most worried about." He sighed. "She'll never get over it."

I wasn't sure where he was taking me, but I dug in hard.

He pulled me across the slick metal. "At least she has Melody."

I twisted hard and kicked the back of his knee. It buckled, and I broke free as he stumbled.

He cried out as I made a break for it—straight down the stands. I lost my heels. I took the seats like they were stairs. I hurtled down, too fast. Too free. Out of control but there was nothing I could do because I had to get free and run and...

He slammed into the back of me, hard.

I tumbled, and he caught me inches before I slammed forehead-first into the seat ahead. He yanked me back and tossed me over his shoulder.

"You can't leave," he barked, gripping me tight around the waist.

"Ellis!" I screamed. "Mom! *Frankie!*"

"Shut up! Shut up!" He dug the bloody handkerchief out of his pocket and shoved it into my mouth.

"Nobody can hear you over here. Nobody can see you."

He lumbered over to the stairs and began a halting descent. "They're not coming this way." My head rattled as he pounded down each step.

Oh my God. Ellis and Mom and anyone who was paying attention was waiting for me to show up at the high school. Frankie was wooing Molly at the dance. He hadn't even seen me go.

Alistair hefted me toward the school parking lot. Was he going to shove me into his car?

At least we were getting closer to the bright lights of the school, to people.

My forehead smacked against his back. I opened my mouth as wide as it would go and tried to force the dry gag out of my mouth with my tongue.

When we got close, I'd call for help. Somebody had to hear me!

But then he stopped. And when he turned, I saw we were at the base of the flagpole.

Alistair slammed me down onto the ground. It knocked the wind out of me, leaving me gasping for air, my lungs burning.

"Sorry, babe. I don't have a lock this time." The metal door squeaked on its hinges as he pulled it back. "But I do need a place to dump your body, and this is poetic justice." Heaving for breath, he let the heavy door fall open. "You care so much about Ashley, you can die like her." He tilted his head. "Or at least be buried like her."

I screamed for all I was worth, praying someone from the alumni dance, someone in the school parking lot, could hear me.

If he locked me in there, I'd escape. I'd done it before. It wasn't like they were bulldozing the time capsule tomorrow. I'd have time to think, to plan a way out. Unless I could manage to avoid going in there at all... I struggled to my feet.

He shoved me backward into the metal hole.

I fell hard on my back, and the stars above grew hazy.

"Ellis!" I screamed. "Mom! Frankie!" Then, at the last moment, I screamed for her. *"Ashley!"*

The metal floor shook as he landed hard next to my head. "Shut up!" He slapped a hand over my mouth and wrapped the other one around my neck, choking me.

I gasped and struggled to draw a breath.

"It's like you're physically incapable of being *quiet,*" he grunted, squeezing harder.

My mind scrambled for something—anything—to do, but I couldn't breathe, and my head swam.

Colored spots dotted my vision. I couldn't afford to pass out.

Overhead, a flock of starlings screamed across the sky.

Chapter Twenty-Four

I woke up encased in blackness. My throat clenched, and I screamed up at the darkened lid of the time capsule.

"She's coming around," Ellis said.

The colored spots dotting my vision came into focus, and I saw stars in the night sky.

Stars?

"You're okay." I felt his hand on my shoulder and realized he'd cradled my head in his lap.

I tried to sit. "I'm fine?" I croaked. It came out as more of a question than a statement. My throat felt like it was on fire. I had been sure I was done for.

"You're going to be all right," Ellis coaxed, "but we've got paramedics coming to look you over just to be on the safe side."

It was then that I became aware of a half-dozen curious faces looking down at us from outside the time capsule.

"Give us some space, you guys," Ellis said. "Harriet, Martin, Clive," he added, calling them out.

"But this is much more interesting than the dance," Clive protested.

"Or the booze in the parking lot," Martin added.

"There's booze in the parking lot?" another asked.

Still, every one of them backed away, with the exception of Harriet, who grinned down at me. "I'm so glad you're all right, Verity."

"What happened?" I managed. My neck ached as I took in my surroundings. Ellis and I were alone in the time capsule, with a party going on outside from the sound of it.

Melody arrived at the top of the hole. "Stop trying to find a ladder, Mom. Ellis doesn't need anybody else in the hole, and she's awake. Are you okay, Verity?"

Mom peeked over the edge. "Oh, baby!" she gushed. "It's so good to see you with your eyes open. How does your throat feel?"

Like I'd been strangled. "Where's Alistair?" I croaked.

"Duranja arrested Alistair," Ellis informed me as I sat up.

"With glee," Melody added.

Duranja didn't do anything with glee. That man was dry as toast.

"Alec was wonderful in a crisis," Mom fluttered. "We may have been wrong about him."

"No, we weren't," I managed.

"Ellis was the real hero," Melody stated. "He jumped straight into the hole. He basically dive-bombed Alistair."

That drew gasps from the lookie-loos. Most had retreated from the hole, but they were still listening.

"Alistair is probably in worse shape than you at this point, Verity," Carl added.

"You found me," I said, holding on to Ellis. If I let go, I was afraid none of this would be real.

"It was your mom who found you for me," Ellis said, looking up at her.

"It wasn't me," Mom said. "It was Ashley."

Wait. "What?"

The paramedics arrived at that moment, and after they

looked me over, they helped Ellis gently remove me from the time capsule.

I had a severely bruised throat and a bloody arm—although most of the blood belonged to Alistair. Somehow, after all that, I was going to be okay.

Ellis sat me on a bench while the police questioned me, and then he told them his side of the story as well. Afterward, he and Carl went to fetch the cars to drive Mom and me home.

Ellis taking his car—and Frankie's urn—away from the town square would mean Frankie got yanked from his dance. But considering he'd been romancing instead of helping me solve Ashley's murder, I figured he'd understand.

At least Molly would.

Meanwhile, Mom sat wearily on the bench next to me. I never thought Mom would ever tire of telling stories, but this time, she didn't say a word. She simply sat, the hem of her red dress stained with mud. For the first time, I noticed she was missing both her shoes.

"I wasn't wrong," she said when she noticed me looking. "This ghost detective work is tough."

I wouldn't argue with that. "What did you mean earlier when you said Ashley found me?"

She smiled softly and fingered the gold pendant at her neck. "You remember how Ashley gave me my starling pendant. How we used it to send coded messages to each other."

"You used it to pass notes in class."

"Well, we were at that dance, waiting for you, and worried about you—I couldn't imagine what was holding you up. As a mother, I feared the worst."

In this case, she'd been right.

"Well, while I was fretting by the door of the gym, driving Carl crazy, I noticed my pendant was backwards. Ashley wanted to pass me a message."

"Or your pendant really could have gone backwards. What made you think it was Ashley?"

"I've had this feeling the entire time I've been in town for homecoming that I'd see Ashley, even after I realized she was no longer with us." Mom nodded to a high school couple sneaking out of the dance. "That reminds me of me and your dad."

"Ew, Mom."

"Anyway, I knew it was her. I just did." She touched the pendant once more. "Carl didn't want me leaving the dance, but I had to do something. I couldn't keep waiting."

"You didn't explain why you took off," Harriett chimed in. "You ran down the front steps of the school like Cinderella and even lost a shoe."

"It's hard to run in heels!" Mom countered.

"Do you mind?" I asked Harriet, who sheepishly retreated toward a group of retirees sharing a cooler in the parking lot.

"I went to the lobby to get some quiet. If Ashley was going to appear to me, I didn't know if she'd do it in a crowd," Mom continued. "Then I heard birds outside. A huge flock of starlings. It had to be a sign."

That was exactly what it had been. I'd seen them, too. "Most people don't see spirits like me." I was still surprised I could do it. "But our deceased loved ones do give us messages in other ways."

Mom nodded, as if she couldn't quite believe it herself. "The birds flew straight over the school toward the football field, and they dipped hard right over the time capsule. It was a sign."

"And you followed it," I said, infinitely proud.

"I ran like the dickens." She grinned. "I told Carl to call Ellis. Ellis was up on the second floor, searching for you."

"Wait. Did you reach me first?"

"Yep. And when I saw Alistair, I fired my remaining shoe at his head." She threw her hands out. "I didn't know what else to do. I clocked him, but he didn't stop, and I was yelling like a crazy person, and then Ellis ran straight past me and jumped into the hole and had Alistair in a headlock faster than you could say *Biscuit football.*"

"You did good, Mom," I said, proud to come from a line of strong women who followed their hearts.

"It amazes me," she said, shaking her head. "I came home hoping to connect with Ashley, and I did. I felt her." She pursed her lips. "It's not the same as what you and Frankie have, but I felt her."

"Not everybody has a Frankie." Thank goodness. "But what you have is just as special. You have a friendship that crosses time and death."

"So you did see Ashley tonight?" Mom asked gently. She'd been there when I'd given a brief account to Officer Ryan, but she must have guessed I'd left out a few details.

I nodded and told Mom the rest.

"Is she close by now?" Mom asked, looking out into the surrounding night.

I stood and walked to the edge of the school parking lot.

"Yes," I said as I saw the faint outline of a ghost in a gown standing under the bleachers. "Want to pay her a visit?"

Mom nodded, and we walked silently down the hill, past the old flagpole and to the place where her friend had died.

Ashley stood waiting for us, her hands folded in front of her. "I listened to you and Alistair," she said to me. "I'm sorry he hurt you." It appeared she'd witnessed enough of my run-in with Alistair to realize what had happened on the night of her death.

"I'm sorry, too," I said. "You deserved so much better."

"Ashley," Mom said gently, "I can feel you here."

"You can?" Ashley asked, touching a hand to the round pendant at her neck.

"I miss you," Mom said. "I think about you every day. All the fun we had."

Ashley smiled. "I remember the year we taped pictures of Kevin Bacon all around the school. Nobody ever knew it was us."

I related that to Mom, and she snarfed. "Oh, my God. Yes. On bathroom walls. Under desks. On the nurse's door."

"Why?" I asked, honestly baffled.

"Because we could." Ashley beamed.

"Well, we both had such a huge crush on Kevin Bacon," Mom reasoned.

"I loved *Footloose*," Ashley gushed.

"We watched *Footloose* about thirty times," Mom said before her face fell. "Oh, Ashley, I miss you."

Ashley stood right next to Mom. "I'm sorry we didn't have more time," she said to her old friend. Then to me, she added, "Thank you for giving me this."

"A chance to catch up? Anytime," I said.

"That"—the ghost dipped her chin—"and, well, a chance to have a happier eternity."

She drew close to my mom, so close Mom's mouth made a wide O as she felt the presence or the love or maybe just a cold spot.

"I think she wants me to know she's okay," Mom murmured as her friend began to rise.

"She's leaving," I said as Ashley began to shine with the most brilliant white light.

Ashley looked down at us with love, with peace, as she rose. She broke into a brilliant smile as she gave up her earthly wanderings and mortal concerns and chose to go to the light.

Mom and I stood in silence afterward.

"Is she gone?" Mom asked.

"She's never gone," I reminded her. "Ashley is going to be watching over you and be with you no matter where she is.

She's a part of your life, just like you were a part of hers." That was how loved worked. It was how life worked.

Mom sighed. "I wish I had your power."

"And sometimes I wish I didn't," I said, catching a glimpse of Frankie on a white horse up in the parking lot. I tried not to groan as he drew Molly up onto his mighty steed. "I think they're ready for us," I added as Ellis appeared at the edge of the lot.

Mom took one last look at the area under the bleachers. "Goodbye, Ashley."

The next day, Mom lent me a pretty scarf to wrap around my bruised neck as we attended the Homecoming Goodbye Brunch in the town square.

"I'm still not sure why they call it the Goodbye Brunch," I said, walking Lucy past the Drama Club donuts-on-a-stick booth. "Everyone will still be here tomorrow."

"It's not like anyone really leaves Sugarland," Mom mused, "except for us," she added to Carl.

"Yes, but I don't think Sugarland ever left you," he remarked, looking sideways at the pink ballgown Lucy wore. Mom had made it special. She'd meant to present it to my skunk on the night of the big dance, but the mood hadn't been right.

We still didn't know who was responsible for the threat to my sweet girl. Alistair had denied it, and he'd admitted to far worse. In any case, I was keeping my skunk close.

Lucy, for her part, swished her pink-ribboned tail and acted like the belle of the ball.

"It's nice to get some peace," Mom said, waving at BreSha Wallice, who was trying to corral two kids determined to run in two different directions. "My phone has been ringing nonstop since last night."

I was surprised she still had anyone left to tell. According to Carl, she'd talked to all of her friends at least twice. She'd held court this morning at the chess tables inside Roan's Hardware, and she'd entertained the waitstaff while we grabbed an early breakfast at Biscuits & Gravy in the old feed store.

"I don't know how I'm going to eat again," I said, passing the 4-H Club chocolate covered bacon booth.

"I'll manage," Carl said, greeting one of his friends at the booth.

A line had formed at the Sugarland Herb Club hangover cure booth. Folks stood in an even bigger line next door at the Garden Club fresh tomato Bloody Mary booth. I lived in a town of optimists.

Mom stopped to talk to Darcy's neighbor Patrice about the events of last night, and I followed Lucy over to a quiet patch of grass between the mayor's office and the town meeting hall.

And there, tucked away, sat Molly on a picnic blanket. A lavish feast—worthy of any Sugarland festival—was laid out before her on tiered trays. A selection of fried plantains, saquitos de empadilla, and Cuban toasties covered one, with a smaller tray of tropical fruits cut into hearts and stars. Champagne chilled in a bucket with two glasses, and a four-piece band played Don Azpiazu's "El Manisero."

Frankie needed to tell her the truth about El Gato, even if she already knew the truth about El Gato. It was the polite thing to do.

I chewed my lip, debating whether or not to say anything, as Lucy danced and tried to draw the attention of the ghost she liked.

To be fair, she liked many of them. Just not Frankie.

Molly didn't notice me or the skunk. Instead, she smiled delightedly at a brilliant yellow butterfly that hovered above her finger. It seemed insects could detect ghosts, same as animals. And she'd found a beauty.

A chill iced my back. "Scram," Frankie said as my skunk made a frantic effort to climb my leg. He wore his El Gato mustache. Again.

"You really need to come clean about this." It would be infinitely better if she heard it from him. "And you're scaring Lucy," I said, taking her into my arms.

"Molly knows the truth," Frankie countered, motioning to Suds, who appeared out of thin air with a fresh moustache on a tray. "We talked it out last night," he added, smoothing the new moustache over the one currently fading on his lip. "But there was one thing I didn't count on from my saucy little filly. She likes it when I play El Gato." He grinned. "It spices up our love life."

"Oh my," I said, not sure I wanted to imagine Frankie and Molly role-playing for good.

"Now hoof it." He waggled his lip to make sure his mustache was on good. "I'm being romantic here."

No problem there. I handed my skunk off to my confused mother and then turned back to Frankie. "I'm out of here. And for the record, I'm glad you two worked things out."

He cast me a cocky El Gato grin. "And I as well, *mi secuaz*."

"All right then," I said as he returned to his love.

"What was that about?" Mom asked when I joined her.

"I don't even know where to begin," I admitted.

"Well, you'll never guess what I learned," Mom said, leading me away. "The school board is going to investigate Mr. Norwood for misconduct. Apparently, it's been going on for a while. That's why Jean has been holed up with those migraines."

"Poor Jean." It wasn't her fault.

We passed Jake and a group of men gathered in a tight circle, laughing. They quieted as we passed.

"Hey," Jake said, stepping out of the crowd. He wore a *Sugarland Biscuits* sweatshirt and a frown. "Can I talk to you for a second?"

My stomach churned. Even though I knew he wasn't a killer, I didn't like the way he was looking at my skunk.

"Okay," I said, picking Lucy up and stepping away from my mom.

He leaned in close, and I could smell the stale-closet scent of his letterman's jacket. "Kiki was arrested at our house this morning for threatening your skunk."

I gasped and instinctively drew Lucy away from him.

"I called the police myself," he added. "She was bragging about it to her old cheerleading friends over drinks last night." He cringed. "She'll be none too happy with me, but it was the right thing to do."

"Your mamma raised you right," I said, stroking my skunk.

He gave a short, quick nod. "Thank you for saying that."

"I can't believe it," Mom whispered as I rejoined her.

Of course, she'd heard the whole thing.

"I wonder if there was some doubt in Kiki's mind as to whether Jake was guilty," I said as we hurried away.

"That, or she's the vindictive terror I warned you about," Mom said. "I mean, all you did was accuse her husband of murder."

"I don't think I said it outright," I mused, trying to remember.

"Well, then I probably did," Mom said, with absolutely no regret. "Make sure you don't cross her in the future," she warned, as if I could control what happened in Sugarland.

"My stars and garters!" I choked out, stopping short as we reached the library.

Duranja and Melody sat on the top step, holding hands, right there in front of God and everybody.

"Noooo," I moaned, giving in to Lucy as she struggled out of my grip.

"Oh, stop that carrying on. I think it's nice," Mom said.

"No, it's not. It's not nice. In fact, I'd been hoping whatever this is," I said, waving a hand at them, "was born of drama and would go away once we learned who broke into the library."

Melody noticed us and waved. "We're going on our first date this Saturday!" she called. "Want to double?"

I was glad to see Duranja pale at that, as I no doubt did.

"If I were in town, I would." Mom smiled at them.

"I—" I had no words.

Duranja kissed Melody on the forehead, and that was my cue to skedaddle.

"You should stay for another week or two," I suggested to Mom as we headed in the direction of Main Street. "Or at least until they open all the items from the time capsule next Saturday."

Mom smiled as she waved at her friend Darcy manning the Sugarland Quilting Society booth. "I love Sugarland, but I've seen you and Melody and everybody else I wanted to see." When I opened my mouth to protest, she added, "I didn't mean what I said in your bathroom. I was worried and angry. I didn't want to see you get hurt, and then I said things that hurt you anyway. Know that I do think about you and Melody all the time, and I did enjoy my visit. But I can't stay forever."

I stopped her under an old oak tree. "I don't understand how you can pack up and leave like it's nothing." Would she even look back when she rolled out of town? "Why don't you like it here?"

Mom took my hands in hers. "I love you, and I love it here," she assured me, "but I also need to roam free."

"Why?" I asked, genuinely baffled. Everyone needed a place to call home.

She dropped my hands and began walking again. "I loved your father and my life here. But I married him straight out of high school, and I never went anywhere."

"It's not like you were trapped," I balked. Lots of people lived in one place their whole lives.

"I had little kids and a husband and your grandma to look after, and now...I don't," she said simply. "I've always wanted to spread my wings, and now this is my time."

"You can do it in Sugarland," I assured her.

She gave me a sad little grin. "No, I can't. At least not right now. Maybe someday."

Which probably meant never.

"I'm still not crazy about you taking so many chances," she added.

I braced myself for the lecture.

"But," she said, "after what I've seen these past several days, how could I expect you to stop following your heart?"

"Thanks, Mom," I said, glad to have her understand.

Maybe I understood her a little better now as well.

"Call me if you ever need any help investigating," she teased. "Maybe I could swing by," she added as Carl walked up holding biscuits and gravy in a cup.

"I'd rather have you here for Christmas," I told them both.

"Oh," Mom said, her hand fluttering to the gold pendant at her neck. "We already talked about going to Florida for the holidays."

"Mom, please?" I pressed. I'd been afraid to hold her to it before, but now I realized I couldn't just let time pass and hope to see her. "It's important."

"It's family," Carl said to her, as if that explained everything.

"You're right," she said as if realizing it for the first time. "I do think we should come back a little more often. And for Christmas this year."

Carl grinned. "Lend me your kitchen and I'll make you my famous brown sugar bourbon baked ham."

"I can make Grandma's corn pudding," I added.

Mom clapped her hands together. "And if Melody is still dating Alec, I'll have him bring his grandma's caramel cake."

"Too soon, Mom."

"I'll ask him about it." She nodded to herself.

I was sure she would.

I could only hope that would scare him away.

Ellis walked up wearing a *Sugarland Biscuits* sweatshirt, off duty for once. "What are you grinning about?"

"It's just nice to have everyone together," I told him, bracing myself as Lauralee bounded up. She looked ready to tackle the whole lot of us.

"I made enough money this weekend to buy my own food truck!" she squealed.

I hugged her tightly while everyone gave their congratulations. Even my sister and Duranja rushed over to share in the good news.

"Here's to a new tradition in Sugarland," Ellis said, raising his Coke can to Lauralee.

She beamed with pride.

"I'll talk to my boss about giving you a permanent spot in front of the library," Melody offered.

"Or you can park in front of the police station," Duranja added. "You are going to make those mini chicken and waffle sliders, right?"

"And lots more," Lauralee teased.

"If you want, I'll bet Roan's can block off a spot for you," Carl suggested. They were right at the busy corner with the police station and the insurance company and lots of businesses nearby.

"There's not much there since the BBQ place went under," I added.

"Well, it's a truck," Lauralee mused. "I can go anywhere."

"You certainly can," I said, pleased to see my friend in charge of her own destiny after working for others for so long.

"Wherever you are, we'll find you," Ellis promised. "Are you going to make those apple pie sticks that you dip in the caramel sauce?"

"Yes," she gushed, "and I'm working on a cheesecake one that you dip in seasonal fruit sauces."

"I'm in love," Duranja declared.

He'd better not be thinking that way—not even about cheesecake.

"We'll have to stop back into town once you're open," Carl offered.

"It'll be worth it," Lauralee promised.

"I adore new beginnings," Melody said as Duranja wrapped an arm around her.

"And keeping family close," Carl added.

"Being there for friends," Mom said, absently touching her necklace.

"And remembering what's important," I said, taking Ellis's hand in mine.

Chapter Twenty-Five

The next Saturday night, we gathered in front of the library for the opening of the time-capsule artifacts. Local restaurant booths ringed the town square, and the loudspeaker played "Celebration" by Kool & the Gang.

Ellis and I sat in plastic chairs in a small VIP area near the bottom of the library steps. In front of us stood a small stage with all of the artifacts wrapped in plastic bags and laid out on the table. Two large television screens stood by to broadcast the findings.

The mayor sat next to me, and behind him, the press.

Bert MacDonald of the VFW newsletter leaned over my shoulder, edging out the reporter from the *Sugarland Gazette*. "And what are you most excited to see, miss?" he asked, even though he was very well aware of my name, my background, and my family history dating back through my grandparents. "I want to see the Class of 1986 box," I told him. If only so I could take pictures for my mom.

She and Carl were already in Nevada, exploring Red Rock Canyon.

The reporter leaned back and wrote while I frowned up at

the main stage. Duranja stood at the edge with Melody, holding her hand.

"She'd better let go of him and do her job," I murmured to Ellis.

"It hasn't started yet," he reminded me.

I vowed to be patient, although I wasn't quite sure where I'd learned how. Or who could have taught me.

A few minutes later, I was rewarded when Melody took the stage.

She wore a simple green dress under a white lab coat and was brilliant as she explained the way the library had sought to catalogue and preserve each box from the time capsule. The audience listened, rapt, as she explained how the archivists had waited until this very night to open them all.

She slipped on white silk gloves, and the crowd *oohed* and *ahhed* as Melody cracked each box open and shared the contents. We saw a homecoming day newspaper from 1945, and the autographed football from the state championship game in 1972. Melody held Darcy Johnson's secret apple pie recipe up for the television monitor, and a blinding flood of cell phone photographs followed. I was glad to see these objects come to light, even if they were originally supposed to be buried for one hundred years.

After all, Alistair had been the only one who had used the time capsule to hide a terrible secret. The rest of us wanted our deeds and our actions and even our recipes to be remembered and passed down, to be talked about and enjoyed.

And as Melody drew the very last box out of its clear plastic wrapper, the entire audience waited in anticipation for the latest treasure, the last glimpse we would have of the past, at least for tonight.

No bigger than a shoebox, the metal container lost flecks of rust as it slid from its wrapper.

"There are no markings on this one," Melody announced.

"And no record of what club or organization left it." She eased back the rusty latch as the large televisions broadcasted her movements. "Everything else has been accounted for," she said as she lifted the lid.

The crowd let out a stuttering gasp. And as the image shone bright on the massive screen, I realized I had a mystery on my hands unlike any I'd seen before.

Note from Angie Fox

Thanks for joining Verity and the gang for homecoming Sugarland-style! Let's hope little Lucy can keep up her wardrobe now that Verity's mother is heading out of town again. Do we perhaps see care packages in Lucy's future?

The next book, Give Up the Ghost *picks up right where this one leaves off — with the mysterious item in the time capsule. It sets off a series of events that even Frankie could never predict.*

If you like these mysteries, and want to know when new ones come out, sign up for my newsletter at www.angiefox.com. I don't email often, but when I do, it's always something good.

Thanks again for reading!

Angie

Don't miss the next
Southern Ghost Hunter book
Give Up the Ghost

Coming Spring 2022!

About the Author

New York Times and *USA Today* bestselling author Angie Fox writes sweet, fun, action-packed mysteries. Her characters are clever and fearless, but in real life, Angie is afraid of basements, bees, and going up stairs when it's dark behind her. Let's face it: Angie wouldn't last five minutes in one of her books.

Angie earned a journalism degree from the University of Missouri. During that time, she also skipped class for an entire week so she could read Anne Rice's vampire series straight through. Angie has always loved books and is shocked, honored and tickled pink that she now gets to write books for a living. Although, she did skip writing for a week this past fall so she could read Victoria Laurie's Abby Cooper psychic eye mysteries straight through.

Angie makes her home in St. Louis, Missouri with a football-addicted husband, two kids, and Moxie the dog.

To receive an email each time Angie releases a new book, sign up at www.angiefox.com. Also be sure to join Angie's online Facebook community where you will find contests, fun facts, general silliness, and special sneak peeks of new books.

Connect with Angie Fox online:
www.angiefox.com
angie@angiefox.com